OR[I...]

'I'll repent,' Dora promised.

'Yes you will.'

'I'll pray for forgiveness.'

'That would be a good start,' the Abbess agreed.

'And I'll . . .'

'You'll get undressed,' the Abbess barked.

Dora stared at her doubtfully, not sure she had heard properly. 'I'm sorry?'

The Abbess bore down on Dora. With her considerable bulk and the forbidding frown that now creased her jaw she presented an intimidating figure, and it was obvious she expected no arguments. 'Get undressed, Sister Pandora. You have a lesson to learn.'

ORIGINAL SINS

Lisette Ashton

This book is a work of fiction.
In real life, make sure you practise safe, sane and consensual sex.

First published in 2003 by
Nexus
Thames Wharf Studios
Rainville Road
London W6 9HA

www.nexus-books.co.uk

Typeset by TW Typesetting, Plymouth, Devon

Printed and bound by
Clays Ltd, St Ives PLC

ISBN 0 352 33804 0

Contents

1 Original Sins   1
2 Idle Hands   26
3 Glutton for Punishment   52
4 The Pride of the Company   90
5 An Envious Lot   130
6 Weight Watcher   188
7 Anger Management   206

1

Original Sins

Dora could feel the sin like the symptoms of an encroaching disease. Its slick warmth fevered her brow; her thoughts were shadowed by dark overtones; and an unnatural warmth seated itself at the top of her legs. Disturbed by the sudden malaise, and worried someone might notice her predicament, she glanced fearfully around the orchard.

The sound of a woman singing – a cheery refrain as light and uplifting as the remnants of the summer's day – travelled from the other side of the apple trees. Dora couldn't see who was there but she felt confident the owner of the voice hadn't noticed her inexplicable plight. Still fretfully scouring the horizon, unnerved by a sensation of being watched that came with her distress, she was shocked to see a man standing on the nearby road.

Tall and dark, he looked undoubtedly sinister with his goatee beard and swarthy good looks. He had no right being there – the road he was standing on was private, barred by wrought-iron gates and liberally planted with signs warning trespassers they were infringing on private property – yet in spite of those precautions denying him access, he still stood there. And, as Dora swallowed the massive lump in her throat, she could see he was watching with the intensity of a practised tomcat stalking a field mouse.

Her insides squirmed as she trembled beneath his gaze. The muscles of her cleft were a turmoil of heat and wetness that she had never previously experienced. Tiny, adorable sparks flurried through her sensitive flesh and she was struck by a greedy need to experience more. Staring at the stranger, sure he was aware of her awakening desire, she wondered if he could satisfy the urge that had suddenly become her driving force. The thought was blackly exciting.

The knowledge of why she felt so flustered, and the ingrained belief that it was deeply and unforgivably wrong, came close to making her faint. She parted her lips, not sure if she was going to call for the unknown man to come to her or shout for assistance from the woman who was singing. Before she had the chance to make either cry the ringing of a hand-bell carried through the apple trees. Dora could have easily ignored the tuneless peal if it hadn't been followed by the direct cry of someone summoning her.

'Sister Pandora! Sister Pandora! It's time for Vespers, Sister Pandora. Hurry along now. You don't want to be late.'

Blushing crimson beneath the shadow of her wimple, Dora raced from the orchard. She was disgusted by the acts she had been contemplating and dismayed by the eager pulse that had accompanied those licentious thoughts. She wanted nothing more than to return to the sanctuary of the convent and yet, even as she hurried to safety, she could feel the weight of the stranger's gaze following her. More disquieting than his interest was the knowledge that a secret part of her liked the effect his attention had provoked.

* * *

Rather than following the sound of prayers coming from the chapel, Dora ran briskly to her cell. The spell of arousal still held her in its thrall and she thought it would be sacrilegious to participate in Vespers while harbouring such obscene desires. She wanted to be naked, her bare body being touched and teased until all her dark urges were satisfied. She yearned to feel the heat of a man against her – and inside her – and, although she had never experienced such an act, she felt certain it would satiate her need. Closing the cell door firmly, then collapsing on her simple cot, she wrapped her arms around her torso and prayed for the torment to go away.

The weight of her forearms pressed against her breasts. She hadn't realised her nipples were standing hard but, as soon as she began holding herself, Dora was acutely aware of the condition. The hard nubs bristled beneath her touch and she was stung by the shrill pain of raw excitement. Even when she moved her hands away echoes of the sweet sensations continued to tease. She knew it would take nothing more than the casual caress of her own hand and she would be wallowing in the blissful experience of those shameful, unbidden pleasures that she had heard were so wonderful.

Diligently, she forced herself to resist.

She considered folding her hands over her lap, then stopped, horrified by the idea of where that might lead. Unable to think of anything else to do with her fingers, she clutched her faithful string of rosary beads and began to recite the practised chants of her Aves, Paternosters and Glorias. The familiar prayers had offered strength and guidance countless times before but on this occasion, instead of giving the comfort she wanted, she could only hear herself mumbling a string of meaningless words. As much as she needed to take security from her beliefs, all Dora could feel was the dull, greedy pounding that hammered incessantly between her legs.

Unwilling to succumb to the burning desire, she invested her prayers with more determination. She tried closing her eyes, to make it easier to concentrate, but the memory of the stranger with the goatee beard loomed large at the forefront of her thoughts. His dark eyes appraised her and his licentious smile twisted with lustful appreciation. There was something demonic in the way he licked his lips and she opened her eyes quickly, fearing that her imagination might play worse tricks if she exposed herself to his memory for too long. Sitting up on the cot, staring miserably at the plain, plaster walls, tears of desperation began to wet her cheeks.

Mumbling the paternoster fervently, pressing her fingers tight against the reassuring shape of each rosary bead, Dora didn't notice when her hands fell into her lap. She had even begun to think that the prayers were finally releasing her from the malady of desire because her thoughts were no longer a tangle of frightened and reluctant denials.

A tranquil calm had come over her and the sensation was so relaxing it was close to being heavenly. It was only when she glanced down, and saw she was rubbing methodically through the coarse fabric of her vestments, that Dora discovered the prayers hadn't helped her to resist the temptation. She considered stopping, pulling her hands away and hurrying to ask the Abbess for guidance and help.

But, far more appealing, was the thought of continuing.

Each time she dragged her fingers up, the eager flesh between her legs shivered. Every subtle pressure was rewarded by pleasures she had never imagined.

The sensations were dark, clearly unwholesome and sinful, but she couldn't deny the enjoyment they brought.

Chugging each breath with quiet force, languishing in the thrill of what she was doing, Dora began to pull her robe up so she could reach beneath. The friction of the coarse twill was invigorating against her thighs but her need demanded something less subtle and more immediate. She quivered with desperation and, when the tips of her fingers met the bare flesh of her leg, the frisson almost made her scream. Panting eagerly, no longer worrying about the shame of what she was doing, Dora smoothed her palm boldly upwards. When her fingertips finally found their target she threw back her head and sighed. The inquisitive caress of her own hand, gently stirring a host of devious delights, was enough to have her hurtling toward a precipice that promised to overwhelm. Frightened to continue, but unable to stop, she teased the tip of her finger against the slippery folds of pink flesh. It would only take the slightest of movements, nothing more than a firm thrust of her finger, and she knew she would experience the penetration that her body so desperately yearned. She was on the brink of satisfying that urge when her cell door opened.

'Sister Pandora!'

The Abbess stood there, her expression changing from concern to shock, and then to mortified horror. 'Sister Pandora!' she exclaimed. 'In the name of all that's merciful, what on earth do you think you're doing?'

And, confused by her desires and responses, and equally shocked by the depths to which she had sunk, Dora couldn't think how best to answer.

* * *

Two hours later, after Holy Mass and while the rest of the convent were away at Compline, Dora still couldn't find words to explain her actions. She sat in the austere warmth of the Abbess's chamber, sipping horribly sweet tea and trying not to feel intimidated by the host of leather-bound tomes that lined the walls. Worries about the repercussions of her actions were taking their toll and her hands clattered the cup and saucer together. She placed the crockery on a corner table and fidgeted unhappily beneath the Abbess's dour frown.

'You didn't attend Vespers.' Even sitting behind her desk the Abbess's huge frame was large and imposing. Her broad face, which could show kindness and patience, was now a mask of staid gravity. The cheeks that were so often ruddy with hale vitality were wan and sunken. 'You didn't attend Vespers, Sister Pandora.'

Dora lowered her gaze to the rug on the floor-boards. 'I was having thoughts,' she explained coyly. 'I was having impure thoughts. Under the circum-stances I didn't think it would be appropriate to offer my prayers at Vespers.'

'You thought it would be appropriate to go to your cell and masturbate?'

The word sat between them like something ungodly. It was distressing to hear the Abbess use such a term and Dora thought it was even more disquieting to know she was to blame.

'Yes. I mean no.' She knew confusion was going to get the better of her and she struggled to explain herself fully. Meeting the Abbess's stern gaze, desper-ately trying to make the woman understand what had happened, she said, 'I didn't go to my cell to mastur . . .' As hard as she tried, Dora couldn't bring herself to say the word. 'I didn't go to my cell for that

6

purpose,' she amended. 'I went there to pray for strength and guidance.'

'Is that what you were doing?' the Abbess asked cynically.

Shamed by the comment, Dora blinked back the threat of tears.

'You neglected Vespers, Sister Pandora. And, as we are a contemplative order, I can't understand why you think it was acceptable for you to renege on one of your day's most important duties.'

Dora lowered her gaze, knowing she wouldn't be able to say anything in her own defence. She could understand the outrage her actions had provoked: she had avoided prayers and been caught wantonly breaking her vow of chastity. She only hoped the Abbess would be able to find sufficient forgiveness in her heart.

'Can you name the heavenly virtues?'

The question was barked so unexpectedly that Dora was briefly uncertain. She glanced around the empty room, not sure if someone else had entered and the Abbess was addressing them.

'Sister Pandora,' the Abbess repeated crisply. 'Can you name the seven heavenly virtues?'

Dora racked her brains to remember her schooling. The answer came in a rush and she recited the list immediately. 'Faith, hope, charity, fortitude, courage, temperance and prudence.' She glanced up, smiling, sure her reply was correct.

'No mention of masturbation?' the Abbess asked frostily.

With each passing second Dora could feel her hopes of being forgiven growing further away. She started to tell the Abbess about the malaise that had come on her, and explain that the urges weren't something she had wanted, but the woman was speaking over her.

'What about the seven deadly sins? Could you name those for me?'

'Anger, pride, envy, gluttony, sloth, greed and lust.' Unable to stop herself, and not knowing why her body should respond in such a way, she blushed a furious crimson when she mentioned the final sin. It wasn't just the burning at her cheeks that told her she was flustered: the deepening of the Abbess's frown informed Dora that her response was inappropriate.

'Do you know why lust is considered a sin?' she asked stiffly.

Dora sat upright, trying to answer the question fully and accurately. 'Matthew five, verse twenty-eight says, "Lust is sin." Romans six, verse twenty-three says, "Sin is death." '

'Lust cripples our ability to give and receive love,' the Abbess concurred. 'Lust blocks God's love from working in us. Lust was Eve's failing, because of which, we all now suffer. Lust is the direct forebear of original sin.'

Dora nodded eagerly.

'Which makes me wonder why you were so eager to succumb to it.'

The statement hung between them for an eternity. The echoes of Compline drifted melodically from the chapel but even the uplifting sound of the prayers couldn't break the chamber's thickening silence.

'I'll repent,' Dora promised.

'Yes you will.'

'I'll pray for forgiveness.'

'That would be a good start,' the Abbess agreed.

'And I'll –'

'You'll get undressed,' the Abbess barked.

Dora stared at her doubtfully, not sure she had heard properly. 'I'm sorry?'

The Abbess levered her large frame from behind the desk and bore down on Dora. With the size of her considerable bulk and the forbidding frown that now creased her jaw she presented an intimidating figure and it was obvious she expected no arguments. 'Get undressed, Sister Pandora. You have a lesson to learn.'

She could think of a million reasons to protest but not one of them was strong enough to make it past her lips. Nudity wasn't condoned at the convent; the Holy See didn't approve of nakedness; and the head of the diocese would surely object. Seeing the determined expression on the Abbess's face, and knowing she would have to do as she was told, Dora toyed reluctantly with her wimple. 'I'm not sure if . . .'

'Undress, Sister Pandora. You're not the first novice to break the chapel's rules with such a sin and I'm sure you won't be the last. I've dealt with your kind before and I don't doubt it will be my sad duty to deal with your type again.'

'But –'

'Undress.'

Knowing she had no choice, Dora pulled the wimple away and then began to remove the remaining clothes from her body. Her underwear was plain, wash-weary white, and she had never felt so much shame as she suffered while removing those underclothes beneath the Abbess's ponderous frown. Her cheeks had flushed furious pink when the Abbess had burst into her cell. But, once she was naked and feeling painfully vulnerable, they blazed dull crimson. Repeatedly she rubbed the heel of her palm against her face to wipe away the steady flow of tears. By the time she had folded the last of her robes into a neat pile on the chair her embarrassment was suffocating. Unhappily she turned toward the Abbess and tried not to think how inappropriate her slender, naked body appeared in the solemn surroundings of the

9

book-lined chamber. Perpetually fingering the rosary offered little solace or comfort but she continued out of ingrained practice.

'You're still plagued by lust, aren't you?'

Dora glanced down at herself, appalled to see her nipples stood flushed and erect. She couldn't see between her legs but she could feel the spreading wetness and wondered if arousal had darkened those feather-like curls that covered the secrets of her sex. Her shame weighed so heavily, the emotion was a torturous block crushing the air from her chest.

'You really are in need of this lesson,' the Abbess said stiffly. Without further word she took hold of Dora's wrist and dragged her from the chamber.

The embarrassment of being naked and taken down one of the convent's hallowed corridors was enough to make fresh tears squirt from her eyes. The humiliation of being led by the disapproving Abbess was even more soul-destroying. 'I will repent,' Dora promised. The words came out in a hurried rush. 'I truly will, Mother Abbess. I truly will.'

The Abbess continued indifferently.

She took Dora past the chapel, toward the kitchens, and out from the sanctuary of the convent's warmth. Before Dora could realise the hard earth was biting into the soles of her feet, or notice that the clement night was not quite so warm against her bare flesh, she saw they were heading toward the cowshed. 'Abbess?' she asked uncertainly.

The large woman said nothing. The last of the day's light was beginning to fade from the sky and had transformed the blossoming night into a beautiful, dark lavender. Because the convent was set in its own remote and exclusive grounds Dora should have had no worries that her nudity might be seen. But fears that the stranger might be lurking out there chilled her with icy excitement. She knew it was foolish to think the man would still be watching – it had been nearly three hours since she had caught him staring at her – but it was hard to shake the idea that he was lewdly appraising her bare form. And, just as unnerving, was the idea that one of the other sisters might see she was having to suffer the shameful indignity. Because she was naked, and because she was stumbling hurriedly after the Abbess, Dora felt sure any observer would easily be able to guess how she had sinned.

'Why are you taking me to the cowshed?'

The Abbess didn't reply until they were in the seclusion of the shed.

The farmland fragrance of animals and waste was overpowering and made Dora perversely aware of her inappropriate nudity. Instead of walking on hard earth her feet were now spiked by stray barbs of hay but she made no further complaint as she was led past the disinterested beasts and into one of the empty stalls at the rear.

'Stay there,' the Abbess said firmly.

Shivering from a combination of cold and fear, Dora remained in the stall. She was beginning to wonder if this was her punishment, and that she would be condemned to spend the night naked and cold and miserable in the stench of the cows. Hurrying through her prayers as she numbly squeezed each bead of the rosary, Dora almost gasped with relief when the Abbess finally returned.

Her hopes of immediate forgiveness began to lessen when she saw that, in one hand, the Abbess held the rusting nozzle of the cowshed's hose. The fattening pipe writhed lethargically behind her and, in an instant, Dora could see what the woman intended doing. She raised her hands, determined to say this was needless and unnecessary.

The spray of water caught her in the chest. Her bare body was buffeted by the raging torrent and Dora couldn't decide if she was holding up her arms for protest or protection. Icy waves blasted her, kneading her breasts and shocking her naked flesh. Each time she tried to gasp for air she found herself swallowing mouthfuls of the spray until eventually she felt light-headed from lack of oxygen. Staggering under the weight of the deluge, she knew she had never felt so cold, so powerless or so humiliated.

When the Abbess finally deigned to stop the hose, Dora was sobbing bitterly.

Even the gently lowing cattle seemed to have fallen silent after the deafening roar of the deluge. The only sounds were Dora's muffled tears and the trickle of the water finding its way down a drain.

'Each of the deadly sins is supposed to have its own specific punishment,' the Abbess reflected.

Her breath sounded laboured, and Dora wondered if the woman was exhausted from the effort of handling the hose, or suffering a lesser degree of the lust that had infected her. She kept the thought to herself, knowing it wouldn't help her situation to voice such a suggestion.

Unaware of Dora's observations, the Abbess continued. 'The gluttonous are supposed to be force fed rats, toads and snakes; the angry will be dismembered alive. For your sin, you should be punished by being smothered in fire and brimstone.' Her voice resounded hollowly from the cowshed walls and Dora thought that grim echo added a disturbing undertone to the woman's words. She dropped the hose to the floor and motioned for Dora to turn around and spread her hands against the wall.

The position reminded her of TV cop shows she had seen as a child but that recollection brought back

12

none of the warm memories Dora usually associated with growing up. Instead, her thoughts were only a nauseating knowledge of how vulnerable her shivering body would appear to her tormentor.

'But I don't think we need to go to the extremes of fire and brimstone,' the Abbess continued. 'Not when I can cleanse the impurity from you with honest soap and water.'

From the corner of her eye Dora could see the Abbess was wielding a stiff-bristled brush and she shrank from the thought of how it would be employed. When she caught the familiar tang of carbolic, she guessed her ordeal had now begun properly. Silently, she hoped it wouldn't be as protracted and painful as she feared.

The Abbess lathered the brush against the soap, mumbling liturgically to herself. 'John wrote, "Do not love the world, or the things in the world. If anyone loves the world, the love of the Father is not in him. For all that is in the world – the lust of the flesh, the lust of the eyes and the pride of life – is not of the Father but is of the world. And the world is passing away, and the lust of it; but he who does the will of God abides forever." '

Dora recognised the words but she couldn't focus on their meaning.

The Abbess stood disturbingly close, the waves of incense coming from her like a perfume. The hem of her habit brushed the back of Dora's thighs and the subtle contact was enough to spark licentious need. She held Dora by one shoulder, her strong fingers burrowing into the flesh and clutching bone. Without any sensitivity, she forced the brush against Dora's hip. The bristles were punishingly abrasive – a million dull needles that scratched a soapy path against her flesh. The contact should have been painful and humiliating but, each time the Abbess scrubbed Dora's body, ripples of pleasure cascaded through her skin. When the soapy brush scoured her nipple, Dora was stung by an exquisite rush of euphoria. Unable to distance herself from the welling excitement, she responded happily when her buttocks and cleft were treated to the same coarse attention. Every punishing caress pushed her closer to an inevitable peak and, not daring to let the Abbess see how she was responding, Dora squeezed the rosary in her fist and shouted her prayers for forgiveness. She supposed, in spite of her desire not to give in to the lust, the symptoms were still blatantly obvious. Her nipples remained erect, their rouged hue as scarlet as a lewd intention. The folds of skin that concealed her sex felt like they were parting hungrily. Her inner muscles remained a turmoil of unfamiliar sensations driven by the urgent desire to experience something forbidden.

'I think you need more cleansing,' the Abbess said solemnly.

Dora begged her not to use the hose again but her cries went unheeded. The Abbess grabbed the hose, released the clamp on the nozzle and deluged her with another endless torrent. Again the icy water pushed and pummelled, teasing Dora's bare flesh and touching her with an intimacy she secretly craved. The flow lasted for an age and, by the time it eventually ceased, Dora was sobbing with heartfelt cries for forgiveness. To her dismay, instead of listening to her pleas, the Abbess started on her again with the brush.

Whereas before the sensations were almost too harsh, Dora's body now seemed ready for the abrasive caress. Every scrub of the bristles promised to take her to an undiscovered plateau of pleasure. The friction of the soap, and the asexual pressure of the

Abbess's burly frame, all pushed her toward an uncontrollable brink that she knew would be climactic.

Unaware she was doing it, Dora squirmed herself against the brush. She languished in the daring thrill of subjecting herself to such punishment and revelled in the dark, masochistic bliss that came from the torment. When the Abbess turned her around, preparing to cleanse Dora's stinging breasts, she yearned for the cruel bite. Eagerly, she closed her eyes and held her chest up. When the expected pain failed to happen, Dora opened her eyes to meet the Abbess's thunderous frown.

'You haven't learnt your lesson.'

Dora shook her head. Suddenly overcome by shame she began begging forgiveness and trying to apologise but the Abbess had already turned her back and was walking out of the cowshed. 'I'm trying not to give in to these urges,' Dora wailed. 'Can't you see that I'm fighting them?'

'You're not fighting hard enough,' the Abbess grunted.

Dora groaned miserably. 'But please –'

The Abbess raised her hand as she walked, silencing Dora's plaintive cry. 'No more,' she called over her shoulder. 'This convent isn't going to humour you any further. Follow me, Sister Pandora.'

Rounding her shoulders, and forcing herself to follow miserably in the Abbess's wake, Dora realised her punishment wasn't over.

She had half-hoped she might be able to deal with the lust herself in the sanctuary of her cell, but the Abbess made swift plans to pre-empt that idea. She took Dora back to her room, told her to lie on the bed, then used cord to tie her hands and feet to the four corners. The bindings chafed her wrists and ankles, and left her unbearably frustrated, but she could understand the Abbess's reasoning. If she had been left alone and unrestrained they both knew what she would have done. Nevertheless, that understanding offered little comfort to Dora in the small hours of the night.

The bondage had been swiftly and effectively accomplished but Dora remembered every glorious moment. She couldn't understand why the memory added fuel to her arousal but she knew the pressure of the Abbess's frame leaning over her, and the sensations of helplessness that came with being tied, had augmented every one of her dark desires.

She spent a fitful night trying to get comfortable in spite of the bindings but, in the end, she didn't manage a moment's sleep. Her thoughts were a turmoil of how vulnerable she was and, when her mind conjectured that the stranger might find her here in this position, her body became a blaze of furious heat. Rationally, she knew he would have no way of gaining access to the convent, and even less idea of where to find her, but those thoughts barely dented her fantasies.

She envisioned him touching her; exploring her; and finally using her. The images were so clear and detailed it was almost as if the experience was really happening. A couple of times she had to renew her grip on the rosary and tell herself that the beads were the only things that weren't coming from her imagination. But it was easier to lose herself in a world where his hands caressed her swollen breasts, and the hardness of his lean, sinewy body pressed against her.

When the first of the morning's light began to bleach night from the sky, and Dora heard the faraway cries of alarm clocks from neighbouring cells, she began to cry tears made bitter by frustration. She knew the Abbess was going to decide her fate today but that was only a small part of her unhappiness. More distressing was the realisation that, with the passing of the night, she was no longer able to enjoy the fantasy of being bound and helpless for the pleasure of the stranger.

It took less than three hours for the Abbess to organise everything. She told Dora she didn't want to damage the convent's reputation with a scandal and said it would be in everyone's best interests if Dora were simply relocated to a corporal order.

Not wanting to cause any more upset than she had already instigated, Dora reluctantly agreed. She packed her few belongings into a suitcase, accepted the train ticket and letter of introduction that the Abbess gave her, and quickly left for a neighbouring diocese. She wondered if the Holy See would have approved of the way her situation had been handled, then realised they would almost certainly have disapproved of the things Dora had done to precipitate the whole series of events.

She might have protested further, or at least argued her case more strongly, if thoughts of lust hadn't still been weighing on her mind. But it was difficult to think beyond the burning need that continued to sear between her legs. Fingering her rosary offered some distraction but she had to concentrate on each of the prayers for fear that her fingers might make their own exploration of her body. And, even when she was forcing her mind on the words of the paternoster, she knew a part of her was thinking about something less esoteric and far more physically fulfilling.

Wilfully distancing herself from the disturbing sensations, not allowing herself to dwell on the caress

17

of her thighs rubbing together or the way her habit lovingly caressed her skin, she made a silent vow that she wouldn't act on the licentious impulses. The gentle motion of the train didn't help and the rocking of the seat beneath her buttocks threatened to transport her to unbridled realms of bliss. Sweating profusely, and near to crying with her need for release, she disembarked at her stop and followed the Abbess's instructions by reporting to the Holy Cross Church.

The priest was an affable, elderly gentleman who greeted her cordially.

Instead of accepting the hospitality he offered, Dora asked if she could visit the public chapel to pray. He obliged her wishes, saying it would give him the time to read the Abbess's letter of introduction. When she said she would like to be alone in the church, he said he understood and gallantly evicted a passing parishioner who had settled herself in one of the pews near the vestry. The tiny young woman, a pretty little thing dressed all in red, cursed bitterly but she eventually left. And, as soon as she was alone, Dora settled herself on her knees in front of the altar.

It was a larger chapel than she had been used to at the convent and the carved pews stretched in empty lines away from the chancel. Dora took a moment to think of the martyred saints immortalised in the stained-glass arches but, not daring to compare their heroic suffering with the paltry torment she was currently enduring, she quickly turned her back on the absent congregation. It was while she was trying to rekindle her faith, staring adoringly up at the ornate crucifix, that she felt the weight of his gaze on her back.

Without needing to turn she knew it was the stranger she had seen outside the orchard. She didn't know how he had found her; but she knew it was him. She didn't know how he had entered the church after the priest had locked the doors behind the woman in red; but she knew he was there. Not sure where the knowledge came from, only certain it was correct, she was held in the thrall of delicious fear as he silently studied her. She didn't need to turn to recognise his swarthy features, or look at him to see the trim, cultivated shape of his pointed goatee. Dora knew it was him without having to look.

She held her breath, trembling beneath the altar as she heard his whisper-soft footsteps approach. The rosary was in her grasp and she tightened her hold on the beads, saying her prayers faster and with more urgency. She continued reciting the same lines repeatedly and rushed the Latin into an inarticulate incantation. When she realised he was behind her, and stepping closer, she tried to invest each line with proper authority. Her nostrils caught a hint of something acrid, a scent of sulphur and dry, suffocating heat. Then he knelt down behind her, pressing himself against her back. Inhaling deeply, making Dora know that he was drinking the perfume of being near her, he placed his arms around her in a loose embrace.

She remained rigid, save for her fingers nervously tugging at the beads. Her heart pounded furiously and she feared it would explode when she watched one of his large, muscular hands cup the shape of her breast.

Dora gasped. He was touching her in exactly the way she had yearned to be touched. But, although she wanted to give in to him, she felt certain some show of resistance was needed. Trying to retain some composure, mustering all the flustered dignity she could manage, Dora asked, 'Is there something I can do for you?'

He chuckled. It was a deep, sonorous laugh that was so pleasant she found it chilling. Because the weight of his mirth rattled through her shoulder blades she was unnerved to find it reminded her of how close he was.

'Yes,' he agreed pleasantly. 'Yes. I'm sure there's something you can do for me.'

She retained her resolve, still fingering the rosary and chanting the prayers inside her mind. Spitting the words through clenched teeth, she said, 'You shouldn't be touching me like that.'

'Are you asking me to stop?'

Dora couldn't finish her prayer.

The conversation was frustrating because he was saying more in the silences. Her own conflicting desires didn't help because, while she didn't want him to be cupping her breast, he was kneading the responsive flesh and coaxing arousal with the skill of a gifted lover. Dora knew he would desist as soon as she gave the instruction but she was scared, if he did stop, she might never know the climactic pleasure that his fingertips promised. Realising there was only one choice open to her, and determined to take that action, she turned slowly around to meet his face.

He watched her with avid interest and she was mesmerised by his large, dark eyes. His smile was curious and patient, the broad lips almost begging her to kiss him. No longer able to resist the urges, and disregarding the potential consequences, Dora pushed her mouth over his. She wrapped her arms around him and rubbed her eager body against his rigid frame.

She couldn't tell if her reaction surprised him, or if this was the response he had expected. His mastery of the situation was greater than her own and she only knew his tongue was gliding into her mouth, tasting and exploring her. He maintained a hold on her breast, at the same time guiding her to the floor so he could lie on top of her. The vestment was pushed up from her legs and the chill air of the church caressed the bare skin of her upper thighs. Not hiding behind pleasantries or teasing he unzipped his pants and she was darkly shocked by the sight of his erection.

'We shouldn't be doing this,' she mumbled.

He nodded agreement. 'No. We shouldn't.' Guiding the tip of his shaft between her legs he grinned demonically and added, 'But we're not going to let that fact stop us, are we?'

She braced herself for the lunge of his entry. The stories she had heard told her she could expect pain but she didn't think that was likely in these circumstances. Even if there was some discomfort, Dora felt sure it would only add to the thrill of this bewildering moment. Pressing her back against the foot of the altar, staring up at the martyred figure of Christ on his cross, she closed her eyes as the stranger's length nudged her hole.

Her cleft was bristling with a greedy need and, feeling sure he would be able to sate that dark hunger, she bucked her hips eagerly to meet him. He pushed forward in the same moment and she felt her virginity tear in one rush of blithe discomfort. She supposed the moment might have merited more reflection but her desire had gone beyond such considerations. He had awoken an urge within her and it was an urge that had treated her to sickly exciting thoughts and helped engineer her expulsion from the convent. Now she knew she was close to satisfying her cravings she was determined not to be distracted by something as immaterial as her chastity.

Repeatedly, he hammered his length into her. Each brutal thrust brought her closer to the pinnacle she needed and, unable to stop herself, Dora held him within her embrace and smothered kisses against his face and neck. The sweet explosion of release was inching ever closer and she matched every penetration with a guileless twist of her hips. When he wrenched open her habit, tugged her underwear aside and then placed his hands against her bare breasts, she was struck by the bliss of her first climax.

The joy was more than she had imagined, buffeting her to an extreme of pleasure that left her simultaneously hot and cold; shamed and elated; exhausted and furiously alert. The inner muscles of her sex clenched spasmodically around him and her grateful cries echoed from the roof of the church. By the time her shrieks had tapered to satisfied sighs, she realised he was slowing down. His length remained inside her, its heat and hardness telling her that he wasn't yet spent. She could feel every excited twitch that pulsed through his member and was stung by the potency of each minor tremor.

'Again,' she murmured, kissing the words against his throat. It didn't matter that what she was asking was sinful and wrong. All that mattered was that he completely exorcise her need. 'Please. Please. I have to feel that again.' She could hear herself begging and wondered if this debasement was another step on the downward spiral her lust had wrought. 'I have to feel that again,' she insisted. 'I have to feel that *and more*.'

He studied her quizzically then placed his hand into hers.

At first she thought he was trying to make a simple, and somehow inappropriate, gesture of affection. It was only when he began to pull the rosary beads from her grasp that she realised he might have something else on his mind. 'You want to feel that pleasure *and more*?' he mused.

Dora nodded eagerly.

Taking the rosary beads from her hand he pushed his fingers to where their bodies met. She could feel the slick wetness that coated her cleft and was struck by conflicting whispers of pride and disgust when she realised she was mainly responsible for that sticky warmth. Meeting his gaze defiantly, not allowing embarrassment or humiliation to spoil the moment, she kept her eyes fixed on his. She even managed to remain calm when he pressed the first of the rosary beads against her anus.

'What are you –?' she began.

He placed a finger on her lips, silencing her with a brisk shake of his head. Slyly, he pushed another bead into her backside.

She had already accepted that the need in her cleft was wrong but, in her quest to achieve satisfaction, she was willing to tolerate that immorality. Yet the unbidden desire to feel more inside her anus was almost too much to accept or understand. She thought of resisting him, fighting and running away, but she knew a refusal now would leave her with the burning lust still smouldering and not completely satisfied. Steeling herself for more humiliation, watching his smile grow more forbidding, she lay beneath the altar as he inserted bead after bead inside her most forbidden hole.

Occasionally he broke from the chore, lowering his mouth to suck on the taut nub of a breast, but for the most part he continued pushing the beads of her rosary inside her rear. When he heard her mumbling a paternoster, he lovingly caressed her cheek and recited the prayer with her.

'What are you doing to me?' she gasped. The question was thick with dull need.

'I'm doing as you asked,' he replied. 'You told me you wanted to feel the pleasure again.'

'But –'

He silenced her with an agile thrust of his shaft. She hadn't realised the length was close to spilling from the lips of her sex but, when he pushed his hips forward and filled her with his hardness, she couldn't speak for fear of screaming ecstatically.

'You wanted to feel all that pleasure and more,' he grunted. He began to ride in and out as he spoke. 'I think we can manage that.'

She clasped a hand over her mouth, sure she would shriek if she didn't find some way to silence herself. She allowed him to continue, caught on a cresting wave of pure indulgence. As the now familiar swell of joy began to rise between her legs Dora was only half surprised to feel his hand return to the mounds of her backside. His fingers slipped between the crease of her buttocks and she knew he was reaching for the few beads of the rosary that still protruded from her anus.

With a blinding flash of inspiration she could suddenly guess what he was going to do and the idea horrified her. She started to say no, determined to tell him that it would prove more than she could accept. Before she could manage the first word the orgasm was on her. The pounding of his length had brought her to the point of no return and she knew this climax was going to easily overshadow the last one.

He slowly wrenched the rosary from her anus as she released her first cry of gratitude. She didn't know how many beads had sat inside the cloying warmth of her backside but the passing of each one spiked a new pinnacle. His shaft continued to plough in and out of her sex, fulfilling her longing and satisfying her desires. But it was the slow, base removal of the rosary that truly met her needs. By the time he was pumping his hot warmth inside her, Dora was beyond feeling anything except an endless crescendo of delight. She whimpered, not sure if the cries came from misery or elation. And, staring up at the crucifix through a haze of glorious euphoria, she began to think that, in some way, she had finally atoned for her sin of lust.

They lay with each other for a while after her climax but Sister Pandora knew it had been that orgasmic moment that had finally quenched the greedy need that broiled between her legs. They exchanged brief pleasantries, and she smiled perfunctorily at his jokes, but she knew her moment of personal crisis had been vanquished and that was the overriding thought that crashed through every other. After he had gone she couldn't recollect if he had given his name and found herself unable to remember anything about him save for his darkly handsome good looks. The only thing she recalled with any clarity was the answer he had given when she asked what he was doing in the town.

'I have business here,' he had said solemnly.

'Business?' The answer stripped him of his air of mystery and made him seem frustratingly mortal. She struggled to hide her disappointment and asked, 'What sort of business?'

His smile was Machiavellian. 'My business is Sinners.*'*

2

Idle Hands

The letter box rattled whenever it was bad news. Stacey could never tell why the sound should be any different – an envelope was an envelope and good news and bad news alike should both have fallen quietly to the coarse coir of the welcome mat – but, for some reason she couldn't fathom, good news slipped in silently and the bad news always rattled.

She listened to the distinctive sound from the luxury of her bath. Knowing it was bad news didn't make her hurry and she sipped her iced tea, took another draw from the hand-rolled cigarette, and continued to bask in the fading warmth of the soapy water. She supposed it was a shame there was nothing stronger than iced tea in her glass, and that the hand-rolled cigarette only contained tobacco, because she felt in a mood for celebrating the change she had instigated in her life. Admittedly, it was a little early in the day for such bold celebrations but the changes were monumental. Gone were the old days of Stacey-the-shiftless. Gone were the days of Stacey-who-couldn't-hold-down-a-job-for-longer-than-two-days. Gone were the days of Stacey-the-lazy-goat. Vowing to put her slothful ways behind her, Stacey was determined that this would be the first day of the rest of her life.

In an ideal world, she supposed the first day of the rest of her life should have happened a fortnight earlier. It would have been embarrassing enough going to her first day in a new job late. But because she would be starting her current job two weeks and three or four hours later than had been agreed at the interview, she expected the atmosphere to be a little uncomfortable.

Not that she let that consideration spoil the luxury of her bath.

She finished the cigarette and thought about shaving her legs. Deciding she could last another couple of days without having to find a fresh razor she briefly contemplated masturbating, realised it might involve more effort than she was willing to invest, and finished the remainder of her iced tea. Another roll-up would have been nice but, knowing wet hands and cigarette papers seldom produced the best results, she elected to choose the health-conscious option.

'The first day of the rest of your life,' she said cheerfully. There was genuine determination in her tone as she added, 'No more idling. No more wasting time and no more frittering life away. From now on it's action and progress all the way.'

She turned the hot tap with her toes and replenished the cooling water with a scalding stream. As far as first days went she thought this one was off to a comparatively good beginning. She would have been happy to relax in the bath a little while longer and it was only the incessant hammering at the front door that roused her. Grumbling unhappily she wrapped a towelling robe around herself, knowing what to expect.

Like the familiar sound of bad news falling through the letter box, the landlord's impatient knock was another unmistakable warning of what she would find when she reached the front door. Stacey brushed wet hair back from her face, collected the post from the mat, then opened the door on Charlie.

He was a repulsive creature, his beer belly exposed by an open Hawaiian shirt and hanging in an unsightly bulge over a pair of baggy shorts. His jaw was unshaven, his smile lacked a full complement of teeth, and his eyes were hidden by aviator sunglasses and the shade of his baseball cap's brim. With her sinuses freshly cleansed by steam from the bath, Stacey could smell the rancid stench of stale sweat emanating from him in waves.

'Rent,' Charlie said gruffly.

Stacey exercised a diplomatic smile, trying hard to feign innocence. 'Is the rent due today?'

'No,' he grunted. 'It was due a month ago.' Uninvited he stepped into her hall and closed the door behind himself. 'I'm here to collect two lots.'

Her plastic smile weakened as she realised it wouldn't be easy to get rid of him this time. Frantically trying to find inspiration, Stacey leafed through the letters that had arrived. Hoping one of them would give her some way of placating Charlie's demands she fumbled past the reminder letters and bills and happily caught hold of a slim, white envelope. The franking label carried the logo of her new employer and she prayed it would be confirmation that her wages had already been paid into her account.

Tearing it open, reading only the first line, she discovered the company had decided to withdraw their offer of employment because she hadn't made any attempt to start on the agreed date. Her hopes for a reprieve began to fade and Charlie's vile smile edged wider.

'We don't need to go through with the usual charade,' he told her. He reached out with one dirty finger and stroked her neck. His touch was as revolting as the caress of a slug and it took all her willpower not to recoil from him. She half expected his fingertip to leave a noxious silver trail in its wake and found herself looking for that mark as his hand slipped down her chest. All she could see was her own bare flesh and his filthy fingers inching precariously close to her breast. Licking his lips, and making no attempt to conceal his actions when he adjusted himself through his shorts, Charlie said, 'We know each other well enough to dispense with the formalities of the game.'

Stacey shook her head. She was struggling not to appear intimidated and wondered if she dared to physically push his hand away. 'It's not a charade,' she insisted. 'And I don't know why you're saying it is.'

'Yes it is a charade,' he argued. 'And it's been the same charade every month for the past year. I come here demanding my rent; you pretend you've not quite got the money; and then we come to an agreeable compromise. Why don't you just pay me my rent the way you usually pay it?'

She wrinkled her nose but, knowing there was no other recourse, Stacey saw she would have to do as he demanded. Hiding her distaste, smiling warmly for him, she reached for the swollen front of his shorts and caressed the stiffness underneath. He was already hard, the thick length inside his pants straining to get closer to her. She could feel the burning warmth of his greedy desire but, without hurrying, she unfastened his zip and snaked her hand inside.

'A quick one off the wrist?' she asked, trying to sound businesslike. 'Will that settle my debt?' As she spoke her hand was encircling him and stroking back and forth. His pulse in her palm beat with frantic need and she expected she could finish him off without taking his erection out of the pants. She had done that before, leaving him to retreat with his spend spreading a wet stain inside his shorts.

'Not this time,' Charlie said thickly. His fingers caught her wrist and he added, 'There's two months' money owing. I think you should give me a fuck.'

She glared at him, upset and offended. Charlie had such a coarse way about him he seldom managed two sentences without making her realise he was bereft of sophistication. She despised the circumstances that had allowed their paths to cross and positively loathed these seedy, monthly encounters. Knowing better than to berate him for his crass language, Stacey resorted to using the same direct vocabulary that Charlie favoured. 'No way,' she told him. 'I'm not giving you a fuck.'

'Just your pussy,' he assured her. He laughed softly as though the idea of a misunderstanding had caused amusement. 'I'm not asking you to take it up the arse.'

She wanted to recoil from him but didn't think that would help to continue her tenancy. She tightened her grip on his erection and said, 'You're not putting this in my pussy. And it's definitely not going up my arse. I'm not giving you a fuck.' The crudeness sounded unnatural coming from her mouth but previous encounters with Charlie had taught her it was the only language he understood. She released her hold on him and tried to pull her hand away but he was strong and kept her fingers against his obscenely warm shaft. 'Not under any circumstances,' she said firmly. 'It's never going to happen.'

He nodded as though the matter was of little consequence. 'Then you can suck me off,' he said generously. 'I'll let you do that.'

She fixed him with a look of darkest loathing, wanting to tell him that wasn't going to happen either. Worried that too many outright rebuffs might make him more determined than ever, scared to push him for fear of the consequences, she stretched a false smile across her lips and said, 'You can play with my tits, if you like. But that's as much as I'm going to offer. If you want anything more then you'll just have to wait until I can pay you in cash.'

'You drive a hard bargain.' Charlie laughed.

He reached for the front of her bathrobe and pulled it open. Stacey steeled herself against a rush of embarrassment and thanked the good fortune that had made her pull on a pair of panties before answering the door. It was bad enough she was exposing her breasts for Charlie's pleasure. The idea that he might have seen her completely naked was enough to churn her stomach muscles.

'If you weren't so good at wrist jobs I'd have thrown you out months ago.'

She said nothing, working her hand up and down his hardness and suffering the indignity of having him maul her bare breasts. This was one of the reasons she kept trying to improve her lot. The search for a better job, and the hollow promises to put her laziness behind her, were all attempts to escape the obnoxious landlord and his salacious demands. Grudgingly she was prepared to concede that he wasn't the most repulsive man she had ever met – and if his splendid, thick cock had belonged to anyone else she would have been more than happy to play with it – but he was coarse and repulsive and there was something inherently unattractive about having to pay her rent with sexual favours.

'Good titties,' he grunted, squeezing one nipple between his finger and thumb. Bending awkwardly, he lowered his mouth to the other breast and suckled hungrily. His tongue was a warm, lithe muscle against the bead of flesh and her sensitive skin responded to him with a reluctant thrill. 'Very good titties.'

She could sense the honesty of his approval from the way his hardness twitched. Releasing him from his pants, exposing the bulbous dome while her hand continued to work back and forth, she shivered with unwanted pleasure. His excitement was infectious and, although she didn't really want to admit as much, he was close to teasing her breasts with the degree of roughness she craved. A little more pressure, and maybe the gentle weight of his teeth, and she knew she would be tempted to submit. Unable to stop herself, she sighed.

'Are you sure you don't want to fuck me?' Charlie whispered.

She couldn't bring herself to answer honestly. 'I've told you I'm not doing that.'

'Then, how about I finger your pussy for a little while?'

She didn't have the chance to say no before his hand was cupping her cleft. His stubby, grubby fingers wriggled against the gusset and she was shocked by the rush of wetness he invoked. It was disturbing to find herself so repulsed and attracted by the same person and she knew she would have to act quickly before giving in to the temptation he was arousing. Dropping to her knees, deliberately pulling her sex from his hand, she knelt in front of him and smiled up.

His eyes were unreadable behind the aviator shades but his gap-toothed grin was repugnant. A wedge of yellowing plaque sat between two of his teeth and his smile seemed designed to expose this unattractive feature. 'You've decided to gobble me?'

She sniffed her dismissal of the suggestion, amazed he could think she would willingly do such a thing. 'Not today,' she said diplomatically. Urging him closer, pulling him by his length, she trapped Charlie's shaft between her breasts and squeezed the mounds of flesh around him. He didn't look best pleased that she wasn't going to use her mouth but she could see he wasn't going to complain. Stacey also thought there was some benefit to pleasing him this way because she didn't have to suffer his hands or his unwashed mouth on her breasts. She was also able to touch her own nipples the way they needed to be handled. Each time she pressed forward, and allowed him to slide up through her cleavage, she tugged on the stiff buds. The sensation surprised her with its intensity and she quickly warmed to the chore of pleasing her odious landlord.

The hairs of his scrotum tickled her chest, and she was uncomfortable with his glans pointing so close to her face each time he pushed into her, but she couldn't deny a growing excitement. If he had deigned to take a bath at some point in his life, and if his way hadn't been so boorish and uncouth, she supposed he could have made a good lover. He was well-built and she idly wondered what it would be like to have such a thickness pounding inside her. The idea excited a fresh surge of warmth between her legs and she clutched her thighs together for fear he might see how she was responding.

She glanced up to make sure her flush had gone unnoticed and was surprised to see his features contorted in a climactic groan. A splash of warm semen doused her neck and jaw, followed by a second spray that hit her eyes, nose and mouth. His shaft continued to pulse between her breasts but she was happy to release her hold on him now that he was spent.

Charlie reached down to grab a fistful of her hair. Pushing her face close to his waning length he said, 'Now suck me hard. Suck me hard so I can fuck that tight little pussy of yours.'

A pearl of grey-white semen grew from the eye of his shaft and she watched it, wondering if she should do as he demanded. The idea was darkly tempting, and might have satisfied the urge he had awoken, but Stacey resisted the impulse. 'No!' She pulled herself from his grip and glared up at him. She could picture her own face, with tears of his semen daubing her cheeks, and didn't know if he would find the sight pitiable or exciting. 'No,' she said with more conviction. 'That's your rent paid for this month. You're not getting anything else out of me.'

'I said I was here to collect two lots of rent,' Charlie reminded her.

Stacey remained defiant. She wanted to wipe the trickle of his come from her mouth because the noxious taste flavoured every breath. Forcing herself not to give in to that urge, sensing it would somehow weaken her resolve, she said, 'I'm not doing anything else for you today. What I've just done covers both lots of the rent that were owing.'

He looked set to argue then seemed to think better of it. Reaching down to hold one of her breasts, squeezing the orb with menacing force, he said, 'Go on then. I'll agree to that. But I should warn you now, your rent goes up as of next month.'

She met his gaze without revealing her inner turmoil. 'I'll have the money for you next month,' Stacey said coldly.

'You better had,' he agreed. 'Because next month, I won't accept a wrist job or a titty-wank as payment. Next month I'll want my money or something much more satisfying.' Dropping a lewd wink, casting his gaze meaningfully in the direction of her cleft, he gave her orb a final squeeze before marching through the door.

Returning to her bath, Stacey decided the time for procrastination was now definitely over. If she wanted to avoid having to completely surrender herself to Charlie, she could see she was going to have to find lucrative employment soon. There could be no more hesitation and she would need to get herself a job immediately. With that decision made, she reached for the tap with her toes, and added a fresh stream of hot water to the cooling tub.

One week later the letter box rattled the announcement of further bad news. As soon as she had finished her morning soak, Stacey collected the post and opened the offending letter. She could see it was from Charlie, and confirmed his intention to increase her rent.

'Damn,' she cursed quietly.

The previous seven days had given her a chance to cool from the idea of rushing into a new job and she had quietly hoped Charlie might simply forget his parting threat. Glumly realising that wasn't going to happen, she decided it would be prudent to seek gainful employment.

Throughout the week she had been half-heartedly looking into various careers. Sister Pandora at Holy Cross Church had proved easy enough to talk to but her advice on becoming a nun cured Stacey of all interest in that vocation. After listening to a description of the daily routine Stacey was happy to admit that she had no true calling. The time spent praying didn't sound like it would be too demanding, and she supposed she could help out with some of the corporal work, if the Abbess deemed it necessary, but getting up at five thirty in the morning was something Stacey knew she couldn't manage.

She had also glanced into some of the shops on the high street, on the off chance that one of the boutiques might be displaying a 'Help Wanted, Apply Within,' card. But, in spite of her numerous visits to the town centre, she had been disappointed to find that none of her favourite fashion outlets were currently recruiting. The only place that did seem to have a vacancy was a new nightclub she hadn't seen before.

The name above the facade read 'Sinners' in garish neon, and Stacey thought it would be a place she might visit the next time she had the admission fee spare. She enjoyed the hubbub of a good nightclub and was all in favour of drinking, dancing and flirting whenever finances allowed.

As she stood admiring the frontage a skinny blonde pushed past her and knocked loudly for admission. A shadowed figure opened the door and allowed her to squeeze past him. Stacey got the impression he was about to close the door when he stepped out into the light and fixed her with a curious smile. 'Are you interested in the vacancy?'

She didn't hear the words properly, mesmerised by the musical lilt of his voice. His dark eyes were so large she was lost in their hypnotic power and, coupled with the Machiavellian charm of his beard and moustache, Stacey couldn't do anything except smile weakly. It took her a full minute to gain control of her faculties and she only realised she hadn't replied when he repeated the question.

'Are you telling me you've got a job vacancy?' she asked.

He hesitated. 'There's a position here and I'm interviewing candidates. Yes.'

She stepped closer and then suddenly had second thoughts. He was attractive, but in a sinister way, and while the thought of working in a nightclub appealed to her she was struck by the idea that it would be a mistake to put herself in the employment of this man. She didn't know where the reservations came from, but she trusted her instincts enough to feel sure they must be right.

'You are looking for work, aren't you?'

A bus roared behind her. The sound was loud, sudden and unexpected and Stacey knew ordinarily she would have flinched away from it. On this occasion she stood unmoved, entranced by his questioning smile. Watching him fired a low, familiar warmth in the pit of her stomach and snakes of arousal began to slither down and through her loins. Inside her bra she could feel the discomfort of her nipples swelling against the restrictive cotton. 'I might be looking for a job,' she agreed warily.

He nodded. 'I'll be holding interviews here throughout the week. But I think I'm just killing time.' Gracing her with a cursory glance, smiling approval, he said, 'Feel free to call in if you think you'd like working here. The job's yours if you want it.'

The memory of his smile still made her shiver and she wondered how he had been able to make such a lasting impression after such a fleeting exchange. Purposefully not thinking about him, determined she wasn't going to put herself into the employment of someone so fundamentally creepy, she wearily started the rounds of job hunting.

Stacey had always thought people made too much of an issue about the difficulty of finding jobs. She knew it was comparatively easy because, in the few short years since leaving school, she had found hundreds.

Being successful in interviews was another skill she had mastered and Stacey felt able to sum up that knack with one phrase: do whatever it takes.

It was a further week before she had secured her first interview but she felt confident of success. She selected a short skirt, a modest top that could be opened to reveal an eye-catching glimpse of cleavage, and a pair of heels that emphasised the shapeliness of her bare legs. Collecting a string of approving wolf-whistles on her way to the interview, she felt sure the job was hers even before she had sat down in the small back office.

The owner of the auction house introduced himself as Robert and explained he was one of the two partners she would be working under. He was comparatively young, bookishly handsome, and his gaze was riveted on her cleavage.

Stacey smiled inwardly.

The walls were cluttered with year planners, memos, notes and photographs but Stacey didn't bother looking at them. She kept her gaze fixed on Robert, hanging on his every word as though it was scripture. At the back of her mind there was an annoying and unidentifiable doubt but she put that down to the characteristic reservations that always plagued her at the start of job interviews. She stretched her legs out, crossing the ankles, but making sure he could see how much thigh she was showing. Casually she placed her fingertips against her chest and fluttered her hand as though fanning herself. The room wasn't particularly warm but the gesture helped draw his attention back to her breasts.

Robert coughed and crossed his legs. 'Do you know anything about the vacancy we have here?'

'Your advert said you wanted someone who could manage general filing and secretarial work,' she breathed. With a knowing smile she winked and added, 'I might be able to manage a little more than that, if it was required.'

His cheeks flushed and when he met her gaze she could see he was smiling excitedly. 'Have you worked with computers before?'

The question made her grin with fond recollections. There had been one month where she worked on an office PC and those two days had sped past in a blur of computer card games and cheeky conversations on the internal mail network. She even remembered, if the keyboard was left untouched for a quarter of an hour, an hilarious screen saver appeared. Stacey had spent several enjoyable hours watching that, and remembering the experience made her feel like something of an expert on the subject of information technology. 'I know how to handle computers,' she assured him. Allowing her eye contact to linger fractionally too long, she added, 'I know how to handle lots of different things.'

He had been consulting a pile of notes but he placed these on the desk and pushed them to one side. Stacey had seen this happen before and knew what was coming. Her heart skipped a beat as the tension in the room turned electric. He didn't need to say another word for her to realise they were both of a same mind.

'How badly do you want this job?' Robert asked.

'Desperately,' she replied. Nodding seriously she added, 'I don't think you could believe how desperate I am.'

His gaze flickered from her legs, to her cleavage, then back to the invitation of her smile. 'What are you prepared to do to secure the job?'

She raised a surprised eyebrow, enjoying the thrill of teasing him, but not daring to play the game too boldly. Winning employment in this way was a delicate balance and past experience had taught her that the terms needed to be laid out before she gave in to any of the interviewer's demands. But that caution didn't mean she had to deny herself the pleasure of a little teasing. 'Whatever do you mean?' she asked coquettishly. 'Are you proposing some sort of arrangement?'

'Karina, the last interviewee, had excellent references, a lot of enthusiasm and potential aptitude for the job that's on offer. All you seem to have is an engaging smile and a line of banter that's quite arousing. Are you just leading me on? Or are you prepared to do more than just prick tease?'

She eased herself from her chair and moved to his side. Running her hands over his shirt, sliding them beneath his tie and then moving them down toward his groin, she placed her mouth next to his ear. 'I need a job badly, Robert,' she whispered. 'And I'm prepared to do whatever is necessary to make this interview a success.' Her fingers reached the waistband of his trousers and she slipped them inside.

He stopped her from delving deeper, one hand gripping her wrist, and she was briefly reminded of Charlie. The memory of her landlord's gap-toothed smile was enough to renew her focus on why she wanted this position so badly. It was so clear she could almost see Charlie's ignoble features imprinted on Robert's bookishly handsome face.

'You might find I'm quite a demanding employer,' Robert warned. 'I'm not unreasonable, but I've had staff complain that I ride them too hard.'

She grinned into his attempt at being stern, sure it didn't really fit his personality. 'I can be pretty demanding myself,' she said lightly. Forcing her hand down, breaking his hold on her wrist, she unfastened his trousers and released his erection. The length stood proud, the foreskin already peeling back from the glans. 'But no one's ever complained that I've ridden them *too* hard.' She smiled.

'What do you think you can do in this office?'

'I can do lots of things,' she said, stepping in front of him. She kept her back to him, glancing over her shoulder so as not to forfeit their eye contact. Slowly, inching the hem of her short skirt higher in tantalising snatches, she revealed the back panel of her panties. Reaching between her legs with her free hand, she stroked the gusset and was rewarded by a flicker of heated anticipation. After pulling the crotch to one side she lowered herself over him. The head of his erection tugged toward her but she held the shaft and simply rested it on the centre of her sex. It was a tantalising moment and Stacey felt sure Robert shared her eager need for penetration. 'I don't know if you've read my CV but it does say I can adapt myself to suit most positions,' she breathed. 'Is that what you're looking for here?'

'I think that's exactly what I'm looking for,' he agreed.

Sure the job was hers, Stacey sat on his lap and slid herself onto him.

His thickness filled her, pushing all the way to the neck of her womb as she wriggled to get him deeper. His hands had been clutching the arms of his chair but he released his hold so he could reach around her and grab her breasts.

She moaned.

Part of the sigh was born from a need to make him think he was pleasing her but a lot of it came from a genuine, growing excitement. Seducing an interviewer was always arousing and, each time she had done it in the past, Stacey had succumbed to the dark thrill of knowing she was doing something truly sinful. She shivered, enjoying the simple sensation of having his shaft fill her aching need, then began to ride her pussy up and down. The muscles slurped hungrily around his thickness and the echoes of that sound added to her excitement.

His fingers tugged her blouse open, exposing her bra, then working to ease her orbs from the cups. It was a half-hearted attempt to release the breasts and, as soon as her nipples were free, he ignored the rest of the flesh and teased the tips between his fingers and thumbs.

She would have been happy to sit on him for the remainder of the interview, delighting in the simple pleasure of each pulse that trembled through his length. Coupled with the blissful torment at her breasts, and the naughty thought that she was cheating better applicants of their rightful position, Stacey knew she could have eventually achieved a drawn out, satisfying climax.

But Robert hadn't been lying when he described himself as demanding.

Levering himself out of the chair, taking Stacey with him, he pushed her over the desk. His length buried deep inside and she shrieked happily as fresh torrents of pleasure were wrung from her hole. Gasping breathlessly, she lay against the cluttered surface as he thrust into her with swift, powerful lunges. The swell of an orgasm built quickly and she encouraged him with heartfelt demands for more.

Continuing at his own pace, Robert held her hips and hammered himself into her again and again. His bulbous end spread her wide, pushing inside so deeply she could feel his sac bouncing lightly against her pussy lips. When he eventually pulled himself out, leaving her frustrated and bewildered, she turned to him with an expression of hurt disappointment.

His smile was appeasing. Reaching down for one leg, he turned her over so her back was on the untidy desk. Pens, pencils and ledgers barbed her spine and shoulder blades but it was easy to ignore those niggling distractions. The burning need at her cleft pulsed with an overriding urgency and she knew she could have stood all manner of discomfort in her quest for satisfaction.

Robert parted her thighs and stood between her open knees. Easily, he slipped his shaft back inside her sex and began to ride with renewed vigour. The head of his glans was scoring delicious friction against her inner muscles and Stacey opened her eyes wide with surprise and elation. She regarded him with fresh respect as each thrust buffeted her toward a pinnacle of pleasure.

Her climax came in a tumultuous rush.

Unable to contain the impulse any longer she gave in to the quickening thrill. Her pussy clenched spasmodically as she wallowed in the blissful joy of release. She didn't doubt it was the electric contractions of her sex that forced him to squirt his seed into her and she was treated to a second wave of pleasure that came from sharing his orgasm.

He chuckled softly as he pulled his spent shaft from her wetness. With casual style, he graced one bare breast with a kiss. 'Congratulations,' he murmured. 'The job's yours if you want it.' Returning his flailing length to his trousers he grinned slyly and added, 'Although you'd best not let my brother know about your talents. He'd probably try to take advantage.'

'Your brother?' She remembered the doubts that had been niggling at the back of her mind since the start of the interview. They had been briefly forgotten during the pleasure of seducing Robert but now those reservations came rushing back with renewed force.

'You have a brother?' she asked, not knowing why the news unnerved her.

'My brother is my business partner,' Robert explained. He pointed to a picture on the back wall and Stacey was sickened by a wave of recognition. 'You might have seen him around town,' Robert continued. 'Charlie's well known locally. He even owns a couple of properties around the area where you live. Maybe you've met him?'

Not knowing what else to say, Stacey told Robert she would consider his offer and get back to him. He seemed nonplussed by her sudden lack of interest but she was beyond caring about pandering to his ego. She simply couldn't work under Charlie and she knew she couldn't. It was one thing to give the occasional wrist job in exchange for the rent, and she didn't think there was anything wrong with using whatever talents she had available to secure employment at an interview. But the idea of putting herself in a job where Charlie's demands had so much control was a sure recipe for misery. Collecting her things, knowing she couldn't work under Charlie without enduring his salacious interest every day of the working week, Stacey thanked Robert and rushed out of the auction house.

The pink light of the Sinners sign blazed out of the darkness. Its magenta hue reflected in the glossy black paving slabs and Stacey wondered why she had chosen that route instead of walking directly home. Deciding her motives were immaterial, and that her situation needed some resolution before the rent was next due, she walked wearily up the steps and knocked on the door. She didn't want to see the sinister owner again and was almost thankful when a vaguely familiar face appeared at the open door.

'Can I help you?'

Stacey remembered the skinny blonde from the day she had first discovered the nightclub. Nodding, she said, 'I was offered a job here. Last week, some guy with a spikey beard, I didn't catch his name . . .'

'I know who you mean.' The skinny blonde grinned. 'It's no wonder you didn't catch his name. He seldom gives it.' She extended a hand and introduced herself as Fiona. Feeling the pressure of the slight woman's fingers around hers, surprised by the formality of the gesture and the way Fiona seemed to imbue the contact with something more meaningful, Stacey remembered the doubts she had suffered when she first encountered the nightclub and its owner. Taking solace from the fact that he wasn't there, and assuring herself that her worries had been groundless, Stacey allowed Fiona to escort her through to the kiosk.

'The boss told me to look out for you,' Fiona said conversationally. 'He said you'd be back, and he said that you'd want the job.'

Stacey shrugged. 'He obviously knows me better than I know myself. I didn't think I'd be back. What job was he offering?'

'He wants you to work here, in the kiosk.' She spread her arm out to indicate the small room with its glass window, open counter and high stool. 'You'll only be needed for four hours a night, five days a week, but the pay is very good.'

Stacey remained unimpressed. 'Is it hard work?'

'If you can sit down and smile, you're overqualified.'

They laughed together and Stacey felt strangely at ease with the woman. 'Why did your boss want me to have this job?'

Fiona shrugged. 'I couldn't say,' she replied.

Sensing some hesitancy in her voice, Stacey realised the answer wasn't the same as Fiona saying she didn't know. Pressing the point, deciding she had nothing to lose if she made her mistrust known, she asked, 'Do you think he might have designs on me?'

'I'm sure he has designs on all of us.' The blonde grinned. 'But I wouldn't let that sway your decision. It hasn't made me think twice. Why don't you give it a whirl and see if you like what's being offered?'

Shrugging her shoulders out of her jacket, deciding it couldn't hurt to consider the position, Stacey made herself comfortable in the chair. 'I'm just expected to sit here and deal with customers as they come through?'

'If the customers want to be dealt with, yes.'

Stacey felt stupid asking so many suspicious questions but the job sounded too much like a dream come true. There was a bar nearby, a nightclub where she could spend her breaks, and all she was expected to do was sit down. The idea that such luxury came with a decent wage packet only made it more difficult to accept and she felt certain there had to be a catch.

'What do you do?'

Fiona smiled slyly and dropped to her knees. 'My job is to fill in on the nights you can't make it,' she explained. 'On those nights when you do come in, the boss has told me to sit under your chair.' Before Stacey could stop her, the blonde was crawling into the small space under the counter. There was barely enough room for a person and, even though Fiona was slender and petite, her arms brushed against Stacey's thighs as she made herself comfortable.

'You just sit there?' Stacey asked doubtfully.

Fiona grinned up and shook her head. 'The boss said there would always be something for me to do while I'm down here.' She winked with obvious meaning and said, 'I guess he was right.'

46

A dagger of dark excitement pushed into Stacey's stomach. She caught her breath, momentarily too shocked to think how to respond. She was so used to being in control of every sexual situation and the woman's forceful submission came as something of a surprise.

'You're not meant to –'

She didn't get to complete the sentence. The blonde had pushed her face forward, easing her forehead under Stacey's short skirt, and the sudden intimacy was overwhelming. Stacey stiffened in the chair, not sure she wanted another woman to do this for her, but unable to resist the warmth of breath against her inner thighs or the caress of a feminine fringe brushing the tops of her legs.

The heat of a warm, wet tongue explored her sex.

She hadn't felt her panties being moved to one side but she knew Fiona was lapping at exposed flesh. The sensation of being licked and tasted was exquisite and, although she couldn't understand why it should be different, the attention of another woman seemed somehow superior to the intimate kisses she had enjoyed from men.

Revelling in the pleasure, Stacey gripped the kiosk's counter and squirmed in her seat.

Fiona's tongue traced the outline of her lips, exciting the labia until the flesh felt ready to melt. Stacey shifted repeatedly in her chair, longing for the pleasure to continue but not sure she could tolerate much more. Her interview with Robert had been satisfying, if ultimately frustrating, but this was something else. Eddies of raw excitement were spiralling up from between her legs, each more forceful than the last, and every one urging her to a sweet, blissful release.

'You're telling me this would be my job?' Stacey grunted. She was trying hard to sound unaffected by arousal and knew her attempts had failed. Her words were carried on a guttural rasp and the tension of every straining muscle could be heard underscoring each sibilant. 'I'd just be expected to sit in this chair, have you lick my pussy, and I'd get paid for the privilege?'

Fiona chuckled darkly and the echoes of her mirth trailed sensuously through Stacey's loins. 'I believe that's what the boss is offering.'

'I must be missing something,' Stacey sighed. It was difficult to keep her thoughts focused on the conversation as fresh shards of pleasure repeatedly erupted from her sex. Fiona had slipped her tongue against the sensitive bead of Stacey's clitoris and explosions of unexpected delight kept intruding on her thoughts. 'What's the catch?'

Fiona said something that was muffled against Stacey's pussy. She moved her face to repeat herself and used the tips of her fingers to tease Stacey's labia while her mouth was away. 'The clientele will know what's happening,' she said. 'No one will be able to see.' She hit the hardwood base of the kiosk beneath the window by way of explanation. 'But, there'll be rumours that Sinners has a kiosk attendant who's having her pussy licked while she serves the customers.'

The information didn't spoil Stacey's appetite for the job. She wouldn't be publicly displaying herself, rumours could always be dismissed as such if it suited her cause, and she thought the role would even afford her the status of a local celebrity. Spurred on by the idea of submitting to this pleasure every night of the working week, she reached down and guided Fiona's head back to her sex.

The blonde attacked her with renewed fervour, eagerly devouring the wet lips, drawing her tongue lovingly against the succulent flesh and greedily plundering. Stacey clenched her teeth in a struggle to resist the pleasure, then decided she didn't want to fight the sensations. Happily giving in to the joy, allowing the rush of euphoria to flow through her, she arched her back into the chair and screamed triumphantly.

After the interview with Robert, and then enjoying Fiona's expert tonguing, she thought her capacity for pleasure would have been spent but the comfort of the position only made her eager for more. She laughed greedily as Fiona continued and anticipated the soaring delight of a further climax.

Through the glass window she saw she was being watched.

The figure with the pointed beard and dark, inscrutable eyes, studied her with a determined expression. His gaze was unblinking and she thought it was like being watched by some repulsive reptile. When she blinked her eyes and shook her head he vanished as though he had never been there. Stacey wondered if she had really seen him, or simply imagined his appearance, but she never got the chance to ask or answer the question.

Fiona had a gift for cunnilingus and she used it with unfailing mastery. She alternated her kisses from the penetrating use of her tongue, to sweet, subtle caresses from her lips. Teasing the labia to a state of bristling need, fetching fresh desire from Stacey's clitoris, Fiona quickly took her to a final, breath-taking climax.

When the orgasm struck, Stacey howled. Her cry echoed around the empty foyer and rattled the glass of the kiosk's window. The joy was so strong that, when she finally came to her senses, Stacey realised she was weeping with pure pleasure. Humbly, she mumbled a thank you to the woman responsible for her satisfaction.

'Do you want the job?' Fiona asked.

Her smile glistened with sultry wetness and Stacey thought she had never seen a more arousing sight. She could have happily relaxed back in the chair and instructed Fiona to lick her again. Sensing that wouldn't be appropriate on this occasion, and realising an answer was expected from her, Stacey tried hard to feign indifference. 'You still haven't said how much the job pays.'

Fiona told her the figure and Stacey beamed. Not only was it the most satisfying, undemanding job she had ever encountered, it also assured her of easily meeting Charlie's increased rent. She thanked Fiona, kissed her a fond farewell, and told her she would start the following evening.

Using her toes to turn the tap, allowing the water to soak into her aching frame, Stacey smiled around the drink of iced tea. It was still hard to believe she had secured such a dream job and she wondered if the small change in her circumstances might precipitate larger benefits. Once the salary started to come in, and a couple of her existing loans were cleared, she guessed she would be able to afford better holidays each year. She thought driving lessons might be fun and possibly – no she decided, certainly – she would find somewhere else to live. The chance to escape from Charlie, and never have to suffer his ugly, leering smile, would be worth the cost of increased rent or maybe even the burden of a mortgage. The thought made her smile with genuine hope for a brighter future.

The rattle of the letter box cut through her thoughts. From the warmth of her bath she frowned, wondering who might be sending her bad news and why. Mentally calculating, she realised it had been a fortnight since her interview at Sinners and she had been expected to start work the following night. Knowing what to expect when she opened the letter, cursing the missed opportunity, she took bitter pleasure from her last draw on the cigarette and flicked it across the room and into the toilet bowl.

She couldn't understand why she had allowed such a dream opportunity to slip through her fingers and knew she had been job-hunting for a reason. When the familiar sound of a fist began to hammer against the door, Stacey remembered what that reason had been.

3

Glutton for Punishment

'Lucky Pig,' Wendy Carstairs mused dryly, staring at the scratch card.

The stiff oblong sheet showed a smiling pig beaming from under a blue sky with clouds shaped like currency. Using the edge of a coin she had scraped away the silver latex covering the first box to reveal three matching symbols: a trio of grinning pigs. Her fingers trembled, making the glossy sheen of the card shimmer beneath the kitchen fluorescent. The amount in the second box told her how much her prize was worth.

'Is that a winner?' Dan Carstairs asked, stepping behind her.

His hands fell to her shoulders and he planted a platonic kiss against the back of his wife's head. He didn't notice that she shrank from his touch, or that she wrapped her silk robe more tightly around her quivering frame. But then, he hadn't noticed that she was sitting stiffly, or that she was clutching the robe high against her throat to completely conceal her neck, chest and cleavage. He also seemed blissfully unaware that she was cataloguing excuses and explanations in preparation for his questions.

'Are you the lucky pig?' he asked. 'Or is that the name of the scratch card?'

Wendy started guiltily, wondering if he knew how she'd come by the card or any of the other sordid details she was struggling to hide. Trying to disguise her inner turmoil, she dared to meet Dan with a smile that felt false and transparent. 'I guess I was saying it for both those reasons,' she said quickly. She had been wafting the card, trying to feign indifference, but she was suddenly worried he might see how much her hands were trembling. Hurriedly she slammed it down against the kitchen table. 'I'm a lucky pig because I just won on a Lucky Pig scratch card. Lucky pig. Lucky pig. Lucky . . .' She allowed her voice to trail off, aware that she was close to an hysterical babble.

'How much?'

He sounded pleased but not overly interested. Because he was already walking to the fridge, she had no qualms about lying to him. The threat of discovery was briefly lifted and her panicked hysteria began to abate. Wendy thought there was a good chance her sins might go undetected, for the morning at least, and she supposed that gave her time to invent an excuse or make appropriate plans for whatever damage control was needed. Reading the figure from the box for him, she said, 'It's only twenty-five pounds, and I know that's not a lot, but . . .'

He glanced up sharply and she wondered if he knew what she was trying to conceal. Instead of damning her with an accusation, he said, 'There's no "only" where twenty-five pounds is concerned. When I left school, the first car I had didn't cost much more than twenty-five pounds. Twenty-five pounds is still a lot of money and, if . . .'

He said more but Wendy wasn't listening. When Dan was off on one of his miserly tirades it was easier to ignore him than try to feign interest in any of his oft repeated diatribes. And, while a part of her screeched fretfully that he might suspect something if she didn't hang on his every word, she knew she had much more important things to brood on than Dan's tiresome rhetoric. She could see where his monologue was going and regarded the well-worn catechisms with the contempt of familiarity.

'Why on earth do we need an Olympic-sized swimming pool, Wendy? Neither of us are that bothered about swimming and it costs a fortune to keep the damned thing heated.

'Why do you need a Mercedes and a Volvo, Wendy? How do you expect to drive two cars at the same time?

'Another pair of shoes, Wendy? What's happening to you? Are you growing more feet?'

Wendy knew all his usual complaints and their resultant monologues and years of practice in their marriage made it simple for her to mentally mute his ramblings from her thoughts. Her head still ached from the previous night but a hangover wasn't the predominant spirit that coloured her mood. She was struggling to maintain a facade of normalcy so Dan would scurry off to his precious office and she could go over exactly what had happened.

'. . . my first week's wage was only a little more than twenty-five pounds . . .'

She wanted to get some Aspirin for her headache but she knew Dan would notice the medicine and ask questions. It would be easy to tell him she felt a little delicate after a night out with Andrea but that would lead to more questions and she wasn't sure how best she wanted to answer. There were parts of the evening that she was still reluctant to remember and she certainly didn't want to go over them with her husband.

'. . . and did I ever tell you about the time I was at an auction and only spent twenty-five pounds on . . .'

'The radio says there are roadworks on the circular route,' she broke in. The radio had said no such thing but Wendy thought it was an inspired lie that might make him leave early. The only thing she had heard the morning DJ say was that the good weather had finally broken and it looked like the summer was over. Somehow that simple statement seemed to contain more truth than her convenient fabrication of the traffic report.

'Whereabouts on the circular route?' Dan frowned unhappily. He was ignoring his orange juice and reaching for his jacket without waiting for an answer. Tutting with exasperation he said, 'You know how busy the roads can get these days. Why didn't you mention these roadworks before, instead of keeping me here chitter-chattering?'

'Getting a word in edgewise was no mean feat on its own,' Wendy retaliated. She spat the words with vicious intent, making sure they struck a chord. 'I only mention them now because, by law, if I'm listening to an anecdote of your usual length, I'm entitled to a twenty minute break every four hours.' It didn't sound like her own voice – the anger and the vitriol sounded as though they came from her best friend, Andrea – but her bitter remarks had the desired effect. Dan closed his mouth, fixed her with an expression that would have better suited a kicked puppy rather than a middle-aged business executive, then started toward the kitchen door. He was mumbling something about PMT, hot flushes and the change, but Wendy wasn't in the mood to rise to such a petty line of arguments. She guessed Dan was still fuming when she heard him slam the door on his Lexus. Patiently, clutching her coffee as if her fingers were glued to the mug, she waited until he had over-revved the engine and sped off down the drive before she got out of her chair and took two Aspirin from the kitchen drawer. Swallowing them down with the last of her coffee she took a deep breath to steady her nerves, and then started up the stairs toward the bathroom.

Every step rekindled some discomfort and she flinched from each memory like she would have recoiled from slaps to her face. Her thighs were stiff from the exertion of unfamiliar use and it was a deep, muscular ache that reminded her of the days when she used to visit a gym. But she knew that pain was the least of her concerns. She stepped into the bathroom, locked the door, tested that it was secure, then she went to the shower cubicle and turned the water to its hottest setting. As soon as the spray had begun to steam up the air she walked gingerly to the mirrored wall beside the bath.

The elegantly tiled walls reflected the steam until it was condensing the mirror into the misty surface of a dream. Nervous tremors shook her reflection and, as she tried to unfasten the silk cord from her waist, she realised her hands were trembling more than ever. The nerves were easy to understand because she didn't know what surprises lurked under her robe. Snatches of the previous night kept recurring to her and each one was more disquieting than the last.

A stranger.

A cane.

Submission.

Surrender.

And more.

Much more.

The woman staring back at her from the mirror had her eyes shaded by haunted circles and Wendy was beginning to realise why. Steeling herself for the shock, knowing that she had to see what marks the night had left on her, she pulled the robe open. Every detail of the previous night came flooding back to her.

The music was so loud it didn't exist beyond an incessant, pounding baseline. Disco lights, lasers and smoke played through the darkened nightclub, illuminating dancers and creating a million disturbing images. Andrea was on the dance floor, her familiar red-clad figure gyrating hips with a blond stranger. She was skinny and young, her narrow features looking pretty when she wasn't sneering haughtily down her nose. Wendy, sitting alone with her slowly evaporating vodka, and the second one she had waiting to replace it, smiled with sad envy at her younger friend's joie de vivre. Andrea had been glum recently, hurt by the indifference of a local priest, but she now seemed to have moved on from that upset.

'You look like you need a little more.'

She glanced up, not sure if she was more startled at being approached, or simply surprised she had heard anything above the raucous roar around her. The man staring down at her wore a goatee beard and an interesting smile. The glint in his expressive brown eyes made Wendy feel unexpectedly desirable and, inwardly, she thanked him for that. His comment confused her and she glanced at the two waiting drinks on her table, not sure how he could think she needed anything else.

'I look like I need a little more what?' she asked.

He shrugged and sat down on the opposite side of the table.

She thought about telling him that Andrea was sitting there but, because her friend was still enjoying the dance floor, she didn't think there would be any point chasing this darkly handsome man away with such an explanation. She also thought about telling him she was happily married, or at least married and unwilling to rock the boat, then decided, for the moment, that was another unimportant detail. He watched her silently from the opposite side of the table and Wendy got the impression he could read the conflicting arguments that were fighting inside her mind. Not wanting the silence between them to stretch out for too long, she eventually asked, 'May I help you?'

He shrugged. 'Quite possibly. Yes. More importantly, perhaps I can help you?'

She laughed, trying to dismiss his earnest tone and the warmth it generated. She didn't think to wonder how he could make himself so effortlessly heard through the noise, or how he seemed able to understand her when she hadn't raised her voice to fight the music. They were inexplicable details but easy to ignore. The one detail she had trouble accepting was the stranger's obvious interest. 'How do you think you can help me?'

'Your life is currently bereft of passion, isn't it?'

'Not at all,' she said indignantly.

He laughed and shook his head. 'All right,' he agreed. 'It's not bereft of passion, but there's not enough for you, is there? You're here with your friend, just pretending to enjoy a drink or two, but you've been hoping you could find someone who can give you the satisfaction you crave.' To emphasise his words he reached beneath the table and placed a hand on her knee.

Wendy stiffened, momentarily lost for words. She glanced around the nightclub, wondering if anyone was watching them, or in a position to see. Fears of Dan suddenly looming from the shadows rushed senselessly to the forefront of her mind. When she realised no one had noticed them, she turned her gaze back to the mesmerising charm of the stranger's smile.

The hand against her leg was an unexpected intimacy and intruded on every thought. She wanted to tell him he had gauged her needs incorrectly, and laugh derisively at his presumptuous arrogance. But the idea that he was right, and that she did crave more passion and satisfaction, made it difficult to build an argument. The pressure of his fingers, the weight shifting ever so slightly against her stocking-clad flesh, was a constant distraction to every objection she quietly considered. The warmth of his touch, the intrusion of his fingers creeping ever so slightly higher, all added impetus to the idea that he might be correct.

'Perhaps I could tend to that craving?' he suggested. 'Perhaps I could offer you some satisfaction?'

She sipped at her vodka and cast a glance in Andrea's direction. Her friend was still in the throes of a dance and oblivious to Wendy. The muscular blond partner she had found was athletic and seemingly possessed by the same lust for life that had captured Andrea this evening. Watching them laugh and grin with one another, Wendy guessed she was only going to intrude on her friend's good time if she didn't accept the stranger's invitation. Coming to a sudden decision, smiling at her own sense of devilment, Wendy smiled across the table. She took a deep breath, savoured the sensation of his fingers stretching the fabric of her stocking, and said, 'OK.'

In the bathroom mirror the woman staring back at her looked like she had been through a battle. Her bared breasts, ripe, plump and swollen, still bore the haphazard lines of a caning. Blazing stripes were slashed across the tender orbs and a clutter of weals criss-crossed over her nipples. The buds were particularly sensitive to her touch but the reawakening of pain also brought with it memories of the dark and twisted pleasure. Her sides were lined by gouges: deep furrows where fingernails had scratched flesh. She remembered every one of those fading scars being inflicted and shivered with the unwanted warmth each recollection generated.

Turning to glance at her back, not sure she wanted to see what was there but knowing she had to look, Wendy bit back a moan. She didn't know if the cry came from disappoint, shock or shame, but she knew it was the same sound she had made repeatedly the previous evening.

Those details were coming back in an unstoppable flood.

He slid to her side of the booth and they embraced like long-lost lovers. One hand remained at her knee, creeping slowly upward, while the other tested the shape of her breast. The fabrics of her blouse and bra hindered the contact but it didn't make the frisson any less exciting. His touch was bold, firm and inquisitive and she could feel him exploring the hardening shape of her nipple. Their mouths met in a hungry exchange and Wendy revelled in the daring of what she was doing. It had been more than ten years since she had kissed someone other than Dan and, the knowledge she could still incite such passion, made her feel younger and more attractive than she had in years. Being wanted, she thought, was a better aphrodisiac than Viagra, and a more powerful beauty treatment than any of the cosmetic surgery procedures she had ever considered, investigated or undergone. She savoured the kneading he administered to her breast and fought a dual conflict of interests as she hoped the hand on her thigh would stay safely where it was and simultaneously willed it to slip higher.

'Your name,' she gasped. It was a crime to break the kiss but she knew she had to stop herself before things

went too far. Already her hands were tracing the breadth of his chest and her fingers longed to drop to his lap and caress the bulge that distended his trousers. 'What's your name?'

He shook his head. 'My name is as immaterial as yours. Call me whatever you will. It won't make any difference.'

She supposed anonymity was sensible, although she didn't think necking with a stranger in full view of a public dance floor was truly anonymous or sensible. Nevertheless, there were more important demands to be met and she concentrated on those rather than something as inconsequential as exchanging pleasantries and labels.

He moved his mouth from hers, kissing her cheek, neck and then her earlobe. His fingers were slipping higher up her leg, stroking her inner thigh and brushing from the denier of her stockings to the receptive skin of her bare thigh. Tingles of need, sparkling sensations of raw desire, began to shimmer from beneath his touch. Her sex felt fetid with longing and her entire body ached with the genuine desire for him to touch more intimately.

'I want you,' he said boldly.

She shivered: unsurprised by the revelation and in complete accord. Aware of the enormity of what she was saying, but knowing that it needed to be said, she told him, 'You can have me.' It was only after a moment's more kissing that she thought to ask, 'But where?'

His fingers reached the cleft between her legs. She had half-expected him to touch there but had been undecided whether she wanted it or if that might be too much to deal with from a stranger. As he brushed the edge of his fingernails against the crotch of her panties she knew he was caressing her exactly as she needed. Giving in to the unbidden pleasure, wallowing in an

61

attention she couldn't recall enjoying for the best part of a decade, Wendy melted in his embrace. Sobbing gratefully, she allowed him to stroke her labia through the thin film of the cotton gusset and relished every delicious nuance.

'Where can we go?' she demanded. 'And when?'

When he raised his mouth from her throat he was panting slightly. 'I have an office behind the kiosk in the foyer,' he breathed. 'We can go there.'

'When?'

'Now.'

As one, they stood up and left the forgotten noise of the dance floor.

The woman in the bathroom mirror traced a finger against the raised flesh that cut into her shoulder blades. The thin lines crossed her back, their frequency increasing as they reached her buttocks, and only beginning to disappear once they had passed the backs of her thighs. The marks on her rear were livid and simply looking at them was enough to make Wendy wince. When she dared to trace a finger against one burning welt, the shock of discomfort burnt like ingrained fire. More disquieting, when she bent forward, trying to see if there were any signs of injury between her cheeks, she could see some of the lines straightened, as though she was seeing them in the same way they had been drawn.

Her pussy lips pouted with sullen contempt. She couldn't recall the last time her sex had looked so flushed and the temptation to touch herself was almost a compulsion. Wendy was only able to resist the impulse because she could also see the distended ring of her anus. The puckered flesh looked swollen from use and she was sickened to find the observation rekindled more excitement.

'What on earth did you do?' she whispered to herself. 'What on earth were you thinking?' But the questions were immaterial. She had only been thinking about satiating a gluttonous demand. And the memories of all that she had done were coming back with full force.

She didn't notice any of the office's decor or furnishings. There was no light, or no need for one, and the walls remained in perpetual shadow. As they entered she saw it had a desk and a chair and she guessed either would do for what they were planning. The rest of the decor was as unimportant as the nameless track that still pounded from the dance floor, or the names they hadn't exchanged.

He took her in his embrace as soon as the door was closed behind them. His hands returned to her body but, rather than continuing to tease and fondle, she was delighted that he began to unfasten her clothes. Her blouse went first, the buttons being pulled open to reveal the lacy secrets of her bra. Then her skirt was tugged off and he was sliding her panties down her hips.

She thought of telling him he was working too fast – that they had all night and there was no need to rush – but his urgency was only a match for her own and she couldn't be bothered trying to resurrect the long-dead ghost of her patience. It had always been her way to get what she wanted immediately, and when the opportunity presented itself, to get more than she wanted. She couldn't see herself making an exception on this occasion and she fervently hoped she would be able to manage more this evening. She supposed it was typical of her avaricious demands that, as the stranger tugged the panties down to her ankles, she was eagerly unzipping his fly and releasing his shaft.

It had been a long time since she had held an erection that didn't belong to her husband and she was enchanted by the urgent heat burning along its length. His obvious desire was apparent in every thrusting twitch and she squeezed her fist around him just to assure herself the whole experience was real and not the product of her passion-barren imagination. Hungry for him, needing to satisfy the libidinous urge that had brought her to the unlit office, she guided him between her legs. Her pussy was sodden with arousal and the lips slid wetly around his swollen end. As she raised her hips slightly, then placed him inside, she was catapulted to a precipice of pleasure. Spasms of joy soared through her sex and, if he hadn't held her by the waist, she knew she would have fallen to the floor in a broken heap of arousal.

The position wasn't suited to meet the urgency of her need but Wendy was prepared to tolerate that annoyance for the moment. Briefly she was content to revel in the joy of having his body pressed against hers, his hands exploring and exciting, while his pulsing length trembled inside her hole.

The stranger reached for her buttocks and lifted her to the edge of the desk.

Wendy allowed herself to be manoeuvred, surrendering to his control and enjoying the fresh sensations being wrought from her sex with each shift in position. As soon as he had her where he wanted he released his hold on her backside and grabbed her hips. She bucked herself onto him and they began to grind their bodies together in a demanding, arrhythmic union. Every thrust pounded new glory through her sex and she jerked against him with a boundless hunger for more. The spasms of pleasure were already growing to a furious pitch and she increased her pace as he lunged with quickening urgency. In the breadth of a few countless moments he had taken her to giddy heights of excitement. She pulled herself onto him and remained rigid as the first waves of splendour rippled upward and outward from her cleft. Her cries of gratitude echoed dully from the walls of their tiny room.

'More?' he asked, murmuring the question between kisses to her throat and chin. 'Do you want me to stop, or do you want me to give you more?'

'More,' she decided, not having to think about her answer. 'Much more.'

His erection had remained hard inside her but he pulled it easily from her shivering depths. Clutching the length in one hand, pulling her slightly forward to meet him, he guided the tip toward her anus.

Her eyes had grown gradually used to the darkness and she could see his gaze with disturbing clarity. He studied her with an unspoken question and she considered her reply sagely before responding. When she did answer, there was no need for words to convey her consent, or sentences to express her desires. It was enough to nudge her buttocks forward and allow her anus to meet the end of his shaft.

The penetration was hard and fraught with pain. But it was no less satisfying because of those sensations. The tight muscle was stretched to new limits, plundered by the alien entry, and then his forbidden warmth was sliding inside her. Wendy wasn't used to such a carnal act – couldn't remember the last time she and Dan had made such a bold experiment in their sex lives – but she realised it had been too long since she succumbed to this unspeakable thrill. Despite the discomfort, heedless to any sense of injury, she pushed herself onto him. All the time she was consciously aware of a need to feel more. His erection filled her, stretching the delicate walls more fully than they had filled her sex, and transporting her to a realm of pure ecstasy. She writhed on him, shrieking back screams of elation as his shaft slid deeper inside. The rush of another climax built all too quickly and she tightened her embrace around him as he pushed himself to the hilt. The darkened room was aglow with the fireworks exploding behind her eyelids and she laughed, screamed and sobbed her way through another blistering climax. The orgasm continued to roar through her as he began to pound in and out.

The woman in the bathroom mirror was crying and Wendy could understand that response. The memories were shaming, still inspiring arousal, but sullied with a bilious self-disgust. She had never been unfaithful to Dan before, although the years of casual neglect had given her every reason, and she was still wondering what had made her fall prey to the charms of the stranger in the nightclub. Stepping into the shower, ignoring the bruises and welts for the moment and trying to rid herself of the remnants of passion-fuelled sweat, she whispered, 'Never again.'

The words 'never again' were so much at the forefront of her thoughts that they underscored every other reaction. She shouldn't have visited Sinners, and would *never again* return. She shouldn't have gone with the stranger that first time, and would: *never again.*

And she shouldn't have returned to him after that first torrid encounter.

'Two words,' Andrea exclaimed cheerfully, *'two bloody words: I've scored.'* She sounded happy and breathless as she returned to her seat. Her face was flushed with so much exertion the cheeks were as scarlet as her dress. *'He's wanting to dance some more but I started feeling guilty about leaving you on your own.'*

Wendy pointed at her drink. 'I'm not on my own. Mr Vodka is keeping me company and I was just on my way to the bar to find Mr Packet O'Cigarettes and Mr Box O'Matches.'

Andrea frowned. 'Don't be like that, Wendy. I felt bad enough . . .'

Wendy shook her head. 'I'm not being like that. He looks like a fun person to be with. You should go and dance together. I'm sure I can find some way to keep myself occupied.' She meant it too because, over Andrea's shoulder, the stranger was smiling at her again. His eyes were creased by genuine appraisal and Wendy could picture a thousand lewd propositions in the lilt of his smile. She only waited as long as it took Andrea to return to the dance floor, and then she was bolting back to the stranger's office, ready to submit to whatever plans he might have.

'You want more already?' he asked. He had to spit the words between her kisses because Wendy was smothering his face with her need. She took him in her arms, rubbing her pelvis against him dryly as she clutched at his buttocks then tried to extract his shaft from his trousers.

'We'll get to that in a moment,' he said, easing her hands away.

Wendy glared at him as though she had been rejected. She was about to respond indignantly when he tugged her close, pulled her blouse open, and planted a hungry kiss between her breasts. Trembling beneath his attention she allowed him to unfasten the bra and let both orbs spill free. She supposed a part of her was worried that someone might come in and catch them but she guessed, given the way the stranger had such easy access to the office, he knew they would remain undisturbed.

'You're a handsome woman,' he murmured.

She enjoyed the praise but told herself she didn't need it. It didn't matter whether he thought she was attractive or if he simply considered her convenient and available. All that mattered was that he had satisfied her initial urge and would be able to cater to the demands of her current need. Allowing him to suck her nipples, savouring the delicious rush that came as each bud was teased, tongued and suckled, Wendy chuckled with dark appreciation.

'You need to feel more than just my tongue against here, don't you?' he whispered.

She held herself still, wondering what he might be proposing. His tongue was a perfect balm against the heat of her desire but she worried he might be trying to take advantage in some way she hadn't anticipated. Fears of him having a friend or two – other men who would come to the seclusion of this dark room to use her – made her stomach muscles squirm. She couldn't decide if the idea excited or repulsed her but her worries didn't abate when she realised she was misjudging his suggestion.

He produced a thin cane from the desk and drew it slowly against her breasts. The friction was an intolerable pulse that sent shivers coursing through her body. 'That first time was good,' he said earnestly. 'But I think we can make this second time better. We can make the pleasure more acute.' Again, he drew the gnarled cane against her sensitive teats.

Wendy almost screamed with excitement. Hungry to feel the punishment he promised, she nodded eagerly. In a hoarse whisper she gasped, 'Yes. Yes please.'

'You're sure?'

She cursed his patient tone and wondered if he wanted her to beg. In her current state of arousal she knew she wouldn't have been beyond humiliating herself in such a way and would happily have fallen to her knees and grovelled at his feet. 'Please –' the word came out as a sob. 'Yes, please.'

Chuckling deeply, he drew the cane back into the darkness, then lashed it across her bare breasts.

She supposed his eyes were used to the impenetrable darkness because he scored her with the accuracy of a marksman. Every blow seemed to catch her nipples, crushing the buds and scorching streaks of searing fire through the orbs. She gasped and shrieked, confident that her cries wouldn't be heard over the nearby thud of the nightclub's music. The pain was bewildering but brought such tormented joy she didn't dare ask him to stop. Each slice shuddered through her frame in an exquisite roar of delight and she called for him to continue until the words hurt her parched throat.

Obligingly, he carried on thrashing her and, although the pleasure was too intense for her to be certain, Wendy felt sure she had climaxed twice during the caning. When he finally threw the cane to the floor she felt weak with longing.

Unmindful of her injuries, the stranger held her by the hips, then placed his mouth around one nipple. His kisses had been exciting before but now, as he suckled the bruised and aching flesh, she realised the pleasure had never felt so intense. He alternated his attention between breasts, dizzying her with anticipation and exciting her greed until she began begging for him to take her.

Not hurrying, treating her to the same brand of slow, disciplined attention he had used before, the stranger released his shaft. He pushed her back against the desk and entered her pussy with one solid lunge.

Wendy screamed. His shaft ploughed into her, bludgeoning her sex in a heady rush of exquisite sensations. As he filled her hole, his hands clawed and pinched at her aching breasts. The contrast of pleasure and pain became intermingled until she couldn't tell one from the other and only wanted the waves of bliss to continue. But it was when he finally erupted inside her that she was treated to the cataclysm of the real orgasm. The explosion started in her loins, spurred on by the thrilling eddies that still lived in her breasts, then travelled briskly to every nerve ending. Every pulse of his climax, every spurt of his burning seed, pushed her to a new limit of joy.

And, even before the first wave of elation had begun to subside, Wendy realised she still wanted more.

The shower removed the cloying scent of their passion but it did nothing for the barrage of red marks that still lined her flesh. She supposed the next few weeks would require careful planning – going to bed after Dan, and wearing some of those all-concealing flannelette nightdresses her mother had given her all those years ago as a laughably inappropriate wedding present. If she had to wear anything remotely revealing, strategically applied foundation would cover the more obvious marks. And, as long as Dan believed she had a headache for the next fortnight, Wendy supposed her indiscretion would remain undetected.

She wrapped the silk robe around her frame again and decided it was time to put the finishing touches to covering her tracks. She went to the bedroom, plucked the bedside phone from its cradle, and tapped in Andrea's number. It seemed unreal to think that so much had happened since their last exchange, in the foyer of Sinners.

'Where have you been?' Andrea cried, stepping into the foyer.

Wendy faltered for a moment, knowing she couldn't tell her friend where she had been but briefly stumped for a convenient lie. Seeing a poster advertising scratch cards she said, 'I fancied chancing a pound on one of those.'

Andrea glanced at the sign and remained characteristically unimpressed. She was heading toward the ladies' loo but paused, placed a hand on Wendy's shoulder, and said, 'Would you mind if I went home with Bruce?'

Wendy thought of asking who Bruce might be, then realised he was the muscular, blond dancer. She smiled indulgently and said, 'Why should I mind?'

'This was meant to be our girls' night out.' Andrea sounded drunk and disappointed with herself. Wendy could hear the first stages of melancholy creeping into her slurred speech. 'But, instead of being a good friend, I've been ignoring you.' She frowned. 'In fact, no. Two words: fuck it. I'm not going home with Bruce. I'm going to spend the rest of the night with you. My best friend, Wendy.'

Wendy caught sight of the stranger standing by the kiosk, watching intently. He met her gaze and raised one eyebrow in a cocky challenge. Melting with sudden need, Wendy nodded for him, then turned to her friend. 'Go with this Bruce guy, Andy,' she said firmly. 'Have fun and think of me while you're doing whatever you're doing.'

'But . . .'

Andrea was calling after her but Wendy couldn't be bothered to listen. 'Call me tomorrow and tell me how it went,' she said. She didn't hear Andrea's reply as she rushed into the darkened back room to press herself into the arms of the stranger's shadow.

'You have a gluttonous appetite,' he observed.

'Is it an appetite you're going to try and satisfy?'

He laughed and span her around. Bending her over the table, he raised her skirt then pulled down her panties. She was glad to have the soiled garment away

71

from her sex because the crotch had been irritating the sensitive lips of her pussy. His spend had begun to leak out of her and it was a relief to be free from the unpleasant reminder that she had been used so copiously. As soon as the underwear was down to her ankles he had his face pushed between the cleft of her buttocks and was working his mouth against her sex. His tongue entered easily, chasing her clitoris then tunnelling deep between her labia.

She hammered her fists happily against the desk, parting her legs so he could get deeper. The arousal he generated was something she had never experienced before and her need for more and more was unceasing. Every time he licked her pussy she screamed for him to continue. In the hateful moments when he paused for breath she cursed the absence of attention. Even when he was touching her, the different demands of her body each seemed perpetually in need. When he briefly turned her over and gnawed against her nipples, her sex hungered for his mouth to return; when his tongue brushed against her pussy, her breasts ached for him to chew against the swollen teats; and, when he stepped away from her, into the shadows that surrounded the desk, her entire body pulsed with a craving for him to come back.

It was only when Wendy heard the deadly swipe of the cane that she fell silent and wondered what to expect next. The stinging blow across her rear answered the question succinctly. It burnt like a line of white fire that blazed across her buttocks.

'Stay still or it will really hurt,' he hissed.

She did as he told her, not daring to move for fear of making the pain more unbearable. He sliced a pair of swift shots, the first scoring her upper thighs, the second cutting deep across her cheeks. Wendy howled with a mixture of shock and excitement and he branded her backside with two more blows.

72

'You want more?' he asked.

She didn't think she could stand the agony but her body yearned for more. He had awoken a desire for suffering that she had never previously known. The blistering heat across her buttocks was spreading to her sex but the caning warmed her in other ways. Giving herself so freely to this stranger, allowing him to humiliate her and demean her with his brutal treatment was the most liberating experience she had ever enjoyed. Each thrash of the cane hurt badly but it also made her feel alive and wanted and desirable.

Knowing she had to sample everything he could offer, she begged him to continue. Laughing quietly to himself, he began to lash the cane hard against her back. A couple of stray shots caught her shoulders and sides but even those pains added to her swelling excitement. However, it was the slices that struck her rear cheeks that pushed her beyond the brink. The untempered weight he threw into every stroke, and the searing anguish that tore through her, had Wendy sobbing with gratitude.

The tears were flowing freely when he finally tossed the cane into the darkness and she knew her pussy was sopping as though the tears were also flowing from there. He tested her with two exploratory fingers, pushing easily into the squelching wetness. Wendy gasped and realised she was close to screaming with her need for him. But, when he did produce his erection, he didn't push it against her sex. As it had earlier in the evening, the rounded end of his shaft prodded at her anus.

The muscle still felt stretched and distended from the last time he had used her and she wanted to tell him that the penetration would be more than she could bear. Not wanting to break the spell of the moment, and needing to have him use her in whatever way best *pleased him, Wendy pushed her buttocks onto his hardness.*

It was a vicious finale to the evening. He was obviously aroused, the thickness of his length bearing testament to that fact, and he hammered into her with a voracious hunger. His hands clawed at her hips and sides, pulling her onto him each time she instinctively jerked away. She could feel his fingertips burying deep beneath the flesh but the pain of each gouge was only another spur to her nearing climax. When his pulse erupted into her dark, tight hole, she found herself collapsing with the enormity of pleasure. She continued to lie slumped across the desk as he carried on riding her until the last remnants of stiffness were expelled from his shaft.

Afterwards he turned the light on so she could find her clothes but it still didn't occur to her to examine the room's decor. She had no intention of returning again – to Sinners, or the stranger – and no need to see what the place looked like. With the courteousness of a true gentleman, he escorted her out of his office and into the foyer. It was deserted save for the blonde in the kiosk. Wendy remembered that when she had first entered the nightclub a couple had been embracing in one corner. They had obviously taken their passion somewhere else and she wondered if they were having half the fun that she had enjoyed.

'Here,' he said, passing her a small piece of card.

Wendy took it from him and asked, 'What's this?'

'You told your friend you were buying a scratch card,' he reminded her. 'You might want to keep hold of it to give substance to your lie.'

Wendy guessed it was meant as a thoughtful gesture, and she accepted it in that fashion. Thanking him, she put the card into her purse and searched for words that might put a definite end to this evening. Turning back

74

*to him, wanting to tell him that, while she was thankful
for what they had shared, it could never happen again,
she was disappointed to find herself alone in the foyer.
There was only the blonde in the kiosk, munching lazily
on a chocolate bar.*

*And, Wendy thought, perhaps that was for the best.
If they had said a proper good night to one another, she
knew her own compulsive nature might have insisted
she arrange to meet her mystery lover again. And,
aware of her gluttonous appetites, she didn't think such
an arrangement would bode well for the future of her
marriage.*

Andrea spent the best part of an hour talking about
Bruce and their sexual antics of the previous evening.
By the time she had finished, Wendy was virtually
convinced that her own indiscretion had gone unnoticed. Still, she knew she had to test the waters
properly before she could relax and consign her fears
of discovery to being a near-miss experience.

'So,' Andrea said eventually. 'Are you going to call
me a depraved slut? Are you going to tell me that a
fiery hell awaits me for my sins?'

In all honesty Wendy thought that her friend's
adventures were quite mundane compared to the
things she had done at Sinners, but she prudently kept
the notion to herself. 'I'm in no position to judge,' she
began carefully. 'I got lucky myself last night.'

Andrea paused. The silence that came from her end
of the phone made her sound briefly aghast. Wendy
held her breath, knowing that this was where Andrea
would either reveal she had suspected something, or
where it would be obvious that her indiscretion had
slipped by unnoticed. Her heartbeat quickened as it
had when the stranger first placed his hand against
her knee.

'You got lucky?' Andrea gasped. 'Who with? Do I know him? Did I see him?'

Laughing, Wendy told her friend to calm her imagination. 'I got lucky with the scratch card I bought,' she explained. 'I won twenty-five pounds.'

'Cool,' Andrea enthused. She sounded pleased but also a little disappointed. 'Maybe we should go there again?'

Wendy said she might, not wanting to pique Andrea's curiosity with an outright refusal. But, as she changed the topic of conversation, and guided them toward settling on their next night out at a different location, the same thought that had been underscoring every other wanted to scream from her lips: *Never again.*

Her sense of personal shame carried a deep burden which she couldn't seem to exorcise. The knowledge of what she had done was degrading and humiliating; the knowledge that she had enjoyed it was even more crushing. Over the following week she treated Dan to his favourite meals, made sure he didn't see her body while the marks were still there, and spent every waking hour cursing the libidinous drives that had driven her into the arms of another man.

The thought of how close she had come to losing Dan, and all the security he provided, was bad. But the shame was worse. She had discovered appetites that she had never previously known and found they were far more pleasurable than she would have imagined. The thrill of submitting to a stranger had been intoxicating, and the punishing delight of each caning had proved a revelation. If she had suspected Dan of having a little more imagination, and if she hadn't feared he might question the source of her newfound interest in discipline, she would have had him striping her backside as soon as the first marks disappeared.

And, if she had thought she would be able to manage the feat without jeopardising her marriage, in spite of the pain and regardless of the cutting shame, she knew she would have returned to Sinners.

Her libido seemed to be operating at a previously undiscovered level. Arousal and satisfaction were constant motives for her actions. Whereas before she had been content to allow Dan his monthly conjugal right, she now found herself driven by a lust that tainted every other thought. If she had dared to let her husband see her naked body she knew she would have worn him out with her excessive demands. Instead, knowing she could only please herself until the last of the welts had faded, Wendy took every opportunity to personally sate her salacious needs. She spent hours in the shower each morning, rubbing and teasing until a climax came with brittle, bitter fury. On an evening she would retire to the bath after Dan had gone to bed and pleasure herself with the scouring hand of an exfoliating loofah mitt. She could endure the water until it had turned cold as long as her fingers were able to tease the weary, sensitive flesh of her sex and she taught herself to experiment with different varieties of penetration and pain. Candles, hairbrush handles and even Dan's toothbrush all found their way into her bath to travel with her on the private journey of self-exploration.

She couldn't prepare vegetables without the shapes of carrots and courgettes reminding her of her indiscretion. Driving became an arduous chore when her fingers curled softly around the bulbous head of the gear stick. The discomfort of sitting had faded within a day but, on those occasions when she shifted position in her chair and reminded herself briefly of the pain, Wendy was treated to the memory of the entire, sordid evening.

But, on reflection, she thought the most annoying aspect of the week had to be the lottery card. The local newsagent wouldn't cash it for her and, although Wendy spent an afternoon visiting various book-makers and department stores in the town centre, she couldn't get any outlet to give her the money she had won. Returning to her local newsagent, she asked the new girl behind the counter for advice.

The name badge on her blouse said she was called Stacey and Wendy couldn't recall seeing her serving in the shop before. 'Lucky Pig lottery cards?' Stacey said. 'I'll go and ask the manager.'

She disappeared from behind the counter, taking the best part of twenty minutes before returning. When she did come back her face looked flushed and her hair was dishevelled. 'Sorry that took so long.' She grinned unapologetically. 'It's my first day here and I didn't know where to find the information.'

Straining to remain patient, Wendy asked, 'So, where would I redeem this card? Did you find out?'

'The manager says Lucky Pig lottery cards are only redeemable in one place.'

Wendy knew what Stacey was going to say before the girl had named the location. She steeled herself for the blow, already working her way through possible ways around the situation.

'It's a nightclub in the town centre,' Stacey told her. 'I don't know if you've been there, or not. I guess you must have if you've got one of their lottery cards. It's called Sinners.'

She had tried to banish the nightclub from her mind, and gone out of her way to put the entire incident behind her. The marks on her back, breasts and buttocks had faded to a memory and, with a couple more sessions on a sunbed, Wendy believed she would have eradicated the last vestiges of evidence.

She might have felt more confident about the declaration if it hadn't come while she was frigging herself to a climax. Sitting on a toilet seat, listening to sounds of others trying to privately go about their business in the neighbouring cubicles, she bit her lower lip as the orgasm soared through her body. It was base behaviour, the sort of activity she associated with seedy little men in tatty raincoats, but the need had come on her with inarguable haste and she couldn't resist the opportunity for satisfaction.

Her fingers scurried wetly against her cleft, tugging at the labia and rubbing frantically against the aching nub of her clitoris. Her sex slurped greedily as she teased a finger inside and, with only a couple of carefully placed thrusts, she was wringing the orgasm from her aching muscle. The heels of her shoes slipped against the tiled floor and she trembled with undiluted euphoria. The release was only minor compared to some of the climaxes she had achieved recently, but it was desperately needed and she wanted to weep with self-gratitude. Taking longer than usual to check her make-up, desperate to make sure no sign of her indulgence could be discerned, she carefully reapplied her lipstick before going back out to the bistro.

'I thought you'd fallen in,' Andrea remarked gruffly.

Wendy ignored the remark and took her seat. Needing to change the topic of conversation, and having being desperate to deal with the one unfinished detail that remained from her night at Sinners, she asked innocently, 'Did you manage to cash that lottery ticket I gave you?'

Andrea reached into her bag and Wendy sighed inwardly. Knowing she was about to receive her prize money was a tremendous weight off her mind. Grinning broadly, she held out her hand, expecting to be given two or three notes.

Instead of handing over money, Andrea returned the card. Shrugging uncomfortably beneath Wendy's darkening frown she said, 'Apparently the cards are non-transferable.'

'Non-transferable? What does that mean?'

Andrea shrugged again. 'It can mean a lot of things but, according to the kiosk attendant at Sinners, it means, if you want your money, you'll have to go there yourself.' She still held the card and, when Wendy made no move to take it from her, she asked, 'Do you want it back? Or should I throw it away?'

Wendy snatched it from her hand. 'You can't throw it away, Andy. It's worth twenty-five quid.'

Andrea laughed. 'But twenty-five pounds is fuck all. We've spent that much on the wine this lunchtime and we're not going to drink it because it tastes like carbonated piss.' She leant forward in her seat, her smile fading to a serious expression as she said, 'It's not worth the hassle, Wendy. If there's some reason you don't want to go back to that nightclub . . .'

Wendy raised her eyes sharply, wondering if Andrea suspected something. She could see no indication of an accusation in her friend's expression but there was always the worry that, if Andrea knew what she had done, she might share the confidence with someone else. 'There's no reason,' she said quickly. 'What makes you think I've got a reason for not wanting to go there?'

'I wasn't suggesting that,' Andrea said honestly. She sat back in her chair, sipped some more of her wine and grimaced with disgust. 'I was just saying, there's no sense in going out of your way, or putting yourself to any trouble for something as paltry as twenty-five pounds.'

Wendy nodded agreement. Despite what Dan might say, twenty-five pounds was next to nothing. It was a feeble sum, barely worth the trip back to the nightclub where it had been won, and almost certainly not worth the risk of losing her marriage, her husband and her home. But, privately, she thought it was still her twenty-five pounds and for that reason alone, she knew she needed to have it.

Seven days later Wendy stood in the nightclub, not sure what she was doing there. The couple she had seen before had returned to their alcove, each munching hungrily at the other's mouth. A steady stream of customers flowed through the foyer and the thump-thump-thump of a heavy bass reverberated through her feet. It had taken a long week of soul-searching before she had decided to make this journey and it was the sight of the Lucky Pigs on the scratch card that finally pushed her. Their contented smiles had mutated into smug grins and she got the impression they were gloating over the fact that she lacked the courage to claim what was rightfully hers. Deciding that cartoon pigs weren't going to get the better of her, and making a mental note not to discuss that thought with the psychiatrist she occasionally visited, Wendy took the scratch card down to Sinners.

However, once she was standing in the hatefully familiar territory of the foyer, what had seemed like the right decision on her drive down there, began to seem like a grave and foolish mistake.

The blonde in the kiosk munched on a chocolate bar. Her face looked a little fuller than the last time Wendy had seen her, and she stared suspiciously through the glass window.

It was something of a relief to see she was alone although Wendy couldn't stop herself from glancing nervously at every shadow and every new face that walked past. Her nerves were taught with trepidation and her stomach felt as though it was being squeezed in a fist. She stepped up to the kiosk, produced her scratch card and said, 'I'm here to redeem this.'

The blonde stared vacantly at the card. After a moment's consideration she leant back in her chair and called, 'We've got a winner here, boss.'

Wendy cringed. If the glass hadn't been separating them she would have put her hands over the girl's mouth, stifled the cry, and told her not to shout for anyone. Panicked, she stared around the foyer like a burglar hearing a key in the lock. No one else was looking at her – no one else seemed to have noticed her – but still she couldn't shake the worry that her secret was about be uncovered.

The man with the goatee appeared from his office behind the kiosk. He smiled with instant recognition when his gaze lit on Wendy. 'A winner?' he said encouragingly. 'Congratulations.' He reached past the blonde and took twenty-five pounds from the petty cash box. After pushing it into Wendy's hand he extended an arm into his office and said, 'Would you care to come in here so I can get your signature for the necessary paperwork?'

She hesitated. 'Do I have to go in there?'

He shrugged, unoffended. 'We can sort it out in the kiosk, if you like.' His voice was smooth and placating and alluded to an innocence that she knew was feigned. 'It's just,' he continued, 'I have all my paperwork in here and it would make things far easier.'

Unable to offer further resistance, Wendy went through to his office. As soon as the door had closed, she found their bodies were pressed together. A part of her wanted to tell him that she hadn't come here for that sort of prize, and that his attention was unwanted. But in all honesty she didn't know which of them had first embraced the other. The only thing she knew for a fact was that he inspired an urge, and past experience had proved he was well able to satisfy it.

His hands were wrenching open her blouse with the same ferocity that she tugged at the zip on his trousers. In the darkness of the office she could hear their combined gasps and grunts as they each hurried to undress the other.

'I shouldn't be doing this,' she told him.

'That's not stopping you.'

'I don't want to be here.'

'Then go. Go and never return.'

Through the fading shadows she glared at him. She was surprised to feel her cheeks wet with unexpected tears. 'I will go,' she decided, 'and I shan't ever return.' She hesitated for a moment, realising there was still unfinished business between them. Despising her own weakness she said eventually, 'Afterwards. I'll go and never return, after we've finished here today.' Not allowing him to argue with her decision, smothering his mouth with her kisses so he couldn't ridicule her change of heart, Wendy reached for the heat of his erection. The sturdy pulse beat rigidly beneath her fingertips and the simple action of holding his shaft reminded her of all the dark pleasures she had been missing.

'Take me,' she demanded.

'No,' he said quietly. 'Not yet.'

She writhed herself against him, despising the fact that he could resist her so easily. If their positions had been reversed, if she had been the man and he had been the woman demanding satisfaction, she knew she wouldn't have been able to show the same restraint. The gut-wrenching need to possess, to use and to satiate were forces she knew she could never control. 'I want you,' Wendy insisted. 'I need you. And I need you now.'

'And,' he said patiently, 'if this is going to be the last chance I have to be with you, I want to make it a memorable experience for both of us.'

The explanation should have touched her with warmth but Wendy could only find it unnerving. She tried peering through the darkness to see if his face gave any indication of what he was planning. 'How are you going to make it memorable?'

He laughed softly. Slipping the blouse from her shoulders, making light work of removing her bra, skirt and panties, he guided her to the desk and bent her over its polished surface. Her breasts squashed against the cool woodwork and she was brushed by the memory of all the glorious indignities he had visited on her the last time she assumed this position. Her backside was held high in the air, exposed, available and vulnerable. She knew her cleft was already sodden and could imagine the wet lips pouting in anticipation. Her legs began to tremble as she tried to decide if she wanted this experience to be less demanding, or more depraved.

'You were very responsive the last time you were here.'

She didn't want to be reminded of that evening but everything he said and did seemed to bring back the whole sordid episode. She was back in the same unlit room, preparing to submit herself to whatever he wanted, and languishing in the thrill of his mastery. Her pussy lips bristled with greedy heat and her inner muscles were already clenching hungrily. When she heard him undress, and caught the unpleasant smell of his sweat and arousal, her need for him only grew stronger.

'Are you going to be as responsive this time?' he asked, sliding his fingers over her backside.

Wendy wanted to scream her devotion to him but instead she simply sobbed against the table. It was impossible to equate the desire he inspired with the tacky circumstances of a stranger and a gloomy office at the back of a tawdry nightclub. But, while she couldn't understand where the need had come from, she couldn't argue that it held her in its thrall. She twitched spasmodically, shivering for him and desperate to feel his touch delve deeper. When he finally deigned to caress the lips of her sex, allowing his fingers to glide seamlessly against her aching labia, she heard herself whisper words of heartfelt thanks.

He slipped two digits inside.

The warm, pink muscles spread easily for him, greedily facilitating his entry and tightening their hold as he plunged deeper. Wendy clawed the surface of the desk, caught in the same throes of abandonment she had been simultaneously dreading and craving. It was wrong; it was shameful; it was bound to be degrading; yet she couldn't bring herself to contemplate leaving. Not until her gluttonous appetite had been satisfied.

The fingers were replaced by his erection. He slid himself easily into her confines, idly slapping her backside before beginning to ride back and forth. The hint of casual abuse – and the complete control he exercised over her – all served to remind Wendy she was there as his willing slave. The idea inspired another series of delicious tremors to cascade through the length of her sex.

'Did you expect me to cane you?' he asked, leaning closer so he could whisper the words into her ear. 'Is that what you've been wanting since you left?'

Torn by shame, guilt, and an honest desire to experience everything he could offer, Wendy couldn't bring herself to answer. She whimpered underneath him as he continued to plough chilling magic through the length of her pussy. Her entire body was ablaze with longing and she didn't care how he used her, as long as he satisfied her need.

Without warning he wrenched his shaft from her sex.

The withdrawal was so sudden and swift Wendy was stung by a crushing sensation of emptiness. Her sense of loss remained while he teased a finger against her anus and she only began to feel a lessening of the emotion when he slid one finger, then a second, into her backside.

There was one hand on the small of her back, holding her in place, and keeping her steady. The two fingers between her buttocks became three before he started to slide them slowly in and out. She revelled in the dark torment, allowing him to spread her open and stretch her wide.

'What are you doing?' she moaned.

'Nothing you won't enjoy,' he assured her.

For some reason she couldn't understand, Wendy knew he was probably right. She tried to relax and give in to the swelling sensations he evoked but the omnipresent threat of danger added a lot to her excitement. The fear that it might not be something she enjoyed, or that he might go too rough, too hard, or try to abuse her without any of the pleasurable side-effects, all accumulated to make the burden of worries a major part of the excitement.

'Stay still,' he insisted.

She remembered, the last time she had been in this room, he had used those words before slicing her back and buttocks with the cane. But she didn't understand what they might precede on this occasion. It was only when he squeezed a fourth finger into her anus that she began to realise what he was doing.

Repeating his instruction for her to remain still, pressing his hand more firmly against her back, he urged his thumb to join those fingers that were already inside her.

Wendy bit back her cry but she couldn't help hammering a fist against the desktop. There was none of the agony she might have expected: in truth there was only a sharp awareness of the joy he was imbuing between her legs. She had never felt so full before and, when she realised his entire fist was nestling in the warm cocoon of her backside, she almost fainted with excitement. When he then decided to return his erection to her pussy, she finally did scream.

It was impossible to gauge time in the darkened confines of the back office. Days might have passed, but more likely Wendy suspected it was a couple of hours at the most. He tied her sitting to the chair at one point, then stroked the cane repeatedly across her breasts. When that punishment had turned her into a sobbing creature, begging for more satisfaction between pleas for him to stop, he released her then refastened her bindings so her backside was exposed for his aim. He thrashed both buttocks, reddening them first, then slicing and beating and taking her to new realms of appreciation.

But, by the time they were both spent, it was the fisting she remembered most prominently. The joy of being stretched, the sensation of being so full and stuffed, was a shameful delight that would live with her forever. Memories continued to shake through her with every step and she knew the experience would be a standard by which she would gauge all others.

And, as she dressed herself afterwards, Wendy thought it was only right she should take a pleasant memory away from this experience. She knew she wouldn't be revisiting the nightclub and had no intention of seeing the stranger ever again. She allowed him to escort her to the foyer and accepted a perfunctory kiss against her cheek.

Walking past the couple who lingered in the corner, ignoring their passionate writhings, she wondered if she would be able to hide her indiscretion from Dan this second time. She believed she might just manage the task, but she also knew it would be a lot harder to keep him at a distance for a second consecutive month. She also thought there was a greater danger he might finally start to grow suspicious about why she was wearing such concealing clothes and her reasons for locking the bathroom door.

'Wait,' the stranger said abruptly.

The sharp tone of his voice made Wendy hesitate as she was on the verge of taking her final step away from Sinners.

'You've forgotten something.' He smiled charmingly. He held it out for her and, unable to resist her own gluttonous desire, Wendy took it from him before leaving.

'Another scratch card?' Dan asked, placing his morning kiss between his wife's shoulder blades. It was a ritual he persisted with, in spite of his protestations about the enforced abstinence and contrary to the mood swings he blamed on 'not getting any'. He didn't notice her pull the robe more tightly around herself, or shrink from something unwanted in his touch.

'It was a complimentary one,' Wendy said, stopping his sermon on the evils of gambling before it could begin. 'They give you a free card along with the prize on every winning ticket.'

He was over by the fridge, pouring himself an orange juice.

Staring at the scratch card, Wendy barely noticed him. She had rubbed the silver latex from the prize box and saw it said she could win fifty pounds on this ticket. Scratching carefully at the first box, she had already revealed two smiling pigs. There was only one space left to uncover and the edge of her coin wavered as she held it over the card.

'Is it a winner?' Dan asked.

She didn't look up when she answered. 'I don't know yet,' she said honestly. And, although she didn't tell her husband, Wendy wasn't sure she wanted to know.

4

The Pride of the Company

'You've been a naughty girl, Stacey,' Julia said crisply.

She sat behind her desk looking like a goddess. Her classical features were marred by a disapproving frown but it was the only flaw in her otherwise perfect appearance. Her jet black hair was tied back in a sleek, businesslike style and her make-up, although subtle, accentuated the aquiline beauty of her face. However, this evening, rather than looking striking, she seemed unnervingly austere. Her lips were thinned with impatience and her eyes sparkled with barely restrained anger.

'You've been a very naughty girl.'

The office, like its owner, smacked of considerable accomplishment. Framed diplomas decorated one wall, rosettes and certificates for show jumping adorned another, while a third was peppered with impressive, mounted photographs. Glancing uneasily at her surroundings, Stacey saw a picture of Julia with the Pope, one of Julia with the Prime Minister and another showing Julia sandwiched between Sir Elton John and Sir Cliff Richard.

'Look at me while I'm talking to you,' Julia snapped. 'You're in enough trouble right now without adding dumb insolence to my list of grievances.'

Stacey snatched her gaze from the pictures and stared miserably at the woman. If she left the room with only a stern dressing down, she knew it would be a lucky escape. Her heart hammered inside her chest and her lungs felt as though they had forgotten how to process oxygen. The prospect of unemployment loomed like a threatening thundercloud and the bleakness of her future was depressing.

'It says here you went to a convent school,' Julia observed. She had been flipping through a manila folder with the word 'PERSONNEL' printed across the top. Looking up from the contents she glanced across the desk and asked, 'Is that correct?'

Stacey swallowed before replying. She didn't know what her education had to do with this end-of-the-day summons to Julia's office but she sensed the woman was trying to make a point. Anxious to appear obliging, she said, 'Yes, miss. That's correct.'

Julia closed the personnel file and placed it on her desk. Sneering, she asked, 'Didn't the nuns teach you that stealing is a sin?'

Stacey started to protest. 'I haven't stolen anything,' she said quickly. 'I would never do that because –'

Julia slapped her hand against the desk. The sound of the impact cut through Stacey's reply. 'Answer the damned question,' she snapped. 'Did the nuns teach you that stealing is a sin?'

There were many nicknames associated with Julia: the nasty cow; the evil one; the ice maiden; and the bitch queen from hell. Stacey had heard them all being whispered during her first day in the office but she knew no one used the insults in front of Julia. Seeing the volatile expression that now rouged the woman's cheeks, she could easily understand why. No one would dare.

Stacey swallowed. Her palms were sweaty, her stomach churned and she felt as though she was fighting a losing battle. She lowered her gaze and said, 'Yes, miss. The convent staff did teach me that stealing is a sin.'

'It's not a lesson you've learnt very well, is it?' Julia said dryly. She raised a hand to silence the argument Stacey was about to make. 'I don't have time to listen to your lies. I have an engagement with Mr York this evening so I intend to make our business swift. Mr Jones, our managing director, paid a visit to your desk this afternoon, didn't he?'

Dumbly, Stacey nodded.

'While the pair of you were chatting he noticed the sales analysis graphs you were producing. He said the pie charts displayed the information with startling clarity and he asked if you were responsible for the program that produced those figures. Did you tell him they were produced by a program that I had written?'

Stacey blushed. She could now understand why she had been summoned to Julia's office and she realised the gravity of her situation. Fervently she racked her brains and wondered if it was possible to talk her way out of the trouble.

'Did you tell him they were produced by a program that I had written?' Julia repeated. Her voice was cracking with the strain of forced patience. 'Or did you take credit from my work?'

'I didn't understand his question,' Stacey said quickly. 'I was surprised that Mr Jones even noticed me with it only being my second day and, when he asked if the charts were my work, I thought he meant –'

'It's bad enough you've been caught stealing praise that was due to me,' Julia broke in. 'Don't make me angrier by insulting my intelligence with your lies.' She rose from her chair, planted both fists on the top of her desk, and glared furiously. 'Bend over, Stacey,' she hissed. 'You've been a naughty girl and it's time you learnt how I hand out punishment.'

Stacey stared at her in disbelief. She wondered madly if Julia was making a joke. It didn't seem likely – the woman was reputed to have no sense of humour – but that explanation seemed more plausible than the idea that she was being serious.

Julia reached into the top drawer of her desk and removed a pair of black leather driving gloves. She pulled them over her outstretched fingers while her malicious smile grew broader. 'Don't make me tell you again,' she said quietly. 'I've already decided this is going to hurt you. Keep pissing me off and I'll make sure you have nightmares about this day for the rest of your miserable life.'

Bewildered, Stacey shook her head. Unaware she was doing it, she placed a protective hand over her breasts. 'You want me to bend over? What on earth for?'

Julia's smile glinted like a blade. She flexed her gloved fingers and said, 'Are you really that stupid? Don't you know? I want to slap your naughty little backside.'

Stacey shook her head and started toward the door. 'You can't do that sort of thing to me,' she decided. 'I have rights and civil liberties. I'm not in the trade union but I'll go and see the managing director if I have to. I'll . . .'

'Take one step outside that door and you're finished here,' Julia said calmly.

Stacey paused with her fingers on the handle.

'Take one step outside that door and I'll see you unemployed. I'll make sure the accounts department screw up with your salary payment. I'll write you a reference that wouldn't get you a position slopping out a prison cell. Take one step outside that door and I'll follow your career for the next twelve months and tell every new employer how you were fired for stealing. The choice is yours, Stacey. One way or another I'm going to hurt you. You can either leave and suffer my wrath for the next year. Or you can bend over and let me slap your backside.'

Shivering with self-loathing, Stacey moved her hand from the door. She turned to face Julia, trying to disguise the venom in her expression as she asked, 'What do you want me to do?'

Julia rolled her eyes. 'Jesus Christ! I've said it enough times, haven't I? How dense are you? I want you to bend over while I spank your backside. It's not the most complicated instruction in the world. I'm sure even a simple little shit like you can comprehend that much.'

Stacey flushed at the insult. Forcing each step, she walked back toward the desk. Her lower lip trembled as she asked, 'Where do you want me to bend?'

'Where you're standing will suffice,' Julia said, stepping from behind her desk. 'Don't try touching your toes. Just bend your knees a little and grab your ankles. That way there's less likelihood of you falling over when I slap your arse.'

Rushing to do as she had been told, scared that if she thought about her actions she would ignore the threats Julia had made and rush heedlessly out of the office, Stacey bent forward and clutched her ankles.

'I'm going to make you sorry for stealing praise that was due to me,' Julia whispered.

Stacey closed her eyes and said a silent prayer.

'By the time I'm finished with you, you'll be begging for forgiveness.'

'Is that what you want me to do?' Stacey blurted. 'If you want me to beg forgiveness I'll get down on my knees and do that now. I'm sorry for taking credit for your work but, please . . .'

'One more word and I'll call my boyfriend in here,' Julia said softly.

Immediately, Stacey stopped speaking.

'He's waiting in the reception at the moment,' Julia explained. 'We're going out together this evening, but I can ring his mobile and invite him to watch while you suffer your punishment. All it will take is for you to say one more word.'

Silently, Stacey fumed. Julia's boyfriend, Mr York, was one of the company's senior directors. Handsome, dark and unquestionably attractive, he was tipped to take over from Mr Jones when the managing director finally retired and Stacey cringed from the idea of him seeing her in this position. It was bad enough having to endure the humiliation beneath Julia's control but she imagined it would be a million times worse if Mr York was in attendance. Picturing that scenario she couldn't imagine a more embarrassing ordeal.

She heard Julia step closer, was tickled by the gentle caress of the woman's skirt brushing against her thigh, and she tensed herself for the indignity that was about to follow. Her heart had been beating briskly before. Now it thundered with violent force.

Gloved hands raised the hem of her skirt. The fabric's movement wafted a small breeze against her buttocks and Stacey almost flinched from the chill caress.

'What a pretty little bottom you have,' Julia mused.

Stacey squirmed beneath the unwanted compliment.

'Stay still while I remove your panties.'

If Stacey had thought the punishment was unbearable before, she didn't know how to describe it now this new level of torment had been introduced. She tried to remain still while Julia hooked her thumbs into the panties and slid them from her hips but it was impossible to staunch an involuntary flurry of shivers. Vulnerability, embarrassment and shame flooded through her in a dizzying whirl. The pulse in her temples pounded ceaselessly and she wondered if she was likely to pass out. The idea didn't worry her too greatly because she thought unconsciousness would be preferable to the intolerable anxiety.

'My, my!' Julia whispered. 'You have a pretty little bottom and a sweet, pouting pussy. I never realised you possessed such attractive assets, Stacey.'

Still fearful that Julia might summon Mr York to observe this humiliation, Stacey said nothing. She clutched her ankles tighter and tried to remain unmoved when a gloved finger traced a line against her labia. The leather was expensive and soft and it instantly etched greedy fire in the centre of her sex. Ignoring the shameful need, Stacey squeezed her eyes more tightly closed until bitter tears began to spill down her cheeks.

'You look wet,' Julia observed. 'I wonder if this means you have submissive tendencies? Perhaps I was foolish to decide a spanking would teach you your lesson. I might have been better rewarded if I'd told you to get down on your knees and lick my pussy.'

Stacey wanted to cringe from the suggestion – it was vile, base and vulgar – but there was something in Julia's phrasing that heightened her arousal. She tried to quell the libidinous urge, hating the fact her body was excited by this punishment, but it was impossible to distance herself from the sensations.

The inner muscles of her sex began to quiver as though she was anticipating a lover.

'Stay absolutely still while I'm doing this,' Julia demanded. 'Don't make a sound, don't move a muscle, and don't even think about trying to stop me.'

Miserably, Stacey vowed to do as she had been told. She held herself rigid, braced in readiness, and wasn't surprised when Julia slapped a palm resoundingly against her backside. The blow landed flat against one cheek and, although it stung, the shame of the punishment hurt worse. Stacey's tears began to flow freely and she bit back a plea for leniency.

Julia smacked a second blow against her. 'This is for stealing my praise,' she grunted.

Stacey clenched her teeth and shivered.

'I'll tolerate pilfering. I'll tolerate your stupid brand of laziness. And I'll tolerate your ineptitude. But I won't have anyone steal praise that should be directed at me.' Landing another blow, forcing a vicious weight into the impact, she said, 'I've never allowed anyone to steal my praise. I won't allow any of the company's directors to take credit for my accomplishments, so I'm fucked if a tacky little shit like you is going to get away with that sort of behaviour on her second day in the office.'

'I'm sorry,' Stacey whispered.

She half hoped the apology would offer some sort of atonement but it clearly did nothing to appease Julia's upset. The woman refrained from delivering another slap to Stacey's punished backside. Instead, she reached down and grabbed a fistful of her hair. Turning and twisting, forcing her to her knees, Julia glared down ferociously into Stacey's upturned face.

'Don't tell me you're sorry until I've decided you're sorry.' The words were hissed with so much passion a spray of spittle freckled Stacey's face.

Anxious to appease the furious figure controlling her, she was ready to apologise again. Before she could think what to say, Julia was pulling harder on her hair. Stacey could see where her face was being directed and, as the woman began to raise the hem of her skirt, she had a sickening premonition of what Julia was planning.

'Don't try and fight me, you little shit,' Julia spat. 'If you don't accept all of this punishment I swear I'll do what I promised before. I'll see you unemployed and you'll spend the next twelve months going from one job to another until I get tired of making your life a misery. Don't try and fight me. Just do as I say.'

Ignoring Julia's threats Stacey tried to resist but the pain in her scalp made her think better of such a futile protest. She could see her strength and position were no match for the other woman's and, eventually, she realised she had no option except to do as she was told.

The crotch of Julia's panties was a white triangle. As she was pulled closer Stacey could detect the tang of musk and secret sweat. Horrified, she watched Julia use her free hand to pull the gusset to one side. The lips of her sex, flushed and glistening with dewy excitement, loomed unnervingly close.

'You needn't bother speaking from this point onwards,' Julia breathed. 'I'm sure you could make more productive use of your tongue if you want to make atonement for your sins.'

Stacey tried to shake her head but Julia's hold was tight and unrelenting. Even though she was trying to resist, her face was continually being pulled closer to the fragrant cleft.

'What's the matter?' Julia asked. 'Don't you want to earn my forgiveness?'

Knowing she would have to surrender, sure Julia wouldn't let go until Stacey had made this sacrifice, she extended her tongue. Squeezing her eyes closed, trying not to think about what she was doing, Stacey pushed her mouth against Julia's pussy. The taste of feminine excitement was disquieting and she loathed the quickening pulse that began to beat between her legs. Even worse, she thought, was Julia's moan of obvious sexual excitement.

'I called you a naughty girl before –' Julia giggled darkly '– but I didn't realise you were this naughty.'

Flushing crimson, Stacey pushed her tongue between the sodden folds of the labia. She squirmed deep inside the throbbing tube of muscle and allowed the wet lips to smother her mouth.

Julia drew startled breath. 'I wish I'd discovered your talents earlier.' Her voice was thick with mounting arousal. 'If I'd known you had a gift for this sort of behaviour I'd have made much better use of you.'

Ignoring the words, knowing they were only being said to make her feel worse, Stacey continued to plunder the wetness with her tongue. The alien sensation of pussy lips against her mouth was disturbingly arousing and she struggled to think past the growing excitement as she tried to follow every instruction.

'Tongue me deeper, you little shit. Deeper.'

Obediently, Stacey did as she was told. She could see no advantage in trying to escape, realising Julia would continue to dominate until she had reached her climax. Every attempt Stacey made to pull away was countered by a short, sharp tug on her hair. She soon decided that staying between the woman's legs was the simplest way to avoid further suffering.

'Go on,' Julia insisted, bucking her sex to meet Stacey's tongue. She panted and spoke in a low rasp that seemed to indicate a nearing climax. 'I'll show you what happens to anyone who tries to rob me of due credit, you little shit. Now, tongue me deeper.'

Sobbing pitifully, Stacey did as she was told. She licked the slippery flesh of Julia's pussy, overcome by the knowledge that the woman's climax was about to strike. A part of her wanted this whole, torturous ordeal to be quickly ended but another part – a part she was loath to acknowledge – was secretly wallowing in the pleasure of submission. Disgusted by that concept, Stacey refused to think about her response.

Julia screamed. She tugged hard on Stacey's hair and shivered through her orgasm. Stacey felt the pussy muscles trembling around her tongue and, heedless of the pain, she pulled her head away. She glanced up and watched the dark-haired woman grimacing happily through a paroxysm of bitter pleasure.

Slowly, Julia regained her composure. She slipped her fingers from Stacey's hair, straightened the crotch of her panties, then brushed down the hem of her skirt. Staring down, she glared contemptuously at Stacey kneeling on the floor. The sneer was only replaced by a smile when she saw the tears falling down Stacey's cheeks.

Seeming satisfied with this response, she stepped back behind her desk, plucked at the fingers on her gloves, then slid the leather from her hands. After tossing them into the open drawer she slammed it closed.

Stacey glanced up as though she had been struck again.

'You can leave now,' Julia said sharply. 'But, before you go, I ought to tell you one more thing.'

Stacey blinked the tears from her eyes. She didn't bother climbing from the floor, sure she knew what

the woman was going to say. Her fears were confirmed when Julia's evil smile grew broader.

'You're fired,' she said simply.

Night sped past the limousine in a blur of golden
street lamps and ruby and emerald traffic lights. The
driver was secluded behind a smoked partition and
Julia and Ted York were able to talk without fear of
being overheard.

'You're joking with me, aren't you?' He sounded
uncertain. 'You didn't really spank her bare backside,
did you? You're just saying that to wind me up.'

Julia sniffed with mock indignation. 'Of course I
spanked her bare backside. The little shit had stolen
praise for my hard work. She's lucky I didn't staple
her pussy lips together.'

Ted shook his head and then grinned uneasily. He
had the bland good looks of a James Bond actor:
strong and masculine but otherwise unremarkable.
After listening to Julia recount Stacey's punishment
his tanned complexion had begun to pale. 'I think
you are joking with me,' he decided. 'You wouldn't
really have done something that could so easily
rebound on the company. You wouldn't really have
risked the scandal of an unfair dismissal claim, a
sexual harassment suit, and God knows what other
litigious actions.'

Annoyed that he was missing the point, Julia rolled
her eyes. She considered Ted to be more of a trophy
boyfriend than a genuine partner. He was a successful
man who could get her invited to the important social
gatherings and, as his girlfriend, she knew she bene-
fited from the status that was sycophantically af-
forded to him. But she only cared for him in the same
way she cared for his limousine: they were both
vehicles to take her where she wanted to go. And, as

useful as he could be in some areas, there were times when Ted's obsession with the company's good name really grated on her nerves.

'I dealt with Stacey,' Julia said firmly. She felt affronted that Ted had such little faith in her abilities to control subordinates but she tried not to dwell on that unspoken slur. She could already sense they were on the brink of bickering and potentially spoiling the night before it had begun. 'The little shit won't cause any trouble because she'll be too scared and too embarrassed. Trust me, Ted. I know how to deal with the drones and insignificants we employ.'

Ted gaped. 'You really did spank her, didn't you?'

Wearily, Julia wondered how it was possible for such a successful man to be so dense. He was one of the most senior directors beneath Mr Jones – tipped to become the next managing director, unless Jones put the company in the hands of his mysterious heir, Andy – yet Ted couldn't seem to grasp this one simple fact. Seeing there was only one way to convince him, Julia took his hand and pushed it beneath her skirt. She guided his fingers to the sodden panel of her gusset and asked, 'Doesn't this prove it? My pussy is sopping. Partly it's from the arousal I got while slapping her arse. Partly it's wet from the tonguing she gave me to make amends. Doesn't this prove I'm telling the truth?'

Ted's mood changed like the flick of a switch. His concern for the company's reputation was brushed aside as his excitement took over. Inwardly smug, Julia marvelled at how easy it was to control him. Like all the men she had encountered on her journey up the corporate ladder, Ted only needed the briefest sexual distraction and she had him exactly where she wanted.

With scant regard for subtlety, he pushed the crotch of her panties to one side. His fingers burrowed easily into her wetness and the labia melted beneath his eager touch. Julia smiled into his eyes and knew whatever argument had been brewing between them was all but forgotten with the promise of passion.

'You should have called me in to watch,' Ted grunted.

She laughed. 'I threatened her with that. I guess the little bitch had a crush on you because she squirmed at the idea of your being present.'

He worked two fingers deep into her hole and began to rub slowly back and forth. His thumb toyed with her clitoris and, caught on a rising swell of euphoria, she writhed against the seat. Parting her legs so he had easier access – hitching her skirt up so she could see what he was doing – Julia asked, 'Does this mean you forgive me for disciplining my subordinates?'

Instead of replying, he unfastened the uppermost buttons on her blouse. The lacy cups of her bra were revealed and he eased one breast free. The coffee-coloured nipple, contrasting starkly with the plump, pale orb, stood hard and responsive. Julia revelled in bliss when Ted lowered his lips over the nub and began to suck. His mouth was a warm, moist haven and she responded ecstatically.

It didn't worry her that the driver might see what they were doing, or that anyone glancing through the limousine's windows could watch Ted using her. She didn't care if they were being observed and felt sure, rather than offending anyone, the sight of her being pleasured was only likely to inspire envy and jealousy. Holding the back of his head, careful not to spoil his well-groomed coiffure, she pressed her breast toward his face and wriggled her sex on his plundering fingers.

'It's a shame you only have dominant inclinations,' he grunted.

She didn't understand the comment at first and had to think past the giddy distraction of arousal to make sense of what he was saying. His fingers were wreaking blissful havoc between her legs, stroking her quickly to a point where nothing existed except her need for satisfaction. When understanding finally dawned Julia stiffened with indignation and placed a steadying hand on Ted's wrist. She tugged on his shirt collar until he moved his head away and met her disapproving frown. 'What the hell do you mean by that?' she demanded. 'What's wrong with my inclinations? I don't see you complaining.'

He rubbed his thumb over her clitoris, silencing her with trembling eddies of pleasure. Julia gasped, sat rigid on his fingers and blinked back a startled cry. She was revelling in delicious excitement but the idea that he thought she was in some way inadequate continued to rankle.

He returned his tongue to her nipple, sparking a raw bolt of pleasure from the tip. His hand continued wriggling soft magic between her thighs and, if not for the gnawing flicker of irritation, Julia would have happily allowed him to continue. With a growl of frustration she pushed his face from her breast and asked him to explain himself.

He laughed at her petulant scowl. 'I wasn't complaining or criticising,' he assured her. 'I was just saying it's a shame you're not more balanced in your sexual appetites. The Pride of the Company are meeting tonight and, if you'd been a little less dominant in your tastes, I'd think they might have welcomed you with open arms.'

Julia stared at him in amazement. Not thinking about what she was doing, she pushed his hand away from her cleft. All thoughts of arousal had suddenly become unwanted distractions and she hurriedly tried to organise her thoughts. 'The Pride of the Company?' she echoed. She had heard the name before: a rumour about an exclusive group of the company's highest ranking executives. Allegedly they dictated corporate trends before they were negotiated in the boardrooms. The gossip she had heard said they secretly made all the company's important decisions. But, when Julia first heard them being mentioned, she had thought it was just someone's paranoid variation on a conspiracy theory. Now, listening to Ted talk about the Pride of the Company, she realised there really was a team of high-fliers who had so far excluded her from their prestigious ranks. 'The Pride of the Company exists?'

His easy grin said more than words. She could tell they did exist and she got the impression that Ted was a member of their upper echelon. 'We're meeting tonight,' he said. 'After the dinner and dance.'

She nodded as though the matter was decided. 'In that case you'll have to take me with you. You simply have to.'

Ted shook his head. 'That's why I was saying it was a shame you only enjoyed domination,' he explained patiently. 'The Pride of the Company includes the most successful executives in the company – we would have invited you to join years ago – but we're exclusively male. There's never been a female member so far and the only women who can attend have to have submissive tastes.'

A finger of dark excitement touched the centre of her belly. Afterwards Julia could never decide if it came from the prospect of submission, or the chance of furthering her career. All she knew was her mind was made up and nothing was going to stop her from getting involved with the secret society of decision makers. 'Take me there,' she insisted.

'I can't.' He sounded genuinely pained at having to refuse her request. 'I've already told you. You don't have the submissive nature that would be required.'

She rolled her eyes with impatience and grabbed him by the arms. 'I can be dominant or submissive,' she explained. 'Give me an instruction. Give me a command. Let me show you how submissive I can be.'

He studied her warily.

'I'm serious,' she growled. 'Give me a command, let me prove I can be submissive, then you can take me to the after-dinner meeting.'

'Go on then,' he conceded. 'If you want to prove your point to me, you can suck my cock.'

She said nothing for a moment, wondering suddenly if he had engineered the entire conversation so she would give him a blow job. If she had been a man, and in his position of authority, she knew it would be a trick that she could happily employ. But she didn't believe Ted had the same qualities of cunning and ruthlessness. Sensing she was running the risk of letting a priceless opportunity slip past her, Julia nodded abruptly. She pushed Ted back in his seat and took advantage of the limousine's spacious interior to kneel in front of him.

Keeping her eyes fixed on his, willing herself to appear pliant and obedient, she stroked the thick bulge that rested inside his trousers. He was hard and twitching under her fingertips and she enjoyed the brief pleasure of tormenting him by simply caressing his zip. Reminding herself she was supposed to be submissive, and there for his pleasure, Julia unfastened his trousers and released his erection.

Ted inhaled sharply.

Excitement had made him swollen. His length was long and thick and his foreskin had peeled back to reveal the meaty dome of his glans. Curling her fingers around the pulsing heat, Julia pushed her face closer and extended her tongue.

'Didn't you know I could be submissive?' she asked innocently.

'It's never been an adjective I've associated with you.'

She giggled softly and teased the tip of her tongue against his fraenum. 'I must have hidden depths that you've yet to explore,' she guessed. 'Get me into the Pride of the Company and perhaps I'll let you discover more of them.' Sure the suggestion must have excited him, certain she was on the brink of achieving membership to the ranks of the company's real decision makers, Julia pushed her face over his shaft.

His thickness was broad enough to stretch her lips wide. The end of his length filled her mouth, and it was a struggle to work her tongue against him and suck at the same time. But Julia endeavoured to tackle the chore with forced enthusiasm. Keeping one hand loosely wrapped around the base of his shaft she stroked her wrist back and forth. Smears of her lipstick bloodied his length and she licked them away with a series of greedy kisses. She continued to work her mouth wetly on him until she felt the first violent shiver tremble through his shaft.

'Am I doing this correctly, sir?' she asked. She held his glans against her lower lip as she asked the question. Carefully, she watched his expression to see if her pretence at servility had convinced him. 'Is there any way I could make this more pleasurable?' she cooed.

He grunted and, sensing his climax was about to explode, Julia pushed her mouth over his pulsing end.

A thick jet of semen spattered at the roof of her mouth followed by a second then a third. Her mouth was quickly filled with his seed but, instead of swallowing the noxious liquid, she held it in her cheeks. She kept her lips around him until he was spent, then indelicately spat the mouthful of come onto the floor of the limousine.

She smiled bitterly to herself when she thought of the driver cleaning up the mess, then brushed the cruel diversion from her mind as she glanced up at Ted. 'How was that for you, sir?' she asked. 'Did I seem servile enough?'

He grinned. 'A true submissive would have swallowed.'

The comment stung but she stifled her instinctive reaction. An argument at this point wasn't going to help secure an invitation to meet the Pride of the Company. 'I suppose you're right,' she conceded. 'I'll have to remember that for the next time.'

Tucking his shaft back into his trousers, Ted graced her with a perplexed frown. 'You really want to go with me after the dinner, don't you?'

'I'd do anything to go with you,' she said honestly. 'Whatever it is you want me to do – whatever it takes – I'll do anything to go. Didn't that blow job just prove how eager I am?'

His smile was humourless as he said, 'I can see that I'm not going to be able to talk you out of this.' Shaking his head in the face of her triumphant smile, he added, 'I just don't think you know what you're letting yourself in for.'

'Where will the after-dinner meeting be held?'

'Not far from the restaurant,' he said carefully. 'There's a nearby club. I expect you've heard of it. It's been going for a couple of years now. It's called Sinners.'

* * *

Lasciate ogni speranza, voi ch'entrate! Julia recognised the quote from Dante, arched over the doorway to Sinners. *All hope abandon, ye who enter!*

But, aside from the forbidding sentiment, she thought the rest of the foyer looked unspectacular. The cloakroom kiosk sold lottery tickets and ciga- rettes; a couple, intimately embracing, lurked in the shadows of an alcove; and the bass thud of nearby music shook the carpeted floor beneath her feet. The pounding vibration was almost like a heartbeat and for an instant Julia was struck by the fanciful image of the nightclub being a living, breathing creature. Brushing the whimsical notion from her thoughts, she drew a breath to steady her nerves and waited for the kiosk attendant to finish dealing with a plump blonde on the customer side of the counter. Their exchange was heated, but conducted in surreptitious whispers and, although she struggled to eavesdrop, Julia couldn't catch any more than the occasional bitter syllable.

The plump blonde walked away from the counter, her crimson expression a knot of twisted emotions. She banged her shoulder against Julia's arm as she marched past and didn't bother to interrupt her monologue of expletives to murmur an apology. It was impossible to tell if she was frustrated, angry or possibly even excited because all those reactions seemed prevalent in her creased brow and shining eyes. Julia couldn't decide what could cause someone to look so perplexed and dismissed the distraction before it added to her worries. She simply decided the plump blonde had more issues to deal with than a dress that was too short and too tight for someone with such an ungainly body.

'I'm here to meet my colleagues,' she said, boldly stepping toward the kiosk.

The dark figure in the booth regarded her with a studied silence. He was unremarkable save for the brilliant white of his dress shirt and the confident way in which he held himself. A whisper of amusement lurked in the corner of his smile but it failed to touch his obsidian eyes.

'I'm with the Pride of the Company,' Julia said, introducing herself. 'I was told you'd be expecting me.'

She had grown quickly bored with the charity dinner. Her table had been filled with drones and insignificants and the chore of making polite conversation, about the benefits of helping the local church, soon became too arduous. Greedily anticipating this moment, looking forward to being accepted by her peers, she had pestered Ted to let them leave early. Eventually he went halfway to relenting and told Julia she should make her own way to Sinners and that he would follow.

But now, intimidated by the alien surroundings and just a little uneasy at the prospect of what might be expected of her, she wondered if she had made the right decision. 'The Pride of the Company,' she said again, nerves exacerbating her characteristic impatience. Speaking with forced patience she explained, 'They're meeting here tonight and I've been invited to join their ranks.'

'Mr York called and said you'd be arriving,' the kiosk attendant remembered. 'If you can wait for my relief to return, I'll happily show you upstairs to their conference suite.'

Satisfied, she nodded and glanced at her surroundings in search of conversational inspiration. With her thoughts distracted by the prospect of meeting the Pride of the Company, there wasn't much she could think to say. 'I've never been here before,' she started.

He raised an eyebrow. 'No. I think I would have recognised you if you had.'

She frowned, wondering if he was building to a pick-up line, then forced the suspicion from her mind. Julia didn't usually get tense before meetings – she prided herself on the ability to remain clear-headed and untroubled by nerves in the most stressful situations – but she knew this evening was going to be more important than any meeting she had ever attended previously. Feigning confidence she nodded at the arched sign above the nightclub's doorway and said, 'That's not the warmest welcome I've ever read.'

His smile was tight-lipped. 'The nightclub is called Sinners. Abandoning hope seemed like sage advice when I placed the quote there.' After a moment's reflection he added, 'Abandoning all virtues seems prudent under the circumstances.'

She didn't understand what he meant and, before she got the chance to ask him to elaborate, a woman was scurrying to his side. Julia recognised her as the plump blonde he had been arguing with moments earlier but, in the time they had taken to begin their faltering conversation, she had changed into a far more revealing outfit than her inappropriately short dress.

'Jesus Christ!' Julia whispered. The blonde's appearance made a lump rise in her throat. The distraction banished all worries from Julia's thoughts and she didn't realise she had made her exclamation aloud. She blinked twice, not sure she was really seeing the outrageous exhibition that the blonde was presenting. Unable to stop herself, she stared after the woman in slack-jawed amazement.

At first glance it looked like the plump blonde was naked. Her bare legs raced quickly through the foyer and, although the image was fleeting, Julia noticed painted toenails and bare feet pushing into the pile of the carpet. She saw a lightly swaying breast – bulbous and somehow unreal in the otherwise normal surroundings – and a glint of something silver. Then the woman had passed by. Julia glanced sharply after her in time to see a bare backside disappearing through the door to the kiosk.

'If you're ready?' the kiosk attendant said, stepping to Julia's side.

She tried to glance behind him, wanting to confirm what she thought she had seen, but he was standing too close and obstinately spoilt her view. Julia caught a glimpse of the blonde's blush, a deep-rooted scarlet that said she was obviously mortified, then the kiosk attendant was holding Julia's arm and guiding her past a sign that pointed upstairs toward the conference suite. Not wanting to cause a scene, and knowing the Pride of the Company meeting was more important than this distraction, she grudgingly fell into step by his side.

'Was she naked?' she whispered.

'Of course not.' He sounded indignant. 'What sort of establishment would this be if I allowed naked women to run around the foyer? Sinners isn't one of *those* sorts of clubs.'

Julia wasn't convinced. 'She looked naked.'

He barked mirthless laughter. 'She might have looked naked but she wasn't. She was wearing her chains.'

Julia swallowed and tried glancing back over her shoulder but they had already turned a corner and were heading up the stairs. The memory of the blonde returned with unsettling clarity and Julia was stunned to realise he was right. A loop of chunky silver links had circled the blonde's swollen stomach, one length dropping between her fat thighs and reappearing

112

from between her jiggling buttocks. Another had been fashioned into a parody of a bra, loosely embracing her ample breasts. Now her mind was beyond the initial shock, Julia found she could recall the details with disturbing ease. But, although she knew he was telling the truth, she didn't want to accept the fact. 'She was "*wearing her chains*"?' she repeated uncertainly. 'What do you mean, "*wearing her chains*"?'

He led her through an anonymous doorway on the first floor before replying. 'You know what chains are. You don't really want me to spell it out for you, do you?'

Flicking a light switch to throw dim illumination on their claustrophobic surroundings, he reached for the hook behind the door and retrieved a length of shiny metals links. 'Chains like these,' he said stiffly. 'That's what she was wearing. They're identical to the ones that you'll be wearing tonight.'

Julia counted to ten before replying, weighing up all the things he had said and trying to think about the implications. They were in a small room, little more than a short corridor, with a door at either end. The exit facing her was labelled with an enamelled sign saying "Conference Suite". Beneath it, repeating the sentiment that had greeted her in the foyer, was the line from Dante she had already read: *Lasciate ogni speranza, voi ch'entrate!* For no reason she could understand, her heart pounded hard and fast.

'You knew you'd be here in a submissive role, didn't you?'

She sneered at him scornfully. 'Of course.'

'And you know what they'll be expecting of you in the conference suite?'

Julia didn't know exactly what would be expected of her, but she had a fair idea. She also had some plans about how to use the evening to her advantage but she wasn't going to explain that much to the stranger from the kiosk. 'I know what they're expecting from me,' she lied defiantly.

He nodded. 'Then you should have no objection to wearing the chains.'

Grudgingly, she snatched them from him. She thought about telling him that, if she had to undress, she would feel more comfortable doing it after he had left. But, reminding herself she was on the verge of presenting herself shamelessly to her peers, she decided his leering presence was something she could abide. Besides, she didn't relish the prospect of being alone with her thoughts and, although she found the kiosk attendant a little disquieting, she was content to let him stay. Also, considering the tangle of metal she was expected to wear, she supposed he might even be able to help her get into the ridiculously revealing costume. Trying not to let natural reservations make her hesitate, she began to undress.

'You're a sinner, aren't you?'

She snorted rudely. 'That's a rich accusation coming from a man who gets his staff to undress for work.' She was down to her bra and pants and congratulating herself for not being disturbed by his lascivious interest. Reaching behind herself to unfasten the clasp on her bra she said, 'One of us must really have our priorities misjudged. You're calling me a sinner and you run an establishment where the women have to wear chains instead of underwear.'

He nodded solemnly. 'The dress code is only an occasional disciplinary measure for some of my staff,' he explained. 'And perhaps, to some extent, I am a sinner. But I'm not in the same league as you.'

She removed her bra and stepped out of her pants, all the time curling her upper lip with distaste.

114

Unmindful of her nudity she glared at him and said sarcastically, 'Oh! Golly gosh! You think I'm a sinner! How can I carry on living a fulfilling life now I know I don't meet the standards of a kiosk attendant? What will become of me?'

He acted quickly and without warning. His hand gripped one breast, cupping the orb and squeezing. There was enough force for the sensation to feel rough but it wasn't so unpleasant Julia wanted to pull away. Eagerly, he stepped closer and pressed himself against her bare body. 'Your sin is pride,' he said quietly.

She started to speak but he silenced her with a kiss. His mouth enveloped hers, his tongue sliding between her lips and gliding over her teeth. Dumbfounded by his audacity, Julia could only stand rigid as he acquainted himself with her nudity. She allowed his fingers to tease the stiffening tip of her nipple and made no protest as he rubbed his upper thigh between her legs. The lips of her sex were caressed by the coarse twill of his trousers and sparks of pure, sharp arousal spat from her pussy. Within moments of him touching her she was in the spell of a dark, greedy excitement.

'Your sin is pride,' he repeated, momentarily breaking their kiss to speak. 'You're guilty of the darkest of all sins and you're so bereft of remorse it's positively chilling.'

Not sure why she was responding to his verbal abuse so eagerly, only aware that she had to have him near her, Julia pulled his mouth back to her face. This time their kiss was more urgent and passionate. When they finally broke for air, she knew their arousal was shared. The swell of his erection pressed through his trousers and weighed with feverish intensity against her stomach. She glanced down at the obscene bulge, smiling at the inordinate size as she licked her lips. Placing a hand over him she squeezed lightly and said, 'My being a sinner isn't turning you off, is it?'

He brushed her hand away, lowered his mouth as though he was going to kiss her face, then moved his lips over her breast. He effortlessly found her nipple, catching the sensitive teat between his teeth, then nibbling.

Julia found herself transported to the throes of unprecedented bliss and bucked herself toward him. Her body's eager response came as something of a surprise but she didn't waste precious moments analysing her lecherous need. Instead, she just gave in to the thrill and relished his commanding authority. Chuckling throatily at the promise of more pleasure, she murmured giddily, 'Where have you been all my life?'

He snorted dourly, before briefly releasing his hold on her nipple. 'It's your pride that's been keeping us apart this evening.'

The words meant nothing to her and she allowed the meaning to wash over her in the same way his hands caressed her curves.

'If not for your injured pride you could have been here an hour earlier instead of slapping your office girl's backside. If not for your egotistical need to join the Pride of the Company, you could have been here a further half hour earlier instead of sucking Ted York's cock.'

She knew he was referring to events that he couldn't have known about, yet even though she understood that fact, Julia couldn't bring herself to respond to the anomaly. He was inspiring such a wealth of delicious responses she could only close her eyes and revel in burgeoning joy.

The darkness was sudden and frightening.

Rather than being in the embrace of the kiosk attendant she suddenly found she was holding something unhuman and demonic. The acrid stench of sulphur rasped against her nostrils and her arms ached from the talon-like grip of his claws biting into the biceps. The mouth at her breast was unnaturally warm and her nipple felt as though it was being chewed away. Whereas before she had been holding an unprepossessing stranger, she now found herself embracing a creature from the blackest of her nightmares.

She struggled, suddenly needing to escape him.

Even when she had opened her eyes – and proved that her imagination had deceived her – it was still hard to shake off the idea that there was more to the kiosk attendant than she had initially imagined. The scent of his warm sweat, so arousing moments earlier, now seemed redolent of bubbling sulphur. With only a little effort, she managed to extricate herself from his arms.

'You're right,' he said, as though agreeing with some unspoken sentiment about restraint. 'There'll be time for that later. Right now we have to get you ready for your meeting, don't we?'

Not wanting to encourage him, or risk the confrontation that might come from a direct rebuttal, Julia said nothing. She was determined there would be no time for whatever he was planning later. She simply wanted to meet the Pride of the Company and put safe distance between herself and the unsettling man. Without speaking she stepped into the chain bra and thong, guardedly allowing him to help her fasten the unfamiliar clasps.

He stepped back to admire her and applauded softly. 'Now you look like you belong.' He grinned.

'Who are you?' she asked uncertainly. 'And how do you fit into the Pride of the Company?' A chilling thought occurred to her and she fixed him with a terrified expression. 'You're not their leader, are you?'

'Me?' His laughter was self-deprecatory. 'I'm no one special. I'm just the proprietor of this establishment.'

He held out his hand but she resisted taking it, partly because she wasn't sure she wanted to touch him again, and partly because she knew the moment of meeting her peers was drawing closer. 'You own Sinners?'

'That's quite a clever way of phrasing the situation.' He smiled. He snapped his fingers and she realised he wasn't going to take the discussion any further. 'It's time for your meeting to begin,' he intoned sombrely. 'You seem like you have your plans ready, so I think we should make our way to the conference suite, don't you?' He started toward the door and added, 'Ted York will be waiting for you by now. As will the others.'

Trying to hide her hesitance, Julia accepted his hand and allowed him to lead her through the door.

Ted was waiting for her in the conference suite but he wasn't the first thing Julia noticed. There were two dozen men gathered in the room and they turned to study her as though they had been eagerly anticipating her arrival. Julia recognised a handful of the company's directors, saw Mr Jones was there with a drink in his hand, and noticed he had been chatting with a couple of the firm's senior consultants.

For an instant she was almost overwhelmed by panic. She was face to face with the company's acknowledged leaders and dressed in nothing more substantial than a few lengths of chain. The strips of metal felt bizarrely uncomfortable against her sex.

They pressed hard and unnatural between her labia and squirmed against her clitoris, but she ignored the sly weight. The kiosk attendant had taken great pains in making sure her nipples poked out from between two links and, if she had glanced down at herself, Julia would have seen the swollen tips jutting through the ovals of shiny steel. Already feeling overexposed and vulnerable she resisted the urge to study herself. Determined that no one would see any doubt in her expression she coolly returned each curious glance. It took a lot of effort to feign nonchalance but, because she desperately wanted to appear unintimidated, she made her act very convincing.

'Julia?'

Dan Carstairs, marketing director, stepped toward her as he repeated her name. His smile was a mixture of disbelief and unabashed lechery. As he passed the managing director he caught the man's arm and encouraged the head of the company to join him.

'Julia? Is that really you?'

She struggled to keep her tone neutral. 'Hello, Dan.'

'Do I take it that you know this young lady?' Jones asked.

Carstairs laughed with the mirth of a practised sycophant. It was an irritating chuckle that only bore a nodding acquaintance toward the concept of genuine amusement. 'We all know Julia,' Carstairs said, reminding Jones of her position within the company. 'She's the one who helped me prepare our most recent target demograph reports.'

'No.' Julia placed her hands on her hips and shook her head. She was nearly naked, had no idea what further surprises the evening might hold, but in this conversation she considered herself to be on familiar territory. 'That's not quite correct, is it, Danny?' she asked sweetly.

He frowned and she could see he didn't like being addressed with such familiarity. Unable to stop herself Julia sneered haughtily. 'I didn't *help* you prepare those demograph reports. *I did all the damned work*. I blew a month's overtime budget having my staff get your job done and then, when the reports were finished, you took the credit for my observations about where you should be targeting your next sales drive.' Satisfied that she had said enough she stopped herself before her voice could turn strident.

Carstairs' smile evaporated. He glared at her with an expression of unconcealed rage and Julia knew, if the others hadn't been there, he would have slapped her across the face. Watching him impotently attempt to conceal his anger was blackly amusing.

Jones glanced from Julia to the marketing director and she was elated to see him regarding Carstairs with what looked like disdain. She had been aching to get even with Carstairs for three months and this unscheduled revenge had been too good an opportunity to miss. As the pair scurried back into the throng, and Jones began to ask questions that sounded painfully embarrassing, Julia had to fight to stop a triumphant grin from splitting her lips.

It crossed her mind that, even if she couldn't inveigle her way into the ranks of the Pride of the Company, the evening had still been a success. Then she reminded herself that such thinking was for losers. Confident in her ability to turn the night to her advantage she believed that, by the end of this evening, the Pride of the Company would be begging her to join their numbers. That achievement alone would be the real hallmark of the evening's success.

She was still smiling at the thought when Ted produced the ball-gag. It consisted of a red rubber ball secured to links identical to those in the chains around her breasts and hips. He stepped nearer, guiding the ball close to her mouth, and she raised a warning hand.

'What the fuck do you think you're going to do with that?'

'It's a ball-gag. You know damned well what I'm going to do with it. I'm going to put it in your mouth.'

Julia shook her head. 'I'm not wearing a gag.'

'If you don't wear it then you'll have to leave.' His voice dropped to a confidential whisper. 'You might think you're in line for membership here, you'll probably be able to swing it knowing your skills at manipulating people, but the Pride of the Company won't let you stay another minute if you're not wearing this gag.'

She wanted to argue the point but some of the group were already gracing her with peculiar glances. Sensing that she was running the risk of spoiling her chances, Julia grudgingly accepted the sphere of rubber in her mouth. She allowed Ted to secure it at the back of her head and wasn't surprised to hear Dan Carstairs make some artless comment about how she should have been gagged before she was brought into the room.

All the time Ted was securing the gag she wondered if this development would spoil her plans. She hadn't anticipated being deprived of the ability to speak but she didn't think forced silence would have a detrimental effect. Guessing why the Pride of the Company met she had already decided she wasn't going to win anyone over with mere words.

Ted secured the final clasp and stepped away from her. Addressing the group he called, 'What are we going to do with her?'

Bolts of unease speared her stomach as Julia realised she was once again centre of attention and

121

excruciatingly vulnerable. Someone blew a wolf-whistle; a couple of others applauded; the rest shouted coarse and vulgar suggestions. With a determined effort she managed to stave off the urge to blush.

'Fuck her!'

'Cane her!'

'Slap the bitch!'

Julia felt sure the last suggestion had come from Carstairs and she narrowed her eyes when she glared in his direction.

Ted acted as though he was playing to a vaudeville audience and cupped his hand around his ear. 'I can't hear you,' he called cheerfully. 'What are we going to do with her?'

Mr Jones stepped forward from the group, still holding his half-drained glass of Martini. He coughed twice to clear his throat and then said, 'I want to see her broken on the wheel.'

Julia started at the remark. Her unease heightened when the managing director's suggestion was greeted by a cheer of approval and cries to second the motion. The group started to settle themselves on a circle of chairs but, as Ted began guiding her into their midst, Julia hesitated.

Ted leant close to her ear, his warm breath tickling the hairs on the nape of her neck. 'Breaking you on the wheel isn't the torment you might think,' he explained. 'We use a lot of euphemisms and metaphors here in the Pride of the Company but we're not into medieval torture. *Breaking on the Wheel* just means we're going to sit round in a circle and you're going to get passed from one cock to the other until we're all satisfied.'

Not only did the explanation make sense but it also warmed her with a slick, black excitement. Julia saw the executives had seated themselves in a loose circle and noted there was a single empty chair waiting for Ted.

Instead of taking his seat, he escorted her to the centre of the group. Standing behind her, he guided her into a bent position and then clutched her buttocks. The twin lengths of chain that covered her sex were pulled apart and her head began to throb as she realised what was going to happen. She heard his zip tugging down, felt the heat of his erection press against her cleft, and then he was plunging into her.

Her pussy muscles clenched around his erection, squeezing greedily as he burrowed into her. She had screwed him before and knew he was a capable lover but this evening he felt even more adept. His shaft seemed thicker, every thrust inspired a response that bordered on orgasm and, within moments of him beginning, she could feel herself being transported to a sleazy plateau of raw pleasure.

A handful of the men began to clap time while others chanted something about the leader's privilege. Their calls meant nothing to Julia as she squirmed herself eagerly onto Ted's engorged length.

She had never considered herself an exhibitionist but, proud of her good looks and desirable figure, she knew she didn't have anything to hide. A part of her wanted to be embarrassed that colleagues and senior staff were seeing her in this submissive position but she wouldn't let her thoughts follow that downward spiral. She knew she could use this evening to her advantage – she felt sure her position as a regular attendee at these meetings was virtually assured – and she was determined to savour every sordid moment.

Fending off the rush of her own climax, she clenched her pussy muscles tightly around his shaft. Not knowing if she was permitted to move, and not caring if she was breaking any of the group's rules, she writhed her buttocks as she held his erection deep inside. Riding herself back and forth on his length, squeezing the pulsing muscles of her sex as tightly as she could manage, Julia willed herself to wring the orgasm from him.

Ted climaxed with an exasperated grunt.

His shaft had left her warm and swollen, his spend dripping greasily from the walls of her sex. Although she hadn't wanted him to bring her to orgasm, she was pleased with the way he had aroused her passion. When he pulled himself free and pushed her to one of the waiting executives, Julia fell on her new partner hungrily.

His shaft was out of his trousers and he remained on his chair as she impaled herself on him. With a greedy need that clearly outweighed her own, he pawed at her breasts as she rode up and down. The chains around her nipples made it hard for him to excite her but Julia was content to rub her clitoris against the stiffness of his erection as they rode together. His gaze was filled with lecherous admiration and she proudly realised that was the expression she had been hoping to see.

Her plan was a model of simplicity and she knew it couldn't fail to work: she intended to provide each member with the most satisfying sex they had ever experienced, then let their greed for more help sway their decision on her membership. Conceitedly sure of her skills as a lover, clenching her muscles and twisting her thighs with every downward thrust, Julia didn't think her scheme could fail. If the expression of adoration on the man she was currently riding was an indicator, she believed her place with the Pride of the Company was virtually assured. She could see his eyes shining with a desire for restraint and it was a close call as to which of them climaxed first.

Julia was only just enjoying the first thrills of orgasmic bliss when he pumped his seed against the neck of her womb. The intimate spurt was so powerful it was enough to drive another shudder of joy from her hole.

Before she had stopped trembling she was being used by another man.

The hand-clapping continued as she went from one to another. The faces quickly became a seamless blur and she couldn't tell if she was being used by someone she wanted to impress, like Mr Jones, or someone she was loath to screw, like Carstairs. For one insane moment she thought the kiosk attendant was there and sliding his engorged length into her sex. Then that image was gone as another faceless executive slipped his shaft into her sodden hole.

She only realised she had completed her first circuit when Ted dragged her back to the centre of the room and gestured for the applause to cease.

The hand-clapping petered away.

'Are we ready to break her?' he called.

She was still panting from the pleasure of the last penetration and didn't think she had heard correctly. Whatever comfort she might have drawn was banished when the group took up a brisk, urgent chant: ' . . . break her . . . break her . . . break her . . .'

Ted's grin was malevolent as he bent her over and slapped a large palm against her backside. The clap resounded loudly and, although she couldn't see, Julia knew there would be a bright red handprint emblazoned on her buttock. She didn't get the chance to object before she was being pushed around the circle to have her backside punished by the remainder of the group.

It only took a few blows before her rear felt inflamed by the chastisement. Her buttocks were a blazing warmth that rekindled boiling fury against her cleft. She was aware that some only tapped her lightly, as though they believed themselves sensitive to her needs, while others struck with a force that was intended to hurt. Determined they wouldn't find her lacking in any respect, Julia happily groaned as she went round the circle.

She stumbled toward Ted's chair, expecting him to tell her she had done well but he only bent her over again, sharply spanked her backside, then passed her back to the next man in the circle. In spite of her best efforts Julia couldn't manage to keep up the facade she believed the Pride of the Company wanted to see. As the hands continued to clap against her bare buttocks it was all she could do to stumble from one chair to the next and greedily await her punishment. By the time Ted had pushed her to begin a fourth circuit she was wondering if the frustrating torment would ever end.

Still, she continued, shuffling inelegantly, presenting her bottom and only moving on when she had felt the stinging indignity of another slap. She honestly believed she would have been able to carry on indefinitely if someone – Carstairs, she thought – hadn't tripped her up and sent her sprawling on the floor.

'She's broken,' Ted cried. 'No more spanking.'

His shout was met with jubilant applause and Julia glanced up at the sea of mocking faces that surrounded her. Ted pushed his way closer, extended a hand to help her from the floor and supported her as she struggled to maintain balance. His arm fell naturally around her waist and she swooned against him like a weary lover.

'The choice is now yours,' he said quietly.

Julia didn't fool herself into thinking the conversation was private because she knew every member of the group had fallen silent and was listening to their exchange.

'Do you want me to unfasten your gag, find your clothes and let you go home now?' he asked. 'Or do you want to take a final circuit on the wheel?'

She glared at him defiantly, unable to believe that he thought he could get rid of her so easily. Not needing to remove the gag to answer, knowing she could say more without using any words, she reached for his zipper and pulled it down. His hardness sprang through the opening and, with an urgency that exposed her insatiable need, she turned around and skewered herself on his erection.

She didn't know when her arousal had become such a potent force but she knew she needed to satisfy the urge. It burnt madly between her legs and, even when she had milked Ted of his climax, she knew she had to feel the penetration of another man straight away.

As they had the first time, the group each took their turn to use her and then pass her on. Her breasts were mauled through the infuriating links of chain and her buttocks were squeezed and scratched without mercy. Fingers intermittently plundered her anus and, beyond any notions of shame or embarrassment, Julia accepted each intrusion as another spur to the blistering climax that was building within her body. Some of them used her with such haste she barely felt their entry before their climax squirted into her hole. Others rode her hard and with energetic vigour. She took thick cocks and thin cocks, accepted the guileless maulings and whispered crudities, constantly shivering through climax after climax.

And then the last of them was pushing her to Ted's feet where she lay panting, breathless and gratefully satisfied. A warm shiver spiralled up from her aching buttocks, trembling through the tingling walls of her pussy. Julia couldn't recall the last time she had received so much pleasure and wondered if it was all down to her skills as a lover, or if part of the night's success could be attributed to the anticipation of earning gratitude and acceptance from the Pride of the Company.

Drained, weary and spent, it was all she could do to embrace Ted's leg as she curled herself at his feet.

'Well done, Mr York,' Jones said, rising from his chair and slapping Ted on the shoulder. 'You never cease to amaze me with the way you train them so well.'

The words snapped Julia from her blissful reverie. She glared at Ted, expecting him to brush the compliment away and explain that he couldn't take credit for her accomplishment. As the moment stretched she wondered if he was going to have the impudence to accept Jones' praise as though he had in some way been responsible for her performance this evening. Fury welled within her and with such intensity that, for a moment, she feared she might explode with rage. If Ted stole her praise for this hard work she would . . . she would . . .

Julia couldn't think what she would do, or how she might be able to get even with the leader of the Pride of the Company. She considered snatching the gag from her mouth but knew, by the time she had managed to release it, the conversation would be over and done with. For the first time in her life she saw she was in a position where she couldn't gain the upper hand and would never have the chance to suitably avenge this theft of her praise.

'Training them is something of an acquired skill,' Ted arrogantly boasted to Jones. He reached out and slapped a playful hand against Julia's buttock. 'I'm glad you noticed how well I worked on this one. I've been training her for months and, I don't mind admitting: it took a lot of pride to get her here.'

5

An Envious Lot

Karina sorely envied the naked brunette.

She was dragged onto the podium to bask in the warmth of a cold spotlight. A murmur of approval wafted through the crowd, someone wolf-whistled, and a couple of others laughed with what sounded like drunken merriment.

Charlie held her by one arm, his gap-toothed smile edged with malicious pleasure. He turned her around so every inch of her bare body was made visible to the audience. The only parts of her skin that remained covered were those strips of flesh hidden by the chains of her bondage.

'Lot sixty-seven,' Robert said calmly. The microphone carried his words over the muttering voices and instilled an expectant silence. 'She's a pleasing specimen of feminine servility, nice titties, good legs and a backside that loves being slapped and slapped again. Her pedigree is uncertain and there's no deeds of indenture, but I do have signed GP certification to prove she's clean and healthy. On that note, I should add she doesn't eat much so, to fulfil all nutritional requirements, her diet is currently being supplemented with canine vitamins.'

Sitting at the back of the auditorium, watching with horror and disbelief, Karina shook her head in silent refusal. She still couldn't believe Robert – quietly spoken, calm, unassuming Robert – was playing the role of auctioneer: it seemed so totally out of character. She had no problem accepting Charlie's involvement. Charlie was a low-life, despicable piece of scum who would do anything for a cheap thrill or a fast buck. Charlie couldn't say hello on a morning without glancing at her cleavage or trying to see above the hem of her skirt; Charlie could seldom manage two consecutive sentences without using the word twat, fuck, shit or bastard; Charlie couldn't help but undress Karina with his gaze and make lewd suggestions at every opportunity. But Karina would never have imagined Robert being involved with a slave auction. Never in a million years.

'She's toilet-trained,' Robert continued blithely. 'She swallows. She swings both ways. And I'm told she likes it in any hole available. According to the seller, she can be bound, gagged, pierced, tattooed or branded, although, as you can all probably see, she's a clean canvas at the moment.'

Karina pressed a hand over her lap and moaned. Ever since they had brought the woman on to the podium there had been a tingling between her legs and now it buzzed like an electric charge. She pressed more firmly against her cleft and was rewarded by a spark of elation. Her nipples stood stiff inside her bra, weighing uncomfortably against the cotton fabric. Growing more excited with every second, she was thankful for the shadows that were keeping her arousal discreet.

'Who'll start me?' Robert asked. 'Who wants to make the first bid for this splendour of feminine loveliness?'

Karina held her breath, glanced around the group, and wondered if anyone might take him up on the

131

offer. She half-expected the auction to be revealed as a hoax – someone would turn the lights on while Robert pointed and they all laughed at her gullibility – but, as the silence crept on, Karina began to realise that wasn't going to happen. She began to accept she was attending a genuine slave auction and Robert – quietly spoken, calm, unassuming Robert – was the auctioneer.

'Who'll start me?' he asked again, wafting his gavel and glancing into the shadows of the auction hall. 'You all know there's only one lot at these "specialist" auctions. Who'll give me the night's first bid?'

Shocked by a thrill of unbidden arousal, Karina gasped with surprise and snatched her hands away from her crotch. She knew, if she continued touching so boldly, it wouldn't be long before she caught herself masturbating. She wasn't prone to pleasuring herself in public places, the idea was so crass it bordered on being repulsive but, with the discretion of the darkness and all that was happening on the podium, the impulse was hard to resist. The urgency of her need, and her body's demand for satisfaction, threatened to override her better judgement.

'Do I hear five hundred from the back of the room?' Robert asked hopefully. 'Do I hear four?'

The woman in the spotlight was a beautiful creature, her bondage displaying every aspect to exciting perfection. Her brunette tresses were tied back, away from her heart-shaped face, in a ponytail that cascaded down her bare back. She stared out at her potential buyers through the slender lengths of chain that triangulated across her face and held the red, rubber ball-gag firmly in her mouth.

Watching intently, Karina shivered. She couldn't decide if the tremor came from a voyeuristic thrill, or the idea of being in the woman's humiliating position. Both were powerful stimulants and brooding on

132

either made the temptation to touch herself even more irresistible.

The brunette's arms were cuffed behind her back and fastened to the collar encircling her throat. Her breasts were fat and swollen and displayed for everyone to see. A steel bar – *a spreader bar*, Karina decided – lay between her orbs. It was suspended by small, shiny clips that bit wickedly into the woman's nipples.

'Do I hear three hundred from the back?' Robert called again. With what sounded like growing doubt he asked, 'Do I hear two fifty?'

'I want to see it working!'

The exclamation came from the rear of the hall and Karina was able to detect the silhouette of the man who had shouted. He reminded her of the kiosk attendant from Sinners nightclub where Robert had taken her the previous week. At the time she had thought the man seemed an unremarkable figure: attractive but nothing spectacular. Yet she now remembered every detail about him and had no difficulty identifying him across the crowded floor of the dimly lit room. She cast her glance from the attendant to the brunette on the podium and wondered if the man was really interested in buying the woman and owning her as his slave. The concept left Karina shivering and she tried vainly to believe that her reaction was inspired by disgust.

'You want to see her working?' Robert repeated slowly. 'I can do that to a degree, but you have to remember all stock coming through here is sold as seen.' He pointed his gavel toward the '*caveat emptor*' sign behind the podium. At the same time, Robert deliberately nodded towards Charlie.

Karina realised the pair were used to this sort of demonstration and she told herself the idea was frightening and not arousing.

Charlie still held the woman's arm and he lifted it slowly. The brunette was forced to lean forward, her knees bending as she tried to remain upright without falling. Not seeming to care about her comfort or balance, Charlie turned her around until she was showing her buttocks to the auditorium. Because he was forcing her to bend further, the brunette's most intimate secrets were exposed in a shameless display. The ring of her anus was presented to the entire hall and, squeezing out from between her thighs, Karina could see the fat lips of the woman's pussy. A shadow of pubic curls darkened the edges of her cleft and, staring with avid interest, Karina thought she could also see a tell-tale smear of wetness.

'Didn't I say she had a nice backside?' Robert muttered.

Karina squirmed against her seat. Jealousy gnawed at her insides as she wished she could experience the thrill of the brunette's humiliation. Hardly aware she was doing it, she stole a hand back between her legs and touched the top of her thighs. Dragging her gaze from the podium for a second, glancing around to make sure everyone was focused on the slave and no one was watching her, she daringly lifted the hem of her skirt.

'A nice backside,' Robert repeated, consulting notes on his desk. 'And it's already been stretched to take a six inch plug.'

Karina swallowed back her surprise and thrust urgent fingers against the crotch of her panties. The gusset was feverishly warm and sodden with dewy wetness. When she pushed the panel of cotton to one side her pussy lips bristled at the touch. The sensation of excitement had never been more powerful and she couldn't recall ever suffering such a strong need for orgasm. Her responses only heightened when Robert passed Charlie a huge, rubber butt-plug.

'You wanted to see her working,' Robert said. His calm tone of voice made it difficult to work out if he was talking to the caller at the rear of the hall or the entire auditorium. 'This might give you an idea of what she can accept.'

Karina leant forward in her seat. The position meant it was difficult to finger herself but she was prepared to make that sacrifice to see the tawdry display on the podium. She still had enough purchase to tease her clitoris and she tormented the bud of flesh while remaining focused on every sordid detail.

Charlie pushed a finger into the brunette's anus.

The penetration was coarse and surprisingly swift.

Karina thought the woman might have moaned in protest but she was never sure if that was her own imagination or a gasp of surprise from someone else at the auction. Thinking about it, she decided she would be unlikely to hear any cry the brunette made around her ball-gag but she also supposed there would be few people at the auction who might be aghast at what was happening. She even worried the cry might have come from her own mouth but that didn't stop her sliding a fingertip against the centre of her spreading wetness. A series of deepening shivers began to emanate from her pussy and she knew the orgasm that was building would be strong and satisfying.

Standing to one side, positioning himself so everyone could see what he was doing, Charlie slipped a second finger inside Lot 67. Her anus was distended to an elongated circle as he worked both digits back and forth. The brunette trembled and came close to losing her balance. Slapping the butt-plug cheerfully against one cheek, Charlie laughed nastily before pushing the length of rubber into her hole. With surprising speed he forced the phallus inside while sliding his fingers free.

Karina's one criticism was that she couldn't see the woman's face. Imagining the slave's distress, and mentally envisioning her tears, seemed like a pretty poor substitute for actually witnessing her upset. She briefly wondered where the cruel thought had come from, and why she was reacting with such a lack of sympathy, before dismissing the response as irrelevant. In her own mind her priorities were suddenly and clearly laid out: she had to see the outcome of the auction; she had to satiate the need between her legs; and then she would have to think about her future with Robert.

Charlie slid the butt-plug inside in a languid motion.

Karina couldn't tell if it was really six inches in diameter, as Robert had suggested, but she knew it was thicker than anything she would be able to accommodate. It stretched the slave, pushed the muscles of her sphincter into a painfully large circle, before wedging impossibly inside her rectum.

Charlie tugged on the slave's arm, encouraging her to stand erect. When she faced the auditorium again, tears glistened freshly against her ruddy cheeks. Her appearance would have seemed abject and downtrodden if not for the stiffening of her nipples and the spreading wetness on her thighs.

'Do you need to see further proof?' Robert asked. 'Do you want us to tit bind her? Stretch her pussy lips? Explore her with a speculum?'

Karina sat forward in her chair, eagerly hoping she might see any or all of those things. The brunette's misery only fuelled her appetite for more and she rubbed hard at the exposed nub of her clitoris. Pleasure washed through her in torrents and she kept her jaw clamped tightly closed for fear of making a sound that might alert those around her to what she was doing.

'Does anyone want to see anything more?' Robert repeated.

'*I do!*' Karina thought eagerly. '*I want to see a lot more!*'

She didn't get to voice the exclamation before Robert was accepting a cry of three hundred pounds from the back of the hall. Bidding went up in quick fifties, swiftly taking the brunette's price past the one thousand mark. The kiosk attendant was a constant bidder, his mellow voice sounding over all the others as he strove to better each increase.

Still enthralled by what she was seeing, and still trembling with the elation of the discovery that this evening had been, Karina rubbed more frantically between her legs. A minor worry niggled at the back of her mind – she told herself she was performing an intimate act in the company of despicables and low-lifes who had no problem trading in human flesh – but those reservations were easily cast aside in the face of her need for satisfaction.

'The bid stands at twenty-eight hundred,' Robert proclaimed. He held his gavel over the desk and glanced shrewdly around the hall. 'It's a reasonable price for any slave even if she is a brunette. Do I hear twenty-eight fifty?'

Karina held herself on the brink of orgasm, not wanting a rush of pleasure to spoil her enjoyment of the sale's conclusion. She couldn't understand why her arousal was so strong but she knew it had been incited by the ordeal of the slave on the podium. The idea of missing the end was unthinkable and she toyed gingerly with her sodden lips while waiting for Robert to confirm the final bid.

'Going once at twenty-eight hundred,' Robert said, raising his gavel.

The brunette stared out at the auditorium. Her eyes shone wetly.

Savouring the woman's expression Karina dared to tease more forcefully against her pussy.

'Going twice.' Robert cast a final cursory glance around the hall.

The slave glanced hesitantly toward him and Karina briefly wondered why the woman was regarding Robert with what looked like panic. It was an expression she had seen at more mundane auctions – usually on the faces of sellers who were either having doubts about the sale or unhappy with the price the auctioneer was accepting – but Karina couldn't understand how either of those reactions could be applicable in this case. Lot 67 was blinking frantically and scowling at Robert. The expression contorted her features into something ugly and unreal.

Robert wasn't acknowledging the slave as he scoured the auditorium for eleventh hour bidders. Seeming to decide twenty-eight hundred was the best price he would be offered, he slammed his gavel against the desk. 'Going three times. And she's sold to the gentleman from Sinners.'

The brunette glared furiously at him but Robert remained indifferent. Karina got a chance to see a haunted look in the slave's expressive brown eyes and then Charlie dragged her from the podium and into a veil of shadows.

'Thank you, ladies and gentlemen,' Robert said genially. 'I trust you'll all be returning for next week's sale and . . .'

Karina didn't hear any more of his closing speech. She squeezed the nub of her clitoris and a wave of joy coursed through her. The orgasm was so strong she barely had enough time to straighten her skirt before the lights were coming back on to indicate that the auction had ended.

And, as she blinked her eyes used to the brightness, her one overriding thought remained the same as at the beginning of the auction: Karina sorely envied the brunette who had been sold to the kiosk attendant.

'What did you think?' Robert asked quietly.

He sat in the small backroom that led off from the main auction house and looked as normal and trustworthy as always. His tie was loosened and the top button of his shirt had been unfastened but, aside from that, he seemed the same as every time Karina had seen him before. He was quietly spoken, calm, unassuming Robert.

'I didn't think you'd believe me if I told you outright. I thought it would be easier for you to accept the truth if you saw what I do.' He lowered his head while he spoke but maintained eye contact. 'Now you know my secret: *I occasionally auction slaves.*'

She hesitated in the doorway as the last of her reservations began to fade. Along with his brother, Charlie, Robert owned a chain of auction houses throughout the county. For the past month Karina had worked for him as a filing clerk. She and Robert had been out together on two dates. So far their relationship had never gone further than a slow dance in Sinners nightclub and a couple of uninspiring goodnight kisses. But she could see that was all going to change now. After the revelation of this evening she could see it had to change.

Boldly, Karina walked towards his chair. She towered over him with her legs slightly apart so she could feel his knees brushing against her inner thighs.

139

'I've never been so turned on in my entire life,' she blurted. Pushing thoughts of shame aside, thinking only of the burning need that still smouldered within her, she said, 'I rubbed myself off while I was watching the auction. I rubbed myself off and I came.'

He glanced up at her and a reluctant grin surfaced on his lips. 'Then, you don't disapprove?'

She tugged the hem of her skirt up and pulled the sodden crotch of her panties to one side. Grabbing his hand and pushing it over her wetness she said, 'I was so excited I rubbed myself off in a hall full of strangers. Doesn't that answer your question?'

His fingers were cool against her warmth but Karina stood defiantly rigid. Studying his face, trying to read what was happening beneath the smile that glinted in his eyes, she remained silent and waited for him to speak.

'We had a two-way deal,' Robert reminded her.

The weight of his fingers shifted slightly, sending spirals of pleasure twisting through her labia. While she thought she had exorcised her need to climax in the auction hall, the urge returned with renewed ferocity.

'I've shared my darkest secret with you,' Robert said coolly, 'and you were going to share your darkest secret with me. Do you still want to do that?'

She didn't have to think about the question, already knowing what she would say. Leaning closer, squirming her sex against his palm, she cupped her mouth over his ear to speak. 'My darkest secret has changed this evening. What I was going to tell you, what I was going to share with you, it's completely different since I saw the auction.'

His smile was etched with understanding but still he asked, 'What's your secret now?'

Karina smiled. 'I was excited. My darkest secret is, I thought the auction was a real turn-on.' Not knowing how he might respond, only sure it was what she had to do, Karina reached for the zipper at the front of his trousers. She pulled his shaft through the fly, stroked briskly until he was hard, then straddled him. Before she was even certain she was going to do it, Karina could feel Robert's length pushing between the yielding lips of her pussy. Her inner walls were succulent and slippery and her sex ate him with a series of greedy squelches.

'Karina!' he gasped.

She covered his mouth with hers and kissed him furiously. His tongue slipped between her lips and, as she rode up and down, one arm encircled her waist and the other hand cupped her breast. The contact was all she needed to be in the throes of climax and Karina arched her back as the orgasm took hold. Spasms shivered through her body. Still writhing eagerly on his length, she broke their kiss to study him.

'Do the slaves turn you on?'

He considered her solemnly. 'Would you think bad of me if I said yes?'

Her pussy muscles clenched repeatedly and the swell of another explosion prepared to burst from her sex. Trying to control her arousal, not sure it was sensible to be so pliant for him, she fought the impulse to give in to the orgasm and tried mimicking his detachment. 'You didn't look overly excited by the slave you auctioned this evening.'

Robert shrugged. 'I was aroused. I was very aroused. But what would you have expected me to do? Should I have screwed her while she was on the podium and under the spotlight? Should I have had her gobble me while the entire auditorium watched?'

Karina groaned and rode him harder. His words conjured up images that were so close to what she wanted it was almost impossible to stave off the impending climax. Breathing heavily, relishing the weight of his arm around her waist and the pressure of his hand kneading her breast, she eagerly levered herself up and down. Hungrily, she smothered him with fresh kisses, savouring his stoical response in the face of her need.

'Not that it's the domination alone that turns me on,' Robert said quietly. 'If I'm being honest, more than the domination, it's the bondage I like.'

His shaft stiffened inside her and Karina could tell it was something that truly excited him. She held herself on the brink and glared at him through a misty haze of euphoria. 'If that's what turns you on,' she whispered, 'then I want you to do it, with me, now.'

He regarded her quizzically. 'I don't think you know what you're asking for.'

She shook her head, unhappy with his condescending tone. 'If bondage and control excite you, then I want you to tie me up. I want you to restrain me.'

His hesitancy only lasted for the moment it took him to study her face and see she was earnest. Without using any force, he took Karina by both arms and eased her from his shaft. After helping her to stand he climbed out of his chair and placed her in the seat.

Almost casually, he tucked his erection back into his trousers.

She stared up at him, aware of how tawdry she must look with her skirt hitched up to her waist, the crotch of her panties pulled to one side and her pussy lips gaping and sodden. Glancing down at herself she saw Robert had unfastened three buttons on her blouse and one plump breast was exposed to the room.

'Are you sure you want to try this?' he asked patiently.

It took an effort of willpower not to growl with frustration. Karina held the arms of the chair, glared up at him and said, 'Of course I want to try it. I wouldn't have suggested it otherwise.'

He reached into the open drawer of his desk, pulled out a roll of broad insulation tape, and yanked a strip away from the central cylinder. 'I'm giving you one last chance to back out.' The solemnity of his tone had an ominous quality that should have unsettled her. 'I take my bondage games very seriously.'

Karina gripped the arms of the chair more tightly and shook her head. 'Don't tease me,' she implored. 'I want you to bind me and you know you want to do it. Please, Robert. Don't make me beg.'

He nodded, satisfied with her response, before using the strip of tape to fasten one wrist to the chair arm. She barely had a chance to think the bondage would be ineffectual before he was securing her other wrist. She tugged tentatively at the bindings and was surprised to find they held strong.

Working swiftly, Robert bound her ankles to the chair's legs, positioning the tape so her thighs were forced to remain wide apart. Standing back, glancing down critically, he tugged her blouse fully open and forced her bra down so both orbs spilled from the cups.

Shocked by his brusqueness, Karina gasped.

'You look good,' he said, rubbing contentedly at his crotch. 'Bondage really suits you.'

She smiled uncertainly at the compliment.

Starting toward the door behind her, Robert said, 'You don't mind if I go and finish my business in the hall before we continue, do you? I can't see it taking more than quarter of an hour.'

She opened her mouth, not sure how to phrase her reservations without making herself sound stupid. Karina had only expected him to tie her and then use her. She hadn't expected him to walk out of the door and leave her in a state of bound frustration. Struggling to find her voice, she stammered unintelligibly until he nodded with understanding.

'How silly of me.' Robert grinned, pulling another strip of tape from the roll. 'The bondage isn't complete without a gag, is it?' Not waiting for her response, displaying an effortless control over her body now she was helpless, he fastened the strip securely across her mouth.

She regarded him with a panicked expression but his gaze was fixed on the sight of her exposed breasts and gaping labia and she knew he didn't see her silent plea for help.

'I'll go and deal with my business, but I'll be straight back,' Robert assured her. With a wicked smile that seemed disquietingly right for his face, he added, 'Don't go running away.'

They were the last words she heard him speak before he stepped out of her sight toward the office door. She tried tugging her wrists and ankles free but the tape was surprisingly tough. Forcing herself to remain calm, trying not to give in to the thrill of panic that threatened to overwhelm her, Karina drew a deep breath through her nostrils.

'You dirty little bitch.'

She tried twisting in the chair, shocked to hear Charlie's voice.

He stepped into her vision, his grin growing broader as he studied her bound and exposed body. 'Nice twat,' he said blithely. One hand worked in

144

agitation against the front of his trousers and he licked his lips in anticipation. 'I always thought you were the sort of slut who'd go for this caper but I never thought I'd get the chance to experience you at first hand.'

Karina struggled to wrench her arms free but the tape held with infuriating effectiveness. Regardless of how hard she twisted and pulled she only hurt her wrists with the effort.

'And what nice titties you have,' Charlie said approvingly.

He reached towards her and she was repulsed to see his fingers edging closer to her breasts. When he finally made contact, when one of his grubby fingernails pressed against a nipple, she shivered with revulsion. If she had been able she would have screamed for him to leave her alone. But, because her mouth was bound with tape, she could only watch in horror as he pawed at her. Worse than the indignity of suffering his touch – worse than the dilemma of being caught in this invidious situation – was the shock of how her body responded. Rather than the cold dread she expected, her arousal grew.

'I've often wondered what your titties looked like,' Charlie said conversationally. He squeezed her nipple between his finger and thumb and twisted until tears of pain spilled from the corners of her eyes. It felt as though he was trying to wrench the bead of flesh away from her breast. 'I've often fancied seeing them like this,' he went on. 'Would you be flattered if I said they weren't a disappointment?'

Struggling not to listen, desperate to escape and end this trauma, Karina tried to move her legs. Frustratingly, the insulation tape held tight.

'And look at your twat,' Charlie breathed. His voice had lowered to a tone that bordered on reverence. Dropping his hand from her breast, finally releasing her nipple from the anguish he had been inflicting, Charlie pushed his dirty fingers towards her cleft. 'Your twat is dripping. I'll bet you're gagging to have something inside there.'

She could guess what he wanted to do – her imagination had already shown her a thousand black images where he used her for his own vile satisfaction – and she was determined not to let any of them happen. Wriggling furiously in her chair, she tried to close her thighs.

Charlie brushed her legs apart with an effortless flex of his wrist. His hand pushed forward and his fingers pressed against the sodden heat of her sex.

Instead of chilling her with the revulsion she knew he merited, Charlie's touch inspired a thrill of sickening pleasure. There was no delicacy or finesse in his caress. He pushed against her labia and, without any gentleness, forced two fingers inside.

But Karina couldn't deny her body was responding as though it needed his despicable attention. As the first tears of shame began to roll down her cheeks he penetrated deeper. Pushing roughly inside, fixing her with his ugly, gap-toothed grin, he wriggled the tips of both fingers against the neck of her womb.

A shock of hateful joy sang from her pussy. The threat of climax inched closer but she resisted with all the willpower she could summon. When he pulled his hand away she wanted to sigh with relief but, seeing the way his cruel smile shone, she knew her torment wasn't finished.

Charlie raised the two fingers to his nose and sniffed them like a connoisseur. 'You really are turned on, aren't you?' he observed. 'I've sniffed hundreds of pussies and I can always tell when they're *really* turned on. When they're really turned on, they smell greasy like this one.' Pushing the fingers under Karina's nose, forcing her to inhale the cloying perfume of her own arousal, he laughed nastily as she cried fresh tears. With scant regard for her feelings, using her as though she was nothing more than an object, he wiped himself dry on her blouse. 'I'll bet you're wanting brother Bobby to come back in here aren't you?'

Karina didn't think she had ever wanted anything so badly in her entire life but there was no way she could say as much to Charlie. If the strip of tape hadn't been covering her mouth she would have screamed for Robert to return and rescue her. Even if it had only allowed her to move her lips a little she would have told Charlie he was violating her with his unwanted attention and the acts he had already committed were tantamount to gross sexual assault.

She glared at him with an expression of the darkest venom but, like his brother before him, Charlie wasn't looking at her face when he spoke. His gaze alternated between her breasts and cleft. 'I'll bet you're wanting Bobby to come back and save you from his nasty brother. But that's not going to happen for a while yet. Brother Bobby's sorting out finances with the guy from Sinners. I imagine he's going to be a fair while yet.'

Slowly, Charlie reached for the front of his trousers and lowered the zip.

Karina regarded him with wide-eyed horror. She had seen he was aroused as he tormented her but she wasn't prepared for the sight of the erection he produced. His shaft was double the thickness of Robert's and at least half as long again. Rolling the foreskin back, exposing the dark purple dome of his glans, his hand was hardly large enough to encircle the thickness.

'The auction turned you on, didn't it?' Charlie muttered conversationally. He rubbed himself while he avariciously studied her breasts. 'I know it did because I saw how turned on you were when you came in here.' He nodded meaningfully at the CCTV camera over the door and said, 'I was in the security office and I was watching. I saw and heard everything, you dirty little bitch.'

Inwardly, Karina groaned. She had known the auction house was equipped with CCTV cameras and couldn't believe she had been so stupid as to forget about them. With her shame compounded, she sobbed fresh misery and tried to silently implore him for leniency.

'But where does this leave you?' Charlie mused with feigned innocence. His erection was fully hard but he continued to massage himself as he strode back and forth in front of her. 'What's brother Bobby going to say if he comes back in here and finds you and I getting together? I imagine you had your relationship with him all planned out, didn't you? I'll bet you thought all your dreams had come true. You'd found a man who was as perverted as you, yet as trustworthy and dependable as good, old brother Bobby. Am I right?'

If she could have answered, Karina knew she would have had to agree. Underscoring all her arousal, emphasising every sordid thought the night had allowed, she had been thinking Robert seemed like the perfect combination of kinkiness and integrity. The idea she could lose that relationship before it got underway was enough to cause further tears to trail down her cheeks.

'But what's Bobby going to say if he comes back in here and finds you and I doing the dark deed together?' Charlie pressed. 'Do you think he'd be upset? Do you think it would be the last time he ever

148

asked you out on a twee little date with him? Do you think it will be the last time he flashes his gold card membership at Sinners for your benefit?' He stopped tugging at his length and allowed it to hover mere inches in front of her nose.

A glimmer of clear pre-come glistened in the eye of his glans. The scents of his excitement and rank sweat evoked conflicting urges of arousal and nausea.

'I think there's only one thing you can do to give yourself a chance of a relationship with Bobby,' Charlie decided. His chequerboard smile resurfaced as he added, 'I think you know what that is as well.' He reached for the tape at her mouth and then paused. Lowering his voice to a confidential whisper, he said, 'I'm going to release your mouth long enough for you to suck my prick. You're going to gobble me, you're going to swallow every drop I shoot into your mouth and, if you do it properly, we won't tell Bobby what's happened.'

She wanted to resist but there was too much at stake. She told herself it would only be proper to defy him; allow him to remove the gag, and then scream until someone came running. But her worries about how Robert might interpret the scene made her reject the idea. Robert might listen to her version of what had occurred – he might even make a show of sympathising with her plight – but, more likely, he would side with his brother's explanation.

And, as loath as she was to admit it, Karina genuinely longed to suck Charlie's cock. After coveting the brunette's predicament on the auction block, the degradation that Charlie offered seemed like a passable substitute for the satisfaction she craved. Despising him for manipulating her in such a way, and hating herself for being so aroused by what he was suggesting, she nodded consent.

With no deference to her feelings, Charlie wrenched the tape away from her mouth. There was a furious sting across her cheek and her lips felt as though they had been scalded. Before she had a chance to gasp for breath, before she had the chance to think about what she was doing, Charlie pushed the swollen dome of his glans between her lips.

A surge of fresh excitement churned through her loins as his erection pressed against her tongue. She held her breath, not wanting to inhale the vile scent of his nearness, and concentrated only on sucking. Never sure if the response came from a temporary madness, or if lack of oxygen was making her dizzy and behave out of character, Karina devoured him with avaricious hunger. She sucked, licked and swallowed, relishing every subtle increase in his length's monstrous pulse.

'That's it, you dirty little bitch!' Charlie grunted. 'You know you fucking want it. Swallow my cock.'

He grabbed hold of her hair and pushed himself forcefully into her face. The end of his length pressed heavily against the back of her throat and Karina had to swallow repeatedly so as not to gag against the unnatural weight. She sucked harder, telling herself she was anxious to get this ordeal over with and that she was gleaning no excitement from Charlie's abuse. The argument would have been more convincing if she hadn't been battling to ignore a swelling orgasm.

'That's it, you cheap, fucking slut! Suck harder. Harder.'

He renewed his grip on her hair, pulling her face onto his shaft and holding her against himself. His climax spattered at the back of her throat and Karina almost choked as her instincts told her to spit the warm wad of semen out of her mouth.

Charlie continued to hold her head tightly while his shaft repeatedly pulsed. He placed one hand under her chin, his fingers burrowing deep into her jaw. 'Swallow it all,' he grunted. 'You don't want brother Bobby finding any trace of my spunk in here. Swallow every damned drop.'

Unhappily, Karina did as she was told. The effort almost pushed her past the point of orgasm but she suppressed the response as she swallowed his lessening pulses.

'Good bitch.' Charlie grinned, pulling himself out of her mouth and fastening the tape back over her lips. He tucked his spent shaft back into his trousers and smiled approvingly. 'You swallow as good as any of the slaves we've ever had through here. I didn't think you'd be that good. It makes me wonder how well you'd ride your arse along my prick.'

She was disgusted to find, rather than sickening her, the praise increased her arousal. She turned her face up to study him and, while she was scared he might see the lust that remained in her expression, she had to see if he was genuinely pleased or only trying to make her feel worse.

Robert stood in front of her. His easy-going smile lilted briefly over her bondage.

Karina glanced frantically around the small scope of the room that her position allowed her to see. She couldn't see Charlie and madly wondered if she had only imagined his appearance. The slimy taste of his semen assured her his presence hadn't been a figment of her imagination but Robert had appeared so suddenly it seemed like the only logical explanation.

'That was close,' Robert said, kneeling before her and gently removing her bindings. He eased the tape from her mouth with more care than his brother had used. 'Charlie almost came in here and I guess you'd have found it embarrassing if he'd caught you like this.'

Not sure how to reply, only aware that her arousal remained as strong as ever, Karina struggled to speak. When she was able to manage words they were carried on ragged whispers of emotion. 'Why are you unfastening me?' she asked quietly. The taste of Charlie's semen flavoured every word and added to her excitement. 'I thought you wanted to –'

'Let's do that back at my place,' Robert broke in. He released her legs and wrists and helped her from the chair. 'I'm sure we can enjoy ourselves an awful lot more if there's less danger of our being disturbed.'

Allowing him to drape an overcoat over her shoulders, and struggling to understand what had happened and why she had found it all so stimulating, Karina never bothered to wonder why Robert hadn't used the same degree of foresight earlier in the evening. All she could think was: she still envied the brunette who had been sold to the kiosk attendant from Sinners.

She half expected the remainder of her night to be overshadowed by what Charlie had done but Robert was too indulgent a lover to allow her to dwell on that. As soon as they were alone he was kissing and undressing her while appraising her body with his eyes, fingers and tongue. After two glasses of wine, and helped by the ambience of light jazz and Robert's luxurious apartment, Karina was naked and on the verge of believing that the unsettling interlude was behind her.

'You looked exquisite when you were bound and gagged.'

She stiffened at the words, not liking the way it made her think of Charlie standing over her, wafting his erection beneath her nose. Shutting the distasteful image from her mind, taking a sip of wine to clear away the remembered taste of his seed, Karina forced a smile and recalled the compliment Robert had given her after tying her to the chair. He had said bondage suited her.

'You like seeing your women tied up?' she teased.

His smile was softened with what looked like fond recollections. 'I like to be assured of being in control. I like to have a woman's absolute submission.'

The words rekindled the envious thrill she had enjoyed during the auction. Karina drained her glass, placed it on a convenient occasional table, then held out her upturned wrists for him. 'If you want my absolute submission, then I'll make it easy for you this time. Do what you want with me.'

'You expect me to cuff you?' His voice was a meld of patronising amusement. 'You're obviously not an aficionado of restraint, are you?'

She shrugged, trying to conceal her hurt. Slowly, she began lowering her wrists. 'I don't know much about being tied up, if that's what you mean.'

He nodded. 'That's pretty obvious.' With startling speed he caught both wrists before she had lowered them to her lap. His grip didn't hurt but it was firm and uncompromising and he easily pulled her from her chair.

Surprised by his strength and speed, Karina stood naked in the centre of Robert's apartment. Her wrists were held in his hand and her heart pounded incessantly.

He tugged her closer and said, 'If you knew anything about bondage you'd know how impractical it is to cuff a woman's wrists in front of her.' Maintaining his hold on her hands he made a pretence of trying to caress her breast.

She had one bicep crushed against the orb and was frustrated when his fingers only touched the bare flesh of her arm.

Releasing his hold on one hand, spinning her around and then catching it so he had both wrists behind her back, Robert said, 'It's far more practical to cuff a woman from behind.' His fingers snaked around her and this time he was easily able to cup the plump orb.

Karina groaned as he squeezed and kneaded. She writhed her buttocks against the thrust of his erection, wishing it wasn't still contained inside his trousers. Her need for him had been broiling for an age but now it screamed with emphatic demand.

'When you cuff a woman from behind,' he whispered, 'you have easy access to all the important places.' After tweaking one nipple his hand moved from her breast and slid slowly down her stomach. He drew his fingers over her belly button and down toward the triangle of her pubic curls. When he finally made contact with her pussy lips Karina almost sobbed with frustrated arousal.

'But I don't rate either as being the proper way to secure a woman,' Robert breathed. While he whispered the words into her ear he continued teasing the sensitive lips of her sex. Deftly, he splayed her then rubbed the tip of his finger against the pulsing nub of her clitoris. 'I think, if you're going to restrain a woman, you need a good length of rope and a comfortable double bed.'

Eager for him, and beyond the reservations she would have felt with any other man, Karina growled, 'If that's what you want, then take me to your bedroom.'

'I was going to do just that.' He laughed easily. Continuing to hold her wrists, controlling every step she took, he guided her out of the apartment's lounge and into the adjacent bedroom. He pushed her onto the mattress and, using ropes that were already tied to the corners of the bed, he fastened her spread-eagled, with her face down and buried in a pillow. 'Not that this form of bondage isn't without its drawbacks,' he mused.

Listening to him, Karina could hear he was undressing while he spoke. She slyly tested the ropes round her wrists and ankles and found they were inescapable.

'Having you tied face down makes it impossible for me to touch you in some places,' he grumbled. 'But it does give me the opportunity to make perfect use of your backside.'

She drew a deep breath, disturbed by the swelling heat between her legs.

Robert stroked a finger against her bristling pussy lips, tracing upwards toward the ring of her anus. With a casual display of strength, he placed his hands on her buttocks and pushed the cheeks apart. 'This is why I like bondage,' he told her. As he spoke, he placed gentle kisses against the nape of her neck. 'You're unable to resist me in this position and I can do whatever I want. If I were to take things too far, if I were to do something you didn't want, all you'd be able to do is wait until I was finished so you could hear me apologise afterwards.'

She wasn't listening, lost in a rapture of pleasure that came from the way he was teasing a finger against her anus. His bare legs knelt between her spread thighs and the end of his erection prodded haphazardly against her backside. The thrill of feeling his forbidden penetration – the moment when he finally squirmed a finger into the confines of her anus – was enough to send her shrieking towards a pinnacle of pleasure.

'Do you do this to the slaves you sell?' she asked. The words were carried on a soft moan of arousal. 'Is this how you treat them before you put them up for auction?'

He withdrew his finger and then climbed from between her legs. 'You really aren't an aficionado of restraint,' he observed. He adjusted the volume on the CD player and then raised his voice to make himself heard. 'If you were an aficionado, I'm sure you'd know it's customary for a bottom to be silent.'

Karina turned her head as much as the bondage would allow and saw he was fumbling through a drawer at the side of the bed. She had no idea why he was calling her a bottom, or what she had done to earn his disapproval but, when she saw him holding a gag and a hood, she guessed he hadn't liked her asking questions about the auction. Under any other circumstances the idea of being forcefully silenced might have annoyed her but, because the gag reminded her of the slave on the podium, Karina could only feel more aroused at the thought of being secured in such a way.

'This should stop you from talking,' Robert said. He fixed the ball into her mouth and fastened it at the base of her skull.

The wedge of rubber sat tightly and, without needing to try, Karina knew she wouldn't be able to make any articulate sound around the gag.

'And this should make the experience even more interesting for you,' he added, pulling the hood over head.

The room became black. He pulled drawstrings to secure the hood around her throat and she was stung by the fear he might fasten it too tight. Once the moment's panic was passed she remained in relentless darkness and realised she wasn't going to see anything else until Robert decided to remove the hood. All she could do was rely on her other senses to tell her he was climbing back onto the bed, positioning himself between her legs and guiding his erection over her anus.

Karina's first climax came with pathetic ease.

Her sphincter resisted his entry but, because Robert seemed insistent, the muscle eventually relented and allowed him to slide fully inside. A rush of adrenaline pounded along her veins – magical twinges of euphoria erupted throughout her body – and she clawed happily against the sheets. The orgasm continued as he rode back and forth and, by the time he was on the brink of erupting into her bowel, Karina realised her climax had been a roar of continuous and undiluted joy.

Robert held himself still as he shot his seed into her backside. His hands clutched roughly against her hips, he was buried deep into her colon, and then he allowed the tip of his glans to spurt endless jets of white hot semen.

It was the exhilarating release she had known it would be.

Because of the blackness within her hood, Karina couldn't work out if she had lost consciousness or if she was simply operating in a timescale of pleasure that moved more swiftly than normal time. It felt as though, as soon as Robert had pulled his shaft from her anus, he was thrusting himself between her pussy lips. She thought there was some movement on the bed – a shifting of the mattress as though he might be either climbing away or returning – but an erection pushed rudely against her sex and then spread her labia wide open.

Elated by the experience, Karina simply groaned and relished the onset of another delicious explosion. Her inner muscles were hyper-sensitive and she supposed that was why Robert's erection now felt thicker and longer than it had before. The only other explanation was that Robert was spent but he was now allowing Charlie to ride her.

A part of her wanted the notion to be repulsive but instead it only conjured up memories of the arousal she had succumbed to at the auction and immediately afterwards.

She tried to shut the thought from her mind, telling herself Robert was too decent to allow such a thing, but the argument held little sway. This evening she had already seen Robert sell a woman to the highest bidder. She had let him secure her to a chair, she had allowed him to tie her to his bed and he had already used her most forbidden hole. While she believed him to be honest and trustworthy, it didn't seem unreasonable to think there was a risk that he and his brother might have an arrangement for sharing any available woman.

The shaft between her legs pounded with renewed vigour. In spite of her resistance, going against her desire not to feel any pleasure, eddies of joy began to wash through her sex.

Karina concentrated intently, wondering if she could discern any change in the man lying on top of her. Beyond the deafening jazz music it was impossible to hear anything except the squelch of her sex muscles greedily accepting the length that repeatedly pushed into her. Wanting to believe she was being ridden by Robert, Karina tried inhaling to see if she could detect the pungent scent of Charlie's sweat. The only aroma she could smell was the heady perfume of her own arousal.

'Squeeze my cock, you bitch! Squeeze it harder.'

Until she heard the gasped exclamation, Karina had never realised how much the brothers sounded alike. She obeyed the command, clenching her inner muscles around the shaft that speared her, and shivered as her body was treated to another burst of pleasure. She tolerated the incessant pounding between her legs, then savoured another blissful release as the length twitched and spurted inside her sex.

'That's it, *you dirty little bitch!* That's it!'

The hands at her hips clawed more vigorously, pulling her onto the length while the erection pulsed at the neck of her womb. Her body was torn between extremes of pleasure and pain that seemed so conflicting it was impossible to believe they were part of the same experience. She grabbed fistfuls of sheets, not sure which of the brothers had brought her to this orgasm, only aware that she was wholly and subordinately grateful. Her sex was sodden with gelatinous spend and the flailing shaft began to dwindle before being withdrawn.

Overcome with bliss, Karina thought it seemed an age before the man above her climbed off the bed and then even longer before the hood was removed and her wrists were unfastened.

Robert smiled at her as she blinked her eyes used to the room's light. He offered her a replenished glass of wine and she drank greedily. Trying not to make her mistrust too obvious, Karina glanced around the room for any evidence that Charlie might have been there. The bedroom door was ajar and she struggled to remember if they had closed it before Robert tied her to the bed.

Sipping at his own glass of wine, Robert sat beside her and placed an affectionate hand on her thigh. He coughed to clear his throat and said, 'Back at the auction house, when I'd secured you to the chair in my office . . .'

Karina stiffened and wondered what he was preparing to say. She could hear hesitancy in his voice and began to fret about where the conversation was leading. Rather than the mellow warmth she normally savoured after climax she found herself basking in unsettling worries and paranoia.

'. . . one of the reasons I was so long this evening . . .'

Her stomach churned with dread while her sadistic imagination cruelly pre-guessed him. *'One of the reasons I was so long was because my brother and I have a special arrangement. One of the reasons I was so long was because I wanted you to suck his prick before I brought you back here to fuck you. Charlie and I share all our conquests, in fact, he fucked your pussy this evening after I'd ridden your arsehole. We do that to every dirty little . . .'*

'One of the reasons I was so long . . .' Robert repeated.

His voice broke through the downward spiral of her blackly exciting thoughts.

'. . . was because this evening's buyer invited me to a party at his club.' He glanced at her warily and asked, 'Would you be interested in attending as my guest?'

Sighing with relief, Karina kissed him gratefully. 'Go to a party with you?' she cried. 'I'd love to.'

Smiling tightly, Robert shook his head. 'I haven't told you what sort of party it is yet. Let me explain the details before you say yes or no.'

With growing excitement, Karina listened and his words inspired another arousal that she demanded he satisfy. But, when she finally drifted to sleep, her last waking thought was a jealous memory of the slave who had been sold to the kiosk attendant.

Robert provided her with a clinging outfit of rubber that adhered to every curve and crease. Squeezing herself into the garment, pulling and twisting flesh until the costume hugged her like an all-enveloping lover, Karina thought she looked more than ready for the perverse party that Robert had planned. But, before leaving for Sinners, he barked a clipped instruction for her to bend over while he shoved a butt-plug into her anus. It wasn't the same girth as the one she had seen used at the auction but it was wide enough to make its presence felt. It stretched the muscle of her sphincter into a wide 'O' and sat uncomfortably inside her rectum. She hadn't been aware it was a vibrating device until Robert turned it on and sent a series of tingling shivers bristling through her colon.

'Is that comfortable?'

She was trying to ease her legs further apart so the plug could fit more easily. It was far from comfortable and sat inside with a pernicious weight that was made more obvious by its constant roar. Rather than answer honestly, Karina asked, 'How long will I have to keep this in?'

'It will stay there all evening. It will stay there until I decide it can be moved.'

The words made her groan and with that sound came the night's first tickle of clear arousal. It started in the over-stretched flesh of her backside and shivered through the taut ring of her anus. Before she had fully exhaled, a rush of excitement sat inside her belly like a bed of warm coals.

'Now lift your head so I can put this on,' Robert insisted.

She half-turned and saw he was holding a ball-gag. With its combination of straps, buckles and a ball it reminded Karina of the one the brunette had been wearing at the slave auction. She hesitated briefly and wondered if, while she still had the chance to speak,

161

she should mention any of the things that had been at the forefront of her mind.

'*About Charlie . . .*'

She coughed and cleared her throat.

'*The other night, when you had me tied to the chair in your office, did you know your brother . . .?*'

Neither of them seemed the right way to begin and she kept a defensive hand in the air as she struggled to think of the proper way to broach the subject.

'*Do you and your brother have an arrangement I should know about . . .?*'

She told herself this wasn't the right time to be thinking about Charlie because the man was like a douche of cold water to her arousal. Admittedly he was able to touch some perverted need inside her and inspire her to despicable heights of pleasure that she couldn't comprehend. But, as a stimulus to her growing arousal, the thoughts of his gap-toothed smile and odious presence added nothing to her mood of sexual daring.

'Is there a problem?' Robert asked. There was only a vague inflection of irritation in his voice. He glanced at his watch and added, 'We're already fashionably late. If we get much more fashionable we'll have missed the entire party.'

'There's no problem,' she decided. '*The other night – when we were in your apartment and you had me blindfolded and tied to the bed – were we alone?*' She couldn't bring herself to ask the question and shook her head, dismissing the whole subject. 'There's no problem,' she repeated. Realising he was watching expectantly, she added, 'But, if I need to get your attention while I'm wearing the gag, how do I do it?'

He thought about the question for a moment, his characteristic half-smile lilting crookedly on his lips. 'I guess a safe-word is hampered by the gag,' he said obviously. 'So, if things start getting too heavy, if there's anything you want to say to me, or anything you want to stop, then blink repeatedly. If you start to blink repeatedly, I'll call a halt to whatever it is we're doing and find a way for you to tell me your reservations.'

It hadn't been the main thing that was worrying her but Karina was pleased Robert had thought of a way for them to play and still leave her the reassurance of a panic button. Taking renewed pleasure from her obedience, she opened her mouth and accepted the gag between her teeth. It held her jaw achingly wide but, because she knew the accessory would complete the image of bound servility, she was proud to wear it. If the gag had allowed her any opportunity to move her mouth Karina knew she would have been grinning broadly by the time Robert fastened the last of the buckles at the back of her neck.

He cuffed her hands behind her back then studied her with a critical expression. Seeming to come to a sudden decision, he pulled a small craft knife from his pocket and placed a hand on her shoulder to hold her steady.

Unable to move away, Karina could only watch as he pushed the blade towards her chest. He moved the razor-sharp steel closer and she could see he was aiming for the swell of one nipple where it jutted against the rubber fabric of her top. With growing terror she shook her head and then remembered the panic button they had just discussed. She blinked her eyes frantically but Robert wasn't looking.

He concentrated intently on what he was doing, pushed the blade into the rubber, and scored a small slit over her breast. When he squeezed the shape of her orb, the cut in the rubber opened and her nipple peeped out.

163

Karina stared down at the exposed nub of flesh, trying not to think about the maiming she had feared he might inflict. A thousand horrific images had rushed through her mind, each one gratuitously violent and all of them underscored by a loathsome wave of arousal. She had decided Robert was as sick and twisted as his brother; realised the pair were in cahoots; seen they had a diabolical plan to enslave, torture and abuse her; and known she was about to experience the first painful, shameful torment.

When she realised Robert was just adding a final touch to her outfit, she felt giddy with relief. The gag didn't allow her to breath through her mouth and she listened to every rasping exhalation as it shuddered noisily through her nostrils. It was disconcerting that he had ignored their newly established panic button but, overwhelmed by gratitude, she was able to think beyond that worrying detail.

With the same meticulous care he had used before, Robert sliced a cut over her other breast. The bead of flesh slipped easily through the hole and he rolled it between his finger and thumb until it sat fully hard. Pulling a pair of clamps from his jacket pocket, he secured one against each nipple and stepped back to admire her.

Gasping from the inrush of pain, Karina was dizzied by a body blow of raw excitement. She felt exposed and tawdry and realised she now looked like the epitome of an easy and available bondage slut. The idea left her more breathless than ever and she struggled uselessly against her restraints.

'You look good,' Robert said reflectively. He teased a finger against the chain connecting her nipple clamps and tugged downwards.

She gasped as both orbs were wrenched by scorching anguish.

'You look a little too good if I'm being honest.'

She furrowed her eyebrows at the remark, wondering how it was possible for her to look too good. She wanted this evening to go well for both of them and didn't want anything to spoil it for Robert.

He laughed at her obvious consternation. 'You look so good I don't want to be bothered with the party,' he explained. 'I just want to fuck your brains out again and again until I'm totally spent.'

If the gag had allowed her to speak she would have told him she wanted that as well. She briefly envisioned him taking her now: screwing her pussy while the butt-plug continued to shiver in her anus. The mental picture was so close to being complete she knew that dwelling on it would probably have her in climactic throes. Purposefully, she shut the idea from her thoughts.

Robert looked to be agonising over his dilemma as he studied her half-naked body. 'And yet,' he reflected, 'I need to put in an appearance at Sinners, if only to keep the proprietor interested in my auctions.' He chewed on his lower lip and said, 'But, which would you rather? The party? Or should I start riding you now, until you're screaming for me to stop?'

Because the gag effectively quashed all communication, Karina could only beseech him with her eyes.

'We'll go to the party,' Robert decided. He draped a coat over her shoulders. 'I can have you all I want while we're there, and maybe some more besides when I bring you back here after.'

The promise of passion was enough to have her squirming and, as Robert led her out of his flat, toward his waiting car, Karina shut the last of her doubts away. She forgot about the easy way he had ignored their newly established panic button, content to wallow in the pleasure of knowing how close her situation compared to the brunette who had been sold at the slave auction.

Not that Karina needed the panic button for the party.

She stood in the foyer puzzling over the foreign phrase that arched above the doorway to the nightclub. Eventually she decided the words probably meant nothing to her and dismissed them in favour of more interesting incidents. A handful of masters and mistresses walked past. Some of the women were on all fours, being led by collars and leashes, while others walked unrestrained but with the inelegant dignity that Karina now associated with the presence of a butt-plug.

She received a handful of glances, ranging from the snooty and scathing through to the lecherously appreciative. But the majority of attendees ignored her as they continued through the foyer and up the stairs toward their party.

Karina watched a plump blonde, wearing only chains, run toward the kiosk. Her cheeks flushed crimson and she mumbled a truculent apology as she relieved the man behind the counter from his position. One glance at the woman's face was enough for Karina to see, unlike the other slaves that had been paraded half-naked through the foyer, the plump blonde was shamed by her near nudity.

'Greedy bitch,' the kiosk attendant grunted.

His words struck Karina as odd because she would have expected him to either berate the plump blonde for being tardy, or surly or anything other than being greedy. The remark seemed so out of place she would have fretted about it if other events hadn't been demanding her attention.

Relieved from his position, the kiosk attendant stepped out to greet Robert. He shook him warmly by the hand, his brilliant smile stretching wider as he glanced at Karina's rubber-clad figure. 'This is a nice one, Bob.' He grinned. 'Where do you manage to find them?'

Karina was comforted to feel Robert's hand clutch her buttock. The contact was exciting and gave reassurance when she felt in greatest need. 'I can't tell you where I find them.' Robert laughed. 'If I revealed my sources, I'd never get your revenue from another auction.'

The kiosk attendant nodded good-naturedly. 'True enough,' he said, still studying Karina. 'But this one is something special. This one is truly splendid.'

He held a hand beneath her chin, twisting her face to the right and the left as he admired her profile. His fingers felt cold and abrasive and, although he made no move to touch her more intimately, Karina knew the threat of that humiliation was never far away. She couldn't understand what it was that made him seem so sinister and repulsive and only knew she didn't like the unpleasantness of his touch. The tips of his fingers drew over her with a dry caress that felt diabolical.

'You can see this one was born to sin,' the kiosk attendant decided. 'She's got the green eyes of jealousy. Perhaps she's been envying some of the stock that's passed through your auction house?'

His observation was so accurate it was chilling. If she had been in a position to protest her innocence Karina would have started to stammer an outraged rebuff to try and detract from the truth. Because her hands were tied behind her back and the gag filled her mouth, all she could do was shake her head in vehement denial.

'Aren't we all guilty of some sort of envy?' Robert asked seriously. 'You envy me my stock of slaves. I envy you your nightclub.'

167

The kiosk attendant shook his head. 'We're envious but I'd wager it's not to the same degree that this one could manage.' He fixed her with the piercing gaze of his jet black eyes and said, 'This one could teach us a new interpretation to the meaning of sin.'

Blushing, Karina looked away.

The silence threatened to stretch out between them until Robert coughed and cleared his throat. 'You left a message on my mobile,' he remembered. 'You said you needed to see me before I went into the party.'

The kiosk attendant dragged himself from his reverie. 'Yes. Our plans for this evening have changed. It's not going to be one of the usual soirées. A couple of clients asked if I could invite a tattooist and a body-piercer. Because I wanted to do something with that slave I bought from you the other night, I thought it would be the ideal opportunity to start making my mark on her body.'

The casual way he declared his intentions made Karina want to shiver. She had always been attracted to the idea of body jewellery and tattoos but never dared to take her interest further. Discovering she was so close to realising another secret ambition tightened a band of anticipation across her chest. She could picture an artistic Celtic band circumnavigating one bicep, or steel rings adorning her nipples and pussy lips. The idea of making such a bold statement on her own body was empowering and arousing and she was suddenly filled with the greedy need to realise that ambition. Diligently, she held herself rigid and tried to appear unmoved.

Robert was frowning and Karina guessed she had missed some of their exchange. 'Are you saying we're not allowed into your party?' he demanded.

The kiosk attendant chuckled and shook his head. 'You know I would never refuse you access in here. I

168

was only warning you in advance.' He cast a furtive glance in Karina's direction then lowered his voice so she had strain to hear him.

'It's common knowledge that you use my parties to showcase forthcoming attractions from your auction block. And I'm aware that your stock fetches a better price when it's free from tattoos or piercings. I thought, rather than exposing this girl to the risk of unwanted markings, you might want to skip tonight's soirée.'

Karina went through the awkward chore of swallowing around the ball-gag. She wondered if it really was Robert's intention to show her off, then sell her at the slave auction, before deciding the idea was too outrageous to be plausible. Admittedly, he did sell slaves, but she couldn't believe he would think of selling her, and felt sure their charade was all part of the game they were playing. She told herself he was only humouring the kiosk attendant and responding diplomatically rather than explaining the nature of their relationship to a comparative stranger. But still, the worry that he was in a position to abuse her trust burnt like acid on her nerves.

A woman slowly approached them and Karina recognised her as the brunette slave she had seen at the auction. The woman's gaze flashed raw venom when she saw Robert but, because she was gagged and had her wrists bound behind her back, all she could do was glare at him impotently.

Conversationally, Robert asked, 'Are you getting this one painted and pierced tonight?'

The kiosk attendant chuckled and pulled the brunette between them. His broad fingers encircled one nipple and he squeezed until the bud grew fat. 'I'll be having both her breasts pierced,' he explained. 'And I think I'll get cosmetic tattoos around her areolae, just to bring out the colour.' As he made the suggestion his fingernail trailed against the puckered ring of flesh.

The slave squirmed beneath his touch, snatching her hate-filled gaze away from Robert so she could glare at her tormentor.

Karina watched with dry-mouthed apprehension. She wasn't sure if the woman was suffering an unwanted indignity, or wallowing in base pleasure and, in her state of mounting arousal, she found she didn't care. It was enough to be part of the decadence and depravity of the whole evening. Seeing someone else's suffering only served to remind Karina that she wasn't the only one enjoying such dark pleasures.

The kiosk attendant released his hold on the slave's nipple and moved a hand between her legs. Pushing his fingers through the dark curls of her pubic mound he plucked at the brunette's labia and held them firmly. She frowned and danced from one foot to the other. Her eyes were wide with mute suffering as she stared miserably from Robert to her cruel owner.

'I'll definitely get her pussy pierced,' he confided, pulling mercilessly on the brunette's sensitive skin. 'But that's only so I can stretch her lips and torment her with weights.'

Watching, Karina couldn't decide if she was struck by delight or disgust. The brunette's predicament looked like an enviable blend of humiliation and suffering. It was impossible to look at her without feeling the pull of jealousy and, even when the kiosk attendant began to lead his property away from them, Karina couldn't stop her gaze from greedily following.

'I'll give you a couple of minutes to make up your mind about tonight's party,' he called over his shoulder. 'I'll just take this one to the tattooist and get my ownership details branded on her rear.'

Robert took advantage of their solitude to place his mouth close to Karina's ear. When he spoke she was relieved to hear compassion in his tone. 'It's your choice,' he whispered. 'We can stay here, if you like. But I think you'd want to consider the decision very carefully before you commit yourself to a body-piercing or a tattoo. If you agree that it will be best for us to go back to my place, nod your head.'

Touched by his concern, moved by the way he was acting with such gallantry when she had been silently suspecting him of all manner of treachery and deceit, Karina frantically nodded.

Robert grabbed her arm and started leading her in the direction of the exit. 'I'll see you at the next auction,' he called toward the kiosk attendant. 'I hope your night goes well.'

The kiosk attendant raised a hand and waved. As they were walking out of the doorway Karina cast a glance over her shoulder to catch a final glimpse of the brunette slave. While she pitied the woman her torment as the kiosk attendant's property, Karina found she still envied the humiliating thrill the woman had enjoyed at the auction. And, as the arousal continued to warm her, she began to wonder if Robert might let her experience that deeply coveted pleasure.

'Do I hear twenty-five hundred?'

The full idea came to her later that week while she was at work. After the excitement of seeing a slave being sold, the ordinary auctions seemed crushingly mundane for Karina. She sat by Robert's side behind the podium, cataloguing the sales and finishing prices, but her mind was elsewhere. The work seemed more difficult than usual but she suspected that was down to the blissful distraction of the dithering butt-plug

171

nestled in her anus. As well as that diversion, she was also allowing her thoughts to trail back to the pleasurable memory of the brunette being sold.

'The last bid stands at twenty-four ninety,' Robert told the crowded hall. 'Do I hear twenty-five hundred from anyone?' He scoured the auditorium from behind his desk and, seeing no one make any move to improve the current bid, he lowered his gavel and called, 'No sale.'

Karina resisted the urge to put a hand on his arm and explain her idea there and then. She could now see how it would be possible for Robert to allow her the thrill of being 'sold' at the slave auction without the worry that she might end up in the clutches of someone depraved like the kiosk attendant from Sinners. The whole scenario seemed so clear she wondered why she hadn't stumbled on it before. 'Did that lot fail to meet its reserve price?' she asked, trying to pre-guess what had happened.

'Kind of,' he said, lowering his voice. 'Charlie said he'd pay five hundred less than the last bid if it didn't go over three grand. Book the lot down as a sale to him.'

It was familiar practice – one of the perks of being part-owner of the auction house, she supposed – and as she scribbled Charlie's name next to the item in her catalogue Karina tried to think of a way to tactfully broach her plan. 'I need to talk with you,' she told Robert quietly. 'It's important.'

He seemed to sense the source of her urgency because his smile lit with a tinge of dark humour. 'Go to the stockroom,' he decided. 'I'll finish the auction alone and come through to you after. There's a surprise waiting for you there and I think you might already have guessed what it is.'

She didn't know what he meant by the comment but his tone was authoritative enough for her to obey without hesitation. Grinning for him, Karina nodded and rushed toward the stockroom at the rear of the auction hall. Walking while wearing the butt-plug was still awkward and a little ungainly but, over the past few days, she believed she had almost perfected the art of surreptitiously retaining the device. Even if her gait did seem a little stilted she relished the thought that someone might be able to guess the cause of her predicament.

Robert slammed his gavel against the desk as he returned his attention to the auditorium. 'No sale on lot one two one,' he said loudly. 'The item failed to meet its reserve price so we'll move on to our next lot. A jade dog, its eyes are inset with emeralds, and it's fashioned to represent one of the seven deadly . . .'

His voice tapered to a faraway drone when she entered the stockroom and closed the door. The scents of disuse and must assailed her nostrils and the background noise of the auction crowd was drowned by the flicker of a dying fluorescent tube.

Sitting on the battered desk that was occasionally used during stock-taking Karina could see Robert had left a box and an envelope. Each had her name printed on them beneath the words 'LOT 68'. Hurrying to find out what he had left for her, she rushed to the desk and tore open the envelope. The page inside consisted of two simple sentences in Robert's familiar scrawl: '*Don't have* reservations. *Not every lot is sold to the highest bidder.*'

She placed a fist over her mouth, sure she would giggle like a lunatic if she didn't make some attempt to stifle her exclamation. Dropping the letter to the floor, tugging the corners of the cardboard box open, she wasn't surprised by the contents. Inside, just as she remembered from when the brunette slave had been up for auction, were collar, cuffs, ball-gag and a spreader bar. In addition, probably because she had admired them on one of the slaves attending the party at Sinners, Robert had included a pair of rubber stockings.

Giddy with excitement, Karina ground her thighs together. She glanced at the fallen note and reread the message: '*Don't have reservations. Not every lot is sold to the highest bidder.*' Her heart hammered faster as she realised Robert must have had the same thought that had struck her. He had underlined the word 'reservations' as a clue to what he was proposing. She guessed he wanted to put her up for sale, and then tell the auditorium she hadn't met the *reserve* price.

The way they both seemed so perfectly attuned could have kept her grinning dreamily but, realising she was close to achieving her most cherished ambition, Karina put the warm sentiment aside. Tentatively, she reached into the box and wondered if she dared to put the items on.

The battery-powered butt-plug continued to tingle inside her anus and she wondered if that delicious torment had anything to do with her eventual decision. Not knowing if she was driven by a dangerous sense of curiosity, a dark desire to satisfy the insistence of her jealousy, or the growing need for orgasm, Karina didn't take long to make up her mind. After glancing quickly around the stockroom, assuring herself that there was no one lurking in the shadows, she began to undress.

She felt strangely confident standing unclothed in the stockroom and her one regret was that there was no mirror. It was exciting to be naked in such a semi-public place and she would have enjoyed the opportunity to see herself as Robert would if he had chosen that moment to enter. But, determined that nothing was going to sour her soaring spirits, she decided she could admire herself later and reached into the box for the rubber stockings.

Rather than garters, or any form of suspender belt, the rubber stockings were fitted with small clips designed to be secured on her labia. The fastenings weren't big but they looked punishingly ferocious for such a sensitive area and Karina couldn't work out whether she should be ecstatic or frightened. However, by the time she had rolled the sleeve of rubber over her legs, a knot of anticipation had tightened in her stomach. Gingerly she clamped one of the clips against an outer pussy lip, then held herself rigid as her body acclimatised to the piercing pressure.

Urged on by growing excitement she quickly stepped into the other stocking and fastened it with the same delicate care. The pain quickly subsided to a nagging tug that charged her arousal with fresh fuel. The constant pressure was disturbed with every movement and even doing something as simple as removing the nipple spreader from the box dragged the skin cruelly and drove her close to the brink of a savage climax.

Whimpering with her craving for satisfaction, sure she was on the verge of a devastating orgasm, Karina applied the clips of the spreader bar to her nipples. They stung as sorely as the clamps on her pussy lips and she marvelled at the blissful way the pain could feel so punishing and, at the same time, so exquisite. Sure it wouldn't take much more to satisfy the tempestuous need in her loins, Karina struggled to secure the gag's fasteners before fixing the collar around her throat. She had slipped one wrist into the attached cuffs, and was cursing the awkwardness that prevented her from securing her other wrist, when she heard a hatefully familiar voice from the shadows behind her.

'Do you need a little help completing your costume?' Charlie asked.

She tried to turn around and face him but he acted too quickly. Snapping her free wrist into the remaining cuff he laughed triumphantly as she was secured by the restraints. With growing panic, she shook her head in silent refusal but he ignored her obvious plea for leniency.

'Don't you look perfect?' He grinned. 'I'll bet you're dressed like this so you and brother Bobby can play at auction games. Isn't that fucking sweet? Can you wait for brother Bobby to turn up? Or do you want me to get you started first?'

His hand clutched her breast, squeezing the orb and rekindling fresh pain from the clamps on the spreader bar. As he tugged one plump mound, the bar pulled the other and sent dizzying waves of anguish through each tingling nub. Breathless with a sudden surge of arousal, Karina could only glare at him.

'You do want me to get you started, don't you?' His gap-toothed smile resurfaced, greedily appraising her near-nudity. Without delicacy or finesse he dropped his hand to her crotch and pushed two fingers inside her cleft. They plundered easily and parted the slippery walls of her sex as he shoved them deep. When he withdrew his hand, he rubbed his finger and thumb together and chuckled malevolently. 'Greasy.' He laughed.

The single word flushed her with shame. She was almost glad when he span her around and bent her over the desk. The chance to avoid looking at his ugly face and grotesque smile was almost as welcome as if he had decided to leave her alone. A part of her was prepared to admit that it was more than welcome because, in spite of the revulsion he inspired, she knew Charlie could satisfy her immediate need. But she didn't let herself think about that aspect for too long. It was enough to raise her hips, relish the interminable tug of the stocking-clips against her labia, and await his rude penetration.

'Butt-plugged as well?' Charlie mused. 'You really are getting a taste for this depravity, aren't you?'

Her cheeks burnt crimson, the indignity intensifying as he began to lever the phallus from side to side. She had thought before that Charlie was like a douche of cold water to her arousal: he was ugly, repulsive, rude and uncouth and incapable of being considered desirable. Yet, while those beliefs still held true, she thought they were made perverse by the way he could inspire a need that had her trembling with greedy desire.

'Let's slip this out of your arse,' Charlie murmured, coaxing the butt-plug free. 'I'm sure we could find something more satisfying to push in there.'

Karina groaned around her gag as the length of rubber slid from her confines. The dithering pressure had been a constant throughout the day and, with its passing, her anus felt hollow and unfulfilled.

He slapped a hand against her backside and stepped between her legs.

The pressure on her overstretched pussy lips was bordering on the unbearable. If not for the gag filling her mouth she felt sure her screams would have alerted someone from the auction on the other side of the stockroom door.

'You're too good an opportunity to pass up,' he mused thoughtfully. 'And, I'll bet this is what you've been wanting anyway, *you dirty little bitch.*'

The words struck her like a slap as she remembered them being used in Robert's apartment nearly a week ago. She wondered if her fears at that time had been correct – if Robert had allowed Charlie the chance to use her on that occasion – and wished the idea of that relationship didn't add to her loathsome excitement. Before her thoughts could properly return to the incident, the end of Charlie's length was pushing at her anus as he prepared to enter her.

She stiffened against the desk, aware that his thickness was going to stretch her to new limits. Although she despised him and would have happily told him as much to his face, she couldn't deny that he filled her with an insatiable greed. Raising her buttocks to meet him, willing herself to relax so that his penetration was as smooth as she needed, Karina shut her mind to the rights and wrongs of what she was doing and prepared to wallow in the pleasure of being used.

'Too fucking tight,' he grunted, burying himself as deep as his shaft could go.

Choked on a scream of agonising euphoria, Karina barely heard the complaint. He was completing the need that had braised within her throughout the day and, with the moment of satisfaction edging ever closer, she knew the orgasm was going to be swift and strong. She pushed herself against him as he repeatedly bucked forward. His hands grasped her hips as he held her steady for each brusque penetration. Their climaxes came in a blistering unison, his twitching, sporadic jerks scouring shards of unprecedented bliss through her bowel. The pleasure was so strong that, it was only when she began to subside from her personal realm of bliss, Karina realised Charlie had extracted his shaft from her behind and replaced the pulsating butt-plug into her anus.

'There you are, darling,' Robert said, entering the stockroom. His understanding smile edged wider as he glanced at her outfit and said, 'I see you found the slave costume I'd set aside for you. You look good as my Lot sixty-eight.'

Surreptitiously, she tried glancing over her shoulder to see if Charlie was still there. It was impossible to see everything without making her concern obvious and she trusted her own belief that Robert had no idea his brother had just been using her.

Her heart was still racing with the after-echo of the orgasm; her anus was blissfully throbbing with the replaced butt-plug and the sticky warmth of Charlie's semen; and she felt sure the pungent smell of sex lingered on her body. But for some reason she couldn't understand, Robert still seemed unaware that his brother was taking advantage of every opportunity to capitalise on her vulnerability.

Robert's compassionate tone added to her conviction that he remained oblivious. 'I did this for you,' he explained, affectionately stroking her breast. 'I remembered that, all week, you've repeatedly told me how much you envied last week's lot at the slave auction. Tonight you'll get the chance to experience everything that she enjoyed.'

Giddily, Karina nodded. She was thankful that the gag stopped her from talking because, she knew, any words she might have said would have come out choked by overwhelming emotion.

Robert glanced at his watch and flexed a lascivious grin. 'But you've put on your costume too early.' He spoke with faux innocence as his hand cupped one buttock and his finger traced the dithering end of the butt-plug. 'What could we do to pass the time for the next hour until the auction begins?'

She wanted to read more from his expression but he was bending her over the desk just as Charlie had done. Above the pounding in her temples she could hear the distinctive sound of a zip being pulled down.

'Don't bother making a suggestion,' he said, teasing the end of his shaft against her sodden pussy lips. 'I've just realised what we can do to kill the time.'

And, as he pushed himself inside her, Karina began to understand why she had envied the brunette who had been sold to the kiosk attendant.

Karina was dragged onto the podium to bask in the warmth of a cold spotlight. A murmur of approval wafted through the crowd, someone wolf-whistled, and a couple of others laughed with what sounded like drunken merriment.

Rather than enjoying the thrill of finally achieving all that the brunette slave had enjoyed, Karina was berating herself for overlooking one obvious detail: Charlie.

She couldn't believe she'd forgotten about Charlie; all the times he'd taken advantage of her; all the times she'd mentally envisioned herself living this moment; and still she'd forgotten about his involvement with the auction. A sliver of black arousal penetrated her loins.

Charlie held her by one arm, his gap-toothed smile edged with malicious pleasure. He turned her around for the benefit of the audience, exposing every aspect of her bondage-clad nudity.

'Lot sixty-eight!' Robert's declaration caused the excited crowd to fall silent. 'We don't have a brunette this week, but this lot is almost as good. Firm breasts, decent legs and she's happy to accommodate an owner in any or all three holes. The green eyes make for a particularly attractive feature.'

Ignoring the pressure of Charlie's fingers burying into her arms, Karina tried to glimpse some of the faces in the auditorium. It was nearly impossible to see anything other than a sea of grey beyond the dazzling light and, when she did make out a recognisable feature – she felt sure she saw the kiosk attendant's distinctive silhouette – fresh tears of shame jewelled her vision.

'This one isn't fully trained,' Robert continued. He sounded almost apologetic. 'But it won't take much effort from a buyer to raise her obedience to show quality standards. She thrives on bondage. There's a rumour that she eagerly awaits to be pierced and branded, although, as you can all probably see, she's currently unmarked and not carrying jewellery.'

Aside from Charlie, or maybe partly because of him she grudgingly conceded, Karina realised the whole experience was the powerful aphrodisiac she had hoped it would be. She was even willing to accept that it was better than her frequent speculations had supposed. The moment was deeply shaming and her cheeks were flushed crimson. If she had been able to touch herself she knew she would be blessed by another stupendous release. She closed her eyes to wallow in the pleasure, then opened them for fear of missing one glorious moment.

'Who'll start me?' Robert asked. 'Who wants to make the first bid for this passable specimen of servility?'

Karina was suddenly struck by a wealth of fears that all added to her arousal. She worried that someone would make an irresistible offer; that the bidding would start before she had a chance to be properly humiliated; and that the bidding would never start because no one would want her. She stared wildly around the expectant sea of faces, panic threatening to overshadow the burgeoning bliss.

'Do I hear two hundred from the back of the room?' Robert asked. 'Do I hear one fifty?'

Karina groaned, wondering how her body could revel in such torment. She was shamefully displayed, the clips on the rubber stockings wringing poignant anguish every time she shifted her weight and her nipples aching from the constant torment of the spreader bar, but she had never felt more aroused in her life. She glared happily out into the auditorium, trying to imagine the lust her presence was inspiring.

'Do I hear one hundred?' Robert asked.

Karina glanced uncomfortably at him, not liking the implication that she was of little marketable value.

'Do I hear seventy-five?'

'Show us what it can do.'

Without needing to look in his direction, Karina knew the cry had come from the kiosk attendant. The thought of him watching added to her shame and she shivered from the idea that he was so close to becoming her owner. It was something of a relief to know that Robert wouldn't really sell her to such a loathsome creature and she turned to reassure herself that he still had her best interests at heart.

Robert wasn't looking at her. He stared out into the auditorium with his concentration seemingly fixed on the pending sale. 'You want to see her working?' he repeated. 'What should I have her do? Do you want to see her gobble Charlie? Or should I show you how wide I've managed to stretch her anus?'

Karina gasped, appalled by both suggestions and squirming with fresh excitement because of them. She knew Robert hadn't been serious about letting his brother use her but, as she enjoyed the fulfilling role she had so eagerly anticipated, the worries of the last week all seemed to be coming to a head.

Charlie turned her around so she had her back to the auditorium. He raised her cuffed wrists so Karina was forced to bend over. Her sex lips were bitten by new anguish and, if not for the gag in her mouth, her scream would have echoed around the hall. She could imagine how her backside looked, with the glistening lips of her sex stretched impossibly by the stocking's clips, and the gaping circle of her recently used anus.

The delicious humiliation cut deeper than ever before.

'Surely that's a sight to raise the bidding?' Robert suggested. 'Surely someone will offer a mere fifty pounds for something so ripe and juicy?'

Karina moaned. If she could have touched herself at that moment she knew her orgasm would have been a blistering release and the first of many that would have shattered through her with slowly accelerating degrees of devastation. Her breath came in ragged gasps as she revelled in the twin pleasures of pain and humiliation.

Robert reached into the drawer of his desk and produced a thick, black phallus. As he handed it to his brother, he told the auditorium, 'She's been trained to hold a plug and, from what I've seen of her, she shouldn't have any difficulty accepting any thickness a new owner cares to use.'

Karina trembled as Charlie tested the length of rubber between her buttocks. It had been less than a week since she first allowed Robert to use her anus and she still remembered those initial agonising moments as her body tried to cope with the unnatural penetration. But now, although the dildo was thicker than anything she had held before, her body accepted it easily and without protest. The moulded shape slipped effortlessly into her forbidden passage and she basked in the base pleasure of its vast presence. Charlie held a hand on her back, and she guessed he was trying to make his role in the proceedings look more necessary, but her backside devoured the length of rubber eagerly.

She remembered Charlie had teased two or three fingers inside the brunette slave and was disappointed that she hadn't had to suffer that same crushing indignity. But, when he began to slide the phallus back and forth, her dashed expectations vanished beneath another cresting wave of joy.

Someone from the audience cheered approval while another began to clap.

Charlie pulled on Karina's arm, encouraging her to stand up and face the auditorium. When she finally found the courage to do as he asked she had to blink to clear the tears from her eyes. Her cheeks continued to burn and the thick length inside her backside languished with a wonderfully hateful weight.

'Does anyone want to see this slave being tested further?' Robert asked.

Karina groaned. A week ago she had almost screamed in answer to that same question, anxious to witness more torment. Now, she hoped the crowd would show the same restraint they had displayed then because she didn't think her body could cope with anything more. It would only take a subtle caress or a casual touch and she knew she would collapse in a shuddering, orgasmic heap.

Robert pointed his gavel toward the '*caveat emptor*' sign and said, 'This is good stock we're selling today. I don't want anyone walking away from here saying this item didn't fulfil their expectations.'

'Two hundred!'

Karina gasped. She clenched her muscles and was rewarded by a shock of undiluted euphoria.

The bidding went up swiftly and she felt all but forgotten amongst the rising voices and Robert's hurried monologue of where the price was standing. Karina could hear the kiosk attendant's mellow voice sounding over all the others as he perpetually bettered each increase. Her worries about the danger she faced began to heighten.

It occurred to her that Robert was in a position where he could easily abuse the trust she had vested in him. She was cuffed and wearing a ball-gag and unable to argue if he decided to sell her to the highest bidder. Remembering the note he had left offered little reassurance because it didn't actually say he wasn't going to sell her. She fretted that the wording might have been a carefully worded lie, designed to make her trust him enough so she would willingly place herself on the auction block.

'One thousand pounds,' Robert called triumphantly. 'Do I hear another fifty?'

'Here,' cried the kiosk attendant.

Karina shivered. Her sex still throbbed with an inarguable pulse but the pleasure was close to being overshadowed by her doubts about a future as the property of the man from Sinners. Another voice tried bettering the kiosk attendant's calls and took the price up to fifteen hundred. Her insides twisted with a snake of fear. She couldn't decide if it would be worse to become the property of someone she had met and reviled, or a stranger whom she had never previously encountered. Neither option had been on the agenda at the start of the evening and she tried to work out when events had started to degenerate to such a level of unpleasant choices. She supposed it was pointless speculation because all she could do was stand and watch as the bidding passed the two thousand mark and then crept higher.

'The price stands at twenty-five hundred,' Robert told the auditorium. The bids had come so quickly he sounded breathless from following their progress. 'Do I hear twenty-six?'

Karina turned to stare at him, suddenly remembering their virtual panic button. She blinked her eyes repeatedly, sending herself dizzy with the way the bright spotlight flashed on and off against her retina. Straining with the effort, she tried to make him see that she was giving the sign to show she had reservations about the way events were proceeding. It was only as an afterthought that she remembered the brunette slave had blinked at him at this same point in the auction.

Robert ignored her. 'The last bid stands at twenty-five hundred,' he said, raising his gavel.

Karina sobbed around her gag. She would have continued trying to blink for him, even though she suspected it was futile. Rather than being allowed the chance to carry on, Charlie tugged on her arm and made her face the auditorium.

'Can anyone better the price I've been offered by the gentleman from Sinners?'

Karina swallowed thickly and shook her head. She wondered when Robert had changed from the considerate epitome of a perfect boyfriend to the sadistic slave trader who now controlled her destiny. Knowing the matter was of no importance, she lowered her gaze and prepared to accept the penalty for her envy.

'No further bids?' Robert asked. He put his gavel to one side and nodded toward Charlie. Speaking genially toward his audience he said, 'I'm sorry, ladies and gentlemen, but we have a no-sale on our hands this evening. The lot failed to reach its reserve price so you'll have to call back next week if you're interested in purchasing one of this auction house's high quality slaves. Thank you for your custom, and I'll look forward to seeing you next week.'

Karina revelled in a wave of grateful relief. As Charlie took her from the centre of the stage she could have collapsed into Robert's arms and kissed him for an eternity. All the black thoughts she had harboured – all the doubts and fears – now seemed ridiculous as she saw they had been misplaced. He waited until they were out of sight from the auditorium before unfastening and removing her gag.

'I'd thought you were going to sell me,' she blurted, hoping he didn't think she was insane. 'I'd thought you were going to sell me to that horrible man from Sinners.'

Robert laughed, a musical sound that should have banished all her worries. 'Sell you to the guy from Sinners?' He sounded aghast. 'I couldn't have done that,' he said seriously. 'Not when Charlie said he'd pay five hundred less than the last bid if you didn't go over three grand.'

Seeming oblivious to the dawning horror on her face, Robert continued to smile. He seemed to be growing smaller and, with sick excitement twisting her guts, Karina realised Charlie still held her by the arm and was now dragging her away.

Her mind fluttered back to the incident that had inspired her envy and the slave who had gone on to become the property of the man from Sinners. The woman was currently suffering a life of branding, piercing and sexual degradation. Yet, compared to her new-found role as Charlie's property, Karina realised she still envied the brunette slave.

6

Weight Watcher

Fiona sucked on her chocolate bar and smiled contentedly to herself.

She knew she had put on a little weight since she first started at Sinners but that thought never moved the smile from her plump face. She knew she was a source of amusement to many and the subject of contempt and ridicule to others. But she never troubled herself with anyone else's opinion. The only things she concerned herself with were her job as the kiosk attendant, and maintaining a regular supply of chocolate bars. They were the only things that mattered.

'You're getting fatter.'

She glanced at the boss, noticing his trim beard narrowed whenever he was frowning. It detracted from his otherwise handsome features and she wondered if she should mention the detail. Considering the care he took over his grooming, and the assured confidence with which he held himself, she thought it most likely that he already knew. She also thought she could sense trouble brewing.

'I didn't think it would be possible to say those words to you,' he continued nastily. 'You've been dangerously chunky for the last couple of months but you're getting even bigger now. You're the size of a pregnant elephant with hormone problems. Should I be getting a structural engineer to design the next chair we buy for you? Your arse is so big that from behind it looks like two sofas having sex in a tent. Why don't you get on a diet, you fat toad? You're carrying more lard than a butcher's delivery wagon.'

Fiona sucked on her chocolate bar and smiled for him. She was unable to resist a tiny shiver which undulated like pond ripples through the vast rolls of flesh covering her frame. Now that she was comfortable wearing chains instead of clothes she had fallen into the habit of watching her own bare flesh tremble in varying states of excitement. Because of the excess weight she now carried there was a lot of bare flesh to study and the quivering response to arousal never failed to make her grin. Her breathing deepened into a husky drawl. 'Is something wrong?' she asked sweetly.

He sneered with revulsion and walked away, but that was all right. Fiona didn't mind whether he stayed or went; just so long as she had her job in the kiosk, and her endless supply of chocolate bars.

It was disappointing that the boss could sometimes be cutting but she knew she could tolerate his occasional lapses into cruelty. He had welcomed her eagerly when Sinners first opened and the memory of those halcyon days still burnt brightly. Some days, when she spent too much time near the boss or when she indulged in a little too much chocolate, Fiona thought the memory burnt so bright it seared.

It had taken a full week of employment before she finally submitted to him but Fiona thought the experience was worth every second of the wait. Simply being near the boss, watching him charm his victims with a blend of animal magnetism and understated style, was

189

akin to enjoying a skilfully produced ballet. The lilt of his smile, and the mellifluous timbre of his voice, combined to make him almost irresistible. Women, who ordinarily would have cowered from the darker aspects of his personality, seemed briefly blind to his many faults. Instead of shying from him, as any sane person should have done, they all seemed desperate to fall under his demonic spell.

And a part of her knew it was truly a spell in the magical sense of the word. He had a way of exercising control that could only be compared to witchcraft or wizardry or something from the dark arts. If she had been superstitious by nature she might have found the discovery disconcerting. Because she was pragmatic and curious she heard herself ask, 'How do you do that?'

He stood in the doorway to her kiosk, leaning idly against the frame. The last of the patrons had only just left and employer and employee usually shared a couple of minutes' conversation and the occasional drink before Fiona followed the customers out of the building for the night. 'How do you do it?' she repeated. 'How do you make people do things they don't want to do?'

He shook his head. 'I've never made anyone do anything they don't want to do. I simply grant wishes.'

She sniffed indignantly. 'That's not what it looks like to me.'

He shrugged as though the distinction was of no consequence. 'I grant wishes. It's not my fault if people don't know what they're wishing for. I can make every lottery ticket a winner for one person. I can help another woman obtain membership to an exclusive gentlemen's club. I can offer a dream job to someone who yearns for something other than the nine to five rut. It's not my fault if they don't know how best to appreciate those gifts.'

Fiona regarded him warily, suspecting there was some truth in what he said but sure it was hidden in something darker. If he genuinely believed he could grant wishes, and all the evidence she had seen indicated that was true, she thought it would be wise to think with clear focus while she was around him.

'It's been a busy night,' he observed, joining her inside the kiosk. He was using the same sultry tone with which he always wooed his victims but, although she was wary of him, Fiona wasn't going to complain. She could have listened to the sweetness of his voice forever and never grown tired. There was something soothing, enchanting and undeniably arousing about the way words rolled off his tongue. His tone had the rich lustre of a polished instrument and every syllable was made musical with sultry resonance.

'It has been busy,' Fiona agreed. Trying to add levity to the moment, she said, 'I've been rushed off my backside.'

He laughed politely and offered her a bar of chocolate from the kiosk display. When she politely declined, he pressed it toward her. 'Go on,' he said, his gaze flitting over her willowy frame. 'You could use a bit of meat on you.'

'I really shouldn't,' she said earnestly. The chocolate bars had been a constant temptation and, when the boss had first told her she could eat as many as she wanted, Fiona had quietly cursed him for the generosity. Dieting had been a constant in her life and, since her teenage years, her existence had been an unhappy state of near-perpetual hunger. To maintain the waiflike ninety-five pounds that best suited her petite figure she tried to avoid anything with a calorie content higher than water. But, from her first day in the kiosk, she knew the bars of chocolate were going to prove difficult to resist.

'There's no sin in indulgence,' he assured her.

The chocolate bar wafted lazily beneath her nose. Although the wrapper was airtight, Fiona imagined she could smell the rich aroma coming from within. She raised a hand, almost took it from him, then pushed her fingers into her lap. Shaking her head she smiled forlornly and said, 'You know how to tempt people, don't you?'

His smile was etched with wry humour and she saw he was suddenly regarding her as a challenge. The idea made her squirm against her seat and she lowered her gaze, fretful he might see a glimpse of the need in her eyes.

'Clearly I don't know how to tempt you,' he murmured. 'You have tremendous willpower.'

She dared to meet his inquisitive smile.

He still held the chocolate bar but now he had torn the wrapper open. The smooth, creamy scents flooded her senses and her mouth was awash with anticipatory saliva. She swallowed twice, aware the action made her seem nervous, then licked her lips. He raised the sweet to his lips, placed his overbite against the top chunk, then bit a small piece from the bar. After making a pantomime show of enjoying the taste he once again offered the packet to Fiona. 'Are you sure you don't want some? It's scrumptious.'

She stared at the chocolate. Her longing was so severe it hurt like a wound. He held the bar beneath her nose for an age and, when she finally shook her head, he sighed sadly and his smile tightened. Fiona thought she could see his resolve settling deeper but she didn't dare look at him for too long. He raised the bar to his mouth, bit off another chunk, and she had to turn away rather than watch him savour the second piece of milk chocolate.

'It's not nice to tease,' she said petulantly. 'In fact, it's downright cruel.'

His laughter was derisive. 'It's not nice to decline hospitality,' he returned. 'But that's what you're doing.'

She lifted her gaze again, ready to tell him she was doing no such thing, but his actions stopped her words from coming. He was opening his shirt, pulling the tails from the waistband of his trousers and nimbly releasing the buttons. Exposing his smooth, hairless chest – the pectoral muscles honed to perfection and the adorable six-pack tight and enticing – he grinned broadly as he pushed the chocolate bar against his breast.

Fiona watched with rapt attention, entranced by the smear of melted chocolate that began to dribble down his chest. She briefly wondered how warm his body had to be to generate so much heat, and what benefits he thought he might gain from tormenting her in this way, and then she was climbing from her chair and pushing her face toward his nipple.

The bead of flesh was only peripheral to her immediate desire. More importantly, she needed to taste the sweet flavour and lap every trace from his body. Feeling his pectoral muscle twitch against her tongue, and knowing his nipple was hardening from the warmth of her mouth, she wondered if he was experiencing a shadow of the same pleasure that held her in its thrall. Once she had licked the last trace from his chest, still savouring the combined flavours of chocolate and his light sweat, she realised he had been pressing the bar against his other breast.

A rivulet of dark fluid ran down his torso. The thick line of chocolate perfumed the kiosk with an intoxicating aroma and, as he moved the bar away, she pushed her mouth against him. This time she grazed her teeth against his flesh, determined to extract every memory of the chocolate from his skin. She sucked hard against him, enjoying the way his nipple stiffened against her tongue, but still concentrating on the flavour of processed and sweetened cocoa beans. Once his areola was cleaned she chased her tongue down his midriff.

'You really have a greed for that,' he observed.

Still licking the flavour from his abdomen, Fiona said nothing.

He reached for his trousers and unfastened them. When he dropped them to the floor she saw his erection stood bold and proud. The revelation didn't shock her because she had seen the way he commanded other women, slyly spied on some of those he had taken, and felt no surprise that he believed himself able to control her. Given the way he had made her suckle against his breast, she supposed he was exerting some degree of domination and she couldn't deny she was tempted to reach down and touch him.

But, with a massive effort of self-denial, she fell back to her chair. She was blushing furiously and mumbling a garbled apology. 'I shouldn't have done that. That was wrong of me and I didn't mean to . . .'

'You know what I can do,' he said softly. He reached down for her face and tilted her chin so she was staring up at him. 'You know I have the ability to make wishes come true. Isn't there a wish I could grant for you?'

She thought of turning the conversation to his demonic talents. It might have broken his spell if she had asked him to explain how he had come by his abilities, and whether they were true powers, or simply her fanciful interpretation of facts and events. But, while she was able to resist some temptations, she couldn't deny herself the excitement of his predatory interest. Raising the only objection she could think of, she asked meekly, 'Isn't it evil?'

'Evil?' He laughed. 'Is it evil to have a dream come true?' Shaking his head he said, 'Not according to any of the Disney musicals I've ever seen.'

She could tell he wasn't taking her seriously and she glared at him miserably. It crossed her mind that she should take her purse and flounce out of the kiosk and away from Sinners nightclub but she believed there was still a chance things might work to her advantage. And she couldn't resist thinking she was briefly the focus of his charm and that undivided attention wasn't something she wanted to give up so easily. 'What wish could you grant for me?' she asked. 'And what penalty would I have to suffer because of it?'

'People pay their own penalties,' he reminded her. 'Would you shoot the Grand National winner if you squandered your prize money? Would you curse the person who sold you a winning lottery ticket if your round the world cruise struck an iceberg? I only have a little control. I only grant wishes. But I can give you whatever you want.'

She continued staring at him and, although she believed what he was saying, she still bided her time before coming to a decision. It was difficult to remain so calm in his presence; he inspired a hunger that brought her close to trembling and the cleft between her legs felt sodden with desire. But Fiona kept her thoughts focused as he stood above her and stared hungrily down.

'You like chocolate?' he asked, waving the bar hypnotically in front of her face. 'Isn't there something you might want to do with that?'

Determinedly, she racked her brains, always coming back to the same idea but never daring to let it take proper form within her thoughts. It was only when his fingers moved from her chin, and lightly caressed the fine hairs that followed her jaw, that she finally made her decision. 'You're right,' she conceded. 'I like chocolate, and perhaps there is a wish you could grant me.'

His smile was eager. Almost too eager. 'Go on. What's your wish?'

She shook her head. 'There's something you need to do for me first.'

He raised an eyebrow and encouraged her to continue.

Climbing out of her chair, she reached out for him and took the chocolate from his hand. Instead of greedily devouring the bar she pressed it back against his chest and held his gaze as it melted against him. As soon as his nipple was daubed with a thick smear of silky brown, she pushed her face against him and worked her tongue at his flesh.

He settled himself on the counter of her kiosk, his erection still swaying between them as she painted him with the bar, then licked the melted residue from his skin. Growing weary of tasting his breasts, she trailed a line down the centre of his stomach to the thatch of curls at his groin. Chasing her tongue down him, eagerly retrieving every sweet smear, she was elated to feel him shiver.

'What was it you wanted from me, Fiona?' he asked.

She placed a finger against his lips, still working her mouth near the base of his shaft. She hadn't dared to touch his erection yet but she could see the length twitched eagerly every time her face brushed close. The responses he evoked with his words and his smile were nothing compared to the arousal that struck her when she saw how much she excited him. It was thrilling to know that she had inspired the erection of such a desirable man and that added to her eagerness as she touched the chocolate against his glans.

The boss stiffened. He blinked back his surprise as she grinned up at him and he watched with obvious disbelief as Fiona darted her tongue against his dome-like end. His smile broadened when she placed her lips around him and gently sucked on the meaty flesh. 'What was it you wanted from me?' he repeated. 'What is it that you need me to do before we can discuss your wish?'

She swallowed the last of the chocolate that had covered the end of his shaft, savouring the salty addition of pre-come, then reluctantly moved her mouth away. 'I want you to give me my most memorable night ever,' she decided.

He looked surprised. 'That's your wish?'

'No!' She shook her head indignantly. 'That's what I want you to do before I tell you my wish. I want you to give me the most memorable night I'm ever likely to have.'

If he had been regarding her as a challenge she now saw he believed himself able to meet her demands. His confidence seemed to swell as his chest puffed out, his erection stiffened, and he reached down to stroke his fingers through her hair. His touch was so gentle she was barely sure the fingers had reached her skin.

'My most memorable night ever,' she reminded him.

He bent down to kiss her mouth. 'I can do that,' he declared arrogantly. 'It will set a standard by which everything else pales.'

The declaration was enough to make her quiver expectantly.

He removed her clothes, not hurrying, but allowing his haste to be made known. Fiona listened to his soft declarations of appreciation as he exposed her breasts, and she melted with gratitude when he sighed at the sight of her bare cleft. When he began to praise her body, using gentle kisses at first, then growing bolder and using his fingers and tongue, she knew the experience would be everything her imagination had hoped.

Their naked bodies writhed together in a dry embrace of desperate need. She refrained from giving herself too eagerly, still savouring his mouth against hers and the shared flavour of chocolate that lingered beneath each kiss. His hands appraised her breasts, touching lightly, teasing the flesh and bringing her close to the point of wanting him.

But she continued to resist.

When he pressed his bare thigh between her legs, his erection nudging at her stomach and his muscular leg squashing the sodden folds of her pussy lips, she almost crumbled. The hairs on his leg scrubbed her sex and the light abrasion made her dizzy with sudden, avaricious need. Her yearning for him was strong, and the promise of satisfaction was never more than a whisper away, but she had asked him to make this the most memorable night she would ever enjoy, and she knew that he wouldn't be the only one responsible for such an immense pleasure.

Instead of begging him to take her, she contented herself with touching him and revelling in his nearness. His hands were a balm to her growing needs, placating at first, then inciting more insistent demands. His fingers teased her hardened nipples, brushed lightly against the thrust of her clitoris and even dared to caress the ring of her anus. Relishing the fear of sensation overload, maniacally fretful that she might explode if she didn't give in to her need, Fiona finally relented.

'Take me,' she whispered, 'and take me well.'

Positioning himself between her legs, he pushed easily into her succulent centre. His shaft was rigid and unyielding – thick enough to hurt and hard enough to show no remorse – but, when he plunged deep inside her sex, she could only sigh with delight. There was more of him than she wanted, but it wasn't too much more and she couldn't deny his size added enormously to her pleasure. As he stroked himself in and out, filling her, then leaving her empty, Fiona knew she had done right to wait and she quietly congratulated herself on her prudence. The self-congratulation was only a fleeting thought and she didn't allow it to make her mood smug. 'Remember,' she gasped.

He paused, listening intently.

'Remember to make it the best ever.'

Laughing arrogantly, he assured her it would be.

And she knew he was being true to his word when he began to ride her properly. He slid repeatedly into her pussy with an easily matched rhythm that reminded her of those professional dancers she had seen on the nightclub's floor. And, while the majority of her pleasure was being wrung from her sex, she knew his hands, mouth and body were also contributing. He didn't leave her breasts unattended, constantly squeezing the orbs or gnawing lightly at the buds of her nipples. When his fingers were free to caress her he managed to excite new erogenous zones that she had never previously considered sexual. He stroked the nape of her neck and the small of her back, inside her elbows and the soft inlet of flesh at her ankles. The constant contact repeatedly reminded her he was in the embrace of a truly skilled lover. The simple action of holding her arms, or squeezing her body against his, brought her to the brink of climaxes which she knew could have been devastating.

But she resisted the urge to succumb to release. She quietly demanded he gave as much as he was able and refused to let him end her pleasure too swiftly. When she gazed into his eyes, and saw his expression set with a look of fervent determination, she realised he was trying to do as she asked and she knew she couldn't have asked for anything more.

And his skills as a lover were tremendous. Her sex was battered by his repeated penetrations but every *entry glided home with a marksman's accuracy. When he eventually withdrew, then turned her over, she marvelled at the myriad fresh sensations that came from the change in position. She wanted to twist and turn beneath him, experiment with new postures and see if other delights could be born from their union but, having faith in his abilities, she knew he would treat her to the best of the pleasures and that he wouldn't disappoint her.*

Again, she could have congratulated herself on her well-placed faith, but she refused to let conceit spoil her satisfaction.

He moved her easily around the kiosk, taking her in her chair, bending her over the counter, riding her from beneath and behind and always pushing her to new heights of elation. She had thought her orgasm would come in a crippling rush but, rather than a furious, fantastic climax, the pinnacle of pleasure seemed a constant that simply eclipsed itself with every passing second.

She knew it had been the most memorable session long before he finally erupted. She knew she would never again know so much passion and skill combined in an effort to take her to new realms of joy and she supposed the thought should have saddened her. But, as the final wave of euphoria began to subside, she only felt as though she had achieved a long sought-after goal.

He stroked his fingers through her hair, then brushed his knuckles against her bare breast. The contact made her shiver and she grinned as she pulled herself from his reach. His copious spend was still dripping from her sex and each sly, wet dribble inspired a further shiver. 'What's your wish?' he asked quietly.

She smiled slyly to herself and took a fresh bar of chocolate from the kiosk display. Sucking on the end, savouring the melted flavour as it spread across her tongue, she said, 'I don't think I need to tell you my wish. I'm sure it will be granted.'

The boss stormed into her kiosk and glared down at Fiona. 'There are field workers in Seville who haven't seen as much orange peel skin as I can glimpse at the top of your thighs,' he grunted.

The observation burst through her thoughts and shook her from her daydream. She took another bar of chocolate from the display, stared at him while she unwrapped it, then pushed it into her mouth and sucked on the end.

Her entire body trembled with a quiver of enjoyment. The links of her uniform chain rattled in a musical after-echo.

'You give fat a bad name,' he decided. 'Do you have clothes specially made? Does it cause a cotton famine every time you need to buy a new pair of knickers? Do you shower on a morning, or do you just walk through a car wash? That's an idea – maybe I can promote the nightclub by renting advertising space on your arse. If you bent over at the wrong time of day we could lose a couple of hours of sunlight.'

'Something's weighing on your mind, isn't it?' she said with genuine understanding. 'Do you want to talk about it?'

He opened his mouth, looked set to say something, then glanced beyond her, through the glass window of her kiosk, and out to the centre of the foyer.

Two women stood there, one of them dressed all in red, the other virtually naked save for chains around her throat, wrists and ankles. Red stripes scored the naked woman's rear, their blazing heat visible even from a distance. Fiona had seen them both before, the woman in red an occasional visitor, the near-naked brunette a more frequent attendee. The near-naked brunette was a tall and arrogant bitch who seemed motivated only by a sense of self-pride. But there was little evidence of that emotion visible in her now. Her shoulders were rounded and she sobbed unhappily against the shoulder of the petite woman in red.

'What's she doing out here?' the boss asked. 'And who the hell is that interfering bitch with her?'

Fiona could tell the questions weren't directed at her so she made no attempt to reply. She only continued to watch as the woman in red retrieved a tissue from her purse and used it to dab tears from the brunette's eyes. She also pulled something else from her bag and, although Fiona couldn't see for sure, she thought it looked like a small jar of cold cream.

'I'm going to see what's going on,' the boss decided.

'They seem to have it under control.' Fiona observed.

Fumbling with the door handle, he ignored her and burst out of the kiosk. Before he had made it into the foyer the naked woman had disappeared. The woman in red remained and she met the boss with haughty defiance. The exchange looked as though it was going to be volatile but the interruption of a telephone call spoiled Fiona's chances of seeing any further developments.

To compensate for missing the unexpected entertainment, she decided to have another chocolate bar.

A week later the boss's mood hadn't improved. He strode into her kiosk and glared at Fiona with a contempt that was galling. 'Retiring Japanese whalers probably haven't seen as much blubber as I can see right now. I saw a documentary the other night that said there are now two manmade monuments that can be seen from outer space; the Great Wall of China, and your fat arse. I thank Christ you never use the lift while you're in here because it's only designed to take the weight of fourteen people.'

She unwrapped a chocolate bar and regarded him solemnly. 'If there's something you want to talk about, you don't need to skirt around the subject. Sweet talk has its place, but we've known one another long enough for you to be straight with me.'

He sat down and glared at her. His composure was usually flawless, but over the past few weeks she had thought he was looking a little fraught. This evening the symptoms were so plain – the redness at his eyes, the narrowness of his beard and the lines that creased his brow – she wondered how she could have missed their dramatic worsening.

'The nightclub is in trouble,' he said flatly. 'I have an appointment to see the company who're currently financing me, but I've been wanting to forewarn you: things are looking bleak.'

It was hard to digest the solemn news while eating and she put her chocolate bar aside so she wasn't smiling when she replied. 'Things are that bad?'

He nodded. 'Maybe that's why I've been a little offhand with you lately,' he mumbled.

Fiona realised she was hearing the closest he could manage to an apology.

'Perhaps I was thinking, if you took offence and then walked out of here all pissed at me, I wouldn't have to tell you that your job here was no longer safe.'

She considered what he was saying, decided it didn't really excuse the inexcusable, but knew she wasn't going to make an issue over the matter. They sat in sullen silence for a moment as Fiona accepted the gravity of the situation.

'I'm not finished yet,' he assured her. 'But I wanted you to know it's a potential danger. If I can't work some sort of magic, Sinners will close, and you'll be out of a job.'

'Can't you just grant your own wish?' she asked suddenly. The idea came in a flash of inspiration, perhaps ignited by his use of the word 'magic' but, once it was fixed in her mind, she felt sure it was a potential recourse. 'You've always told me you can grant wishes. It's an ability that you have. Can't you just wish for more money, or more customers or more of whatever it takes?'

He shook his head. 'I don't think that would work.' He glared bitterly at her and said, 'I haven't been able to grant every wish that's been made of me. Perhaps my abilities are beginning to fade.'

It was only when she was lumbering home at the end of that evening that Fiona realised he meant her. She stopped in her tracks, shocked that he thought he had failed to grant her wish. On that long ago evening she had been careful to focus her thoughts on exactly what she wanted and the boss's reward had been the perfect fulfilment of her most heartfelt desire. It had been exactly what she wanted.

Every time she ate a chocolate bar, the texture and taste took her back to their evening of passion: each time she ate a chocolate bar, she relived every blissful sensation of the whole, glorious experience.

Unwrapping one of the three emergency bars she kept in her purse, Fiona resumed her journey home, smiling fondly at his misunderstanding. She made a mental note that, tomorrow evening, if she remembered, she might tell him he had granted her wish. It would probably pander to his conceit, and she knew it might make him insufferably arrogant but, if she remembered, she was determined to tell him.

He had granted her wish and it still held true.

7

Anger Management

'Two words,' Andrea said dreamily.

She was only half awake but the phrase was so familiar it was second nature to say it as soon as consciousness returned each morning. She reached across the bed to Ted's sleeping form. Her manicured nails scratched lightly over the sheets, the scarlet polish contrasting against the ivory silk. As soon as her fingertips had found him she yanked his ear until his eyes opened in startled surprise.

'Two words,' she repeated. This time she was more alert and spat the phrase with characteristic venom. 'Fuck me.'

Ted was fully awake in seconds. He shook away his sleep like a dog shaking off water. Lumbering on top of her, positioning himself between her spread thighs, he moved his mouth toward hers.

Andrea placed her hand over his face and forcefully directed his head away. 'Don't kiss me, you pillock,' she growled. 'You've only just woken up. Your mouth will taste like shit. Didn't I tell you to fuck me? Why are you pissing about with your feeble attempts at foreplay?'

Abruptly, he shoved his erection against her sex.

Andrea reached between their bodies and gripped his shaft in one hand. Holding him tight, squeezing

206

until his expression changed from a snarl to the beginnings of an apology, she guided him to the wetness between her legs. The head of his dome rested against the soft centre of her spreading warmth and she teased the end against her slippery lips. 'Do it,' she demanded, releasing her punishing grip. 'And do it well. Fuck me.'

Responding obediently, Ted bucked his hips forward. His shaft plunged easily inside, furrowing through her inner muscles as he hurriedly entered. It was a vicious penetration and Andrea barely had time to raise herself to meet his brusque assault. When she did lift her buttocks from the bed their pelvises clapped together like the first hard blows in a fist fight.

They both grunted: primordial sounds that precipitated pending conflict.

'Bastard,' she cursed.

'Ice bitch,' he returned.

She scowled, wrapping her arms around him and holding his broad shoulders. Ice bitch was one of the titles she had inherited when she arrived in the office and she had specifically told Ted she didn't like the name. As he continued to bombard her with arrhythmic thrusts, Andrea clawed her nails down his back. Ted grimaced, his expression more pained than usual, and she guessed she had opened one of the many wounds she had inflicted previously. The thought brought a sadistic smile to her lips and she clenched her muscles tight around his thickness.

'Ride me harder,' she demanded. 'Ride me harder; ride me faster; and ride me better.'

He spread his shoulders, forcing her to move her hands away. Catching a fistful of her long, blonde tresses, he pinned her head against the pillow. Seeming confident he was now in control, he forced

Andrea to remain beneath him while he pounded his erection between her pussy lips.

She bit back a cry of discomfort, meeting and matching every furious thrust. Holding his other arm, burying her fingernails deep into the fading cuts on his bicep, she used him with the same ferocity he was using her. She clenched her muscles tight around him, squeezing and writhing in an attempt to wring the climax from his shaft. In perfect synchronisation their hips rose and fell as each tried to defeat the other with the force of their passion. Shards of pleasure, inadvertent side-effects from their vigorous union, doused them both with sweat. Droplets of perspiration beaded Ted's brow then sprinkled down onto Andrea's upturned face. She found herself swathed in a meld of their combined sweat, her back and shoulders were drenched, and she relished the tactile bliss of so much slippery heat.

'Make it good, Teddy,' she growled. She knew he liked the appellation 'Teddy' as much as she relished being called 'the ice bitch'. 'Make it real good.'

'I always make it good,' he grunted.

Their gazes locked briefly.

Her flintlike expression gave nothing away except for a lustre of excitement and a glimmer of unconcealed fury. She could see her reflection mirrored in his eyes and fancifully imagined scarlet sparks sputtering from the steel-grey pupils. It was entertaining to realise, even though he held the superior position and even though he was the muscular and dominant macho man, Ted's confident grin was underscored by a flicker of doubt. He continued to hammer his shaft between her thighs and each vigorous penetration pummelled dull pleasure from her sex. But, scowling up at him, Andrea knew which of them was in control and she could see that Ted knew exactly the same thing.

'Faster,' she grunted, repositioning her hips so his broad girth rubbed against her clitoris. A rush of fresh fire surged through her sex and she gripped his arm more tightly. The frantic promise of a swift release inched closer and she almost choked on a cry of raw elation. 'Do it faster,' she insisted. 'Didn't you hear me?'

Their climaxes came in a blistering explosion. He took her briskly to a peak of pleasure and continued pumping into her as she writhed joyously against the sheets. His shaft etched daggers of dark beauty through her pussy and, when his own eruption came, he carried on thrusting his flailing shaft until they were both fully spent.

Andrea glanced at the bedside alarm clock, her momentary smile disappearing as she noticed the position of the hands. Pushing Ted's limp body away, she threw the sheets aside and strutted naked from the bedroom.

'Where are you going?' he called.

Exertion and the early hour were apparent in his voice and she wondered if she shouldn't be trading him in for a younger, more athletic model. She had used him as much as she was able and didn't think there was any point in keeping him around for anything other than sex.

'What's wrong?' he grumbled. 'Where are you going?'

'Two words,' she shouted back. 'Monday morning.'

Andrea's morning routine was a brisk one: coffee, cigarette, shower, then quickly dressed and off to work. Her wardrobe contained a choice of red or naked and she selected a vibrant suit that clung to her slender, petite contours. The blazing colour was

bright and attention-grabbing and she nodded approval at her reflection before heading out to her car.

Like her choice in clothes, her MG was blindingly
scarlet and she thought its compact size and stylish
lines mirrored her personality. The sporty convertible
was fitted with a horn that bellowed like a jugger-
naut's klaxon and she used it frequently to indicate
her displeasure with those drivers and pedestrians
who offended her through the rush-hour journey.
(*'Two words, you fucking arsehole! Two words: High-
way Code.'*) In a rare moment of introspection, she
wondered if the contrast between the vehicle's eye-
catching beauty and its powerful roar reflected something about her personality. But, because she was
anxious to make a start on the day, and because she
could never see an advantage in analysing her own
actions, she didn't give herself any time to dwell on
the matter.

She pulled into the reserved bay of her parking
space, pleased to see that it had now been painted
with her name and position: A Jones, Managing
Director. Grinning tightly, she killed the convertible's
engine and started toward the lifts that would take
her into the office building.

The car park was a concrete forest of light and
shadows with overhanging heating pipes and flutter-
ing fluorescents. The floor was painted with abstract
tyre marks against a background of oil and dirt, and
the whole area was perfumed with filth and petrol
fumes. Disliking the squalor, Andrea usually walked
briskly to the lifts while trying to ignore the decay
that was settling into the underbelly of her father's
former office building. Ordinarily she kept her gaze
focused on the permanently burning lamps near the
lift doors, never looking to the left or the right, as she
tried to make her way safely into work. But move-

ment glimpsed from the corner of her eye made her alter her routine this morning.

A couple stood in the shaded seclusion of a dimly lit corner.

He had his back against a concrete support while she stood immediately facing him. Their arms were wrapped around each other and their mouths were joined in a frenzy of eager exploration. With legs intertwined and their pelvises writhing sporadically, they presented a spectacle of barely tamed arousal that was almost spilling into full blown passion. They caressed and embraced, either ignorant or oblivious to Andrea and the sharp click of her stilettos striking hollow notes on the floor. They didn't respond to the slowing pace of her steps, or see her as she cautiously approached. Nor were they aware of Andrea when she stopped two yards away, folded her arms and stood watching. The first time they noticed her was when Andrea's mobile phone piped a shrill ring into the shadows. Then they both turned to glare at her. Their startled expressions – indignant and accusatory – quickly melted to fear when they realised who she was.

The reaction didn't surprise her. Andrea knew that, as the company's new managing director, she had a reputation for volatility and she supposed their obvious fear was well-placed. If she had been in their position, she knew she would have had every reason to be terrified.

Andrea glanced at the caller display screen on her phone before accepting the call. 'What is it, Julia?' she barked. She pointed a finger at the couple, silently indicating they should stay where they were. 'Make it quick,' she snapped into the phone. 'I'm just about to start something here.'

'The gentleman from Sinners is in your reception.' Julia spoke eloquently but the underground reception was so poor she had to repeat herself twice before Andrea could understand. 'He says he has an appointment with you this morning,' she continued, 'and he says you should have –'

'Two words,' Andrea broke in. 'I'm late. This morning the traffic was a bigger bitch than I am. Give him a coffee and –'

'He's already had a coffee.'

Andrea bristled at the interruption. The hierarchy in the company was well-defined and Julia was in no position to interrupt a superior. 'If he's already had one coffee, then give him a second,' she said testily. 'And keep him in your reception. I don't want him fawning all over me before I've got a chance to reach my desk.'

'But, he doesn't seem very happy to –'

Andrea sighed impatiently and strummed her fingers against her thigh. 'If you want to see him happy, suck his cock. If you want to see me happy, do him another coffee and keep him in your reception. Christ, Julia! Don't you have any pride in yourself? Can't you manage your own job without having me explain every detail of what I expect you to do?'

'But –'

'One word,' Andrea said coolly. 'Goodbye.'

She severed the connection by pressing her thumb on the keypad. Before the dull light of the phone had expired she was smiling at the couple in the shadows.

They had been watching guardedly as she barked her conversation into the Nokia and their wide-eyed gazes reminded Andrea of those tragic rabbits she had so often caught in the headlamps of her convertible. She noticed the pair were holding hands, trying to extract comfort from the reassuring presence of one another, and she was momentarily touched by the sweetness of the gesture. It was so rare to see such signs of affection, she had forgotten how delightfully exploitable they could sometimes prove. 'Don't stop on my account,' she said softly.

The couple exchanged a nervous glance.

He was somewhere in his early twenties with gelled blonde hair spiked into a punkish style that sat incongruously with the collar and tie of his business suit. She looked a little more respectable, a couple of years younger than her boyfriend, and wearing a modest skirt and sensible blouse. If she hadn't been wearing a pair of ludicrously high platforms, Andrea would have thought the girl looked like a model of how all her office staff should dress for work. 'Don't stop doing that on my account,' Andrea repeated. 'In fact, I insist that you carry on.'

'Miss Jones . . .' he began.

'We weren't . . .' the girl started.

Andrea shook her head. 'You weren't talking to me. You were kissing each other. You were kissing each other, here, in the dank seclusion of a dirty, underground car park.' She laughed bitterly to herself, wondering if they would understand the irony if she made a glib comment about the art of romance obviously not being dead. Guessing they were too young and too nervous to appreciate such humour, she folded her arms and said, 'Carry on with what you were doing.'

Hesitantly, the pair exchanged glances and shuffled uncomfortably beneath Andrea's wrathful glare. 'We kind of lost track of the time,' the girl said.

'And we don't want to be late,' her boyfriend added quickly.

Andrea shook her head. 'I'm being nice here,' she explained. The patience in her voice was as thin as a cleaver's edge. 'And I'm asking you to take the easier of two choices. I could go into my office, call your

213

line managers, and tell them why you were late this morning. Or, you could do as I've asked, and carry on with what you were doing.'

The girl paled.

Her boyfriend looked like he wanted to remain defiant but Andrea could see he was going to be chivalrous and go with his lover's decision. Again, she was enchanted by the sweetness of the couple and her perpetual sneer inched into something that nearly resembled a smile.

'We . . .'

'Miss Jones . . .'

'Two words,' Andrea cooed softly. 'Carry on.'

They returned to their clinch after exchanging a final hopeless glance. Their mouths met in a parody of what they had previously been doing but without the same greedy need. When they caressed it was like watching bad actors rehearse.

'You were doing it much better before,' Andrea snapped. She unfolded her arms and began to bark orders as she circled them. 'You, boy: fondle her breasts. And kiss her like you want to kiss her. Girl: you were rubbing your thigh against his crotch before. Do that again. He seemed to get off on it.'

Andrea was warmed by the venomous looks they gave her but knew neither would disobey her instructions. Her imposing grin changed to smug satisfaction when the spikey-haired boy gingerly cupped his hand over his girl's breast. The girl gasped, cast a furtive glance back and forth from his face to Andrea, then seemed to realise there was no other option. Resignedly, she allowed his hand to stay where it was and placed her thigh between his legs. Despite the show of reluctance she maintained, Andrea knew the girl was enjoying some pleasure because she writhed her hips with an eagerness that couldn't have been faked.

There was a sultry curve to the way she gyrated herself against him and Andrea guessed the boyfriend had already inspired a dull desire between his lover's legs. He placed his free hand over one of her buttocks, clutching the mound of flesh through the skirt and drawing her closer to himself. Their mouths continued to meet and separate in a greedy union of shared desire.

Andrea's upper lip curled with growing excitement. 'Now I want to see more,' she decided. 'Now, I want you to turn up the passion a little.'

They parted from their kiss and both turned to worriedly study her.

Andrea pointed directions as she gave her commands. Her voice came out in a clipped, curt staccato that was so sharp it could have pierced flesh. 'Boy: put your hand inside her blouse. Properly fondle her. Girl: unzip his trousers and touch him. You know he wants that.'

'You're not serious,' the boyfriend scoffed indignantly. His girl placed a hand on his shoulder but he puffed out his chest and seemed determined to make some show of defiance on this point. 'You're not seriously expecting us to get so . . . so . . .'

Andrea rolled her eyes as he struggled to find the right word.

'You're not seriously expecting us to get so *intimate*, are you?'

'I'm not renowned for flights of whimsy,' Andrea replied caustically. She plucked her phone from her bag and added, 'I have the building's entire directory stored in this mobile. I don't have to wait until I get up to my office. Do you want me to call your line managers now?'

The girl placed her mouth close to her boyfriend's ear and Andrea guessed she was cautioning him against saying anything further. His truculence eased – not quite abating – but he nodded grudging consent. Still glaring belligerently at Andrea, almost as though it was an act of defiance, he placed one hand inside his girlfriend's blouse while allowing her to unfasten the zip on his trousers.

'Do it properly,' Andrea snapped. 'You weren't faking it when I first saw you so I don't expect either of you to fake it this time. Let yourselves go. Enjoy what you're doing. Arouse each other.'

Neither of them replied but there was no questioning their obedience. The girl released her boyfriend's erection from his trousers and stroked her fingers smoothly up and down the rigid flesh. He seemed to enjoy the attention in spite of the situation's peculiarity because his frown began to fade. Investing more sensuality into his groping, he massaged his girl's breast until she was drawing urgent, needy breaths. Still retaining a hold on her behind, he hitched her skirt up and teased his fingertips inside the elasticated band of her snow-white panties.

Andrea continued to watch. Her features were outwardly inscrutable but inwardly she wore a broad, satisfied grin. They were both young and attractive: his erection was nothing spectacular but, with the foreskin rolled back and the purple dome glistening, she could sense his mounting excitement. The girl's arousal was evident from the shallow rasp of each exhalation and the damp stain that darkened the gusset of her panties. Relishing the gratuitous display they provided – and enjoying the way they were stimulating each other at her command – Andrea toyed with the idea of ingratiating herself between them. She could have happily joined the pair, fondled the girl, teased the boy and then had them both pleasure her until she climaxed. His erection was unremarkable but it would be sufficient to fill the need that smouldered slickly between her legs. The girl's tongue had seemed agile enough when she had been kissing her lover and Andrea guessed it could be more gainfully employed if she simply removed her own panties and barked a couple of authoritative instructions.

Both would be likely to raise perfunctory objections but, ultimately, neither would refuse. If the location had been somewhere more conducive to her mood than a mouldering corner of the car park, Andrea might have acted on the impulse.

The girl's fingers encircled her boyfriend's shaft, sliding back and forth with a pace that only faltered when his hand buried deeper inside the veil of her panties. Occasionally she broke her kiss to glance at their tormentor and it was those glimpses of nervous uncertainty that truly sent Andrea's pulse racing. The girl's expression was a combination of deep arousal and encroaching shame. The doubt that glistened in the whites of her eyes said she was frightened of being punished for doing something naughty but unable to resist continuing.

Andrea revelled in the girl's turmoil. The knowledge that she was controlling everything, and that the couple were having to do exactly as she said, was an arousing power trip. Regardless of the squalid surroundings, unmindful of the stench of dirt and petrol fumes, she could feel her desire growing to such a strength she knew she was going to make best use of the pair and have them take her to a plateau of satisfaction. Inveigling herself between them would be easy enough: stepping silently beside them; helping the girl massage her boyfriend's length; lightly kissing a tear from the girl's cheek while giving her rump a reassuring squeeze . . .

And she had taken her first tentative steps toward them when the shrill ring of her mobile piped through her thoughts. The couple continued to embrace, caress and tease, not needing to hear any instruction for them to continue. Andrea's frown deepened when she read Julia's name on the caller display screen and she stamped her thumb against the answer key with bitter impatience. Making no attempt to mask her annoyance she simply barked, 'What?'

'Your appointment is beginning to get pissed off.'

'Why?' Andrea sneered. 'Do you keep calling him while he's busy doing something else?'

Julia sounded defensive. 'I was only calling you to –'

'Get some perspective on the situation, Julia. He has an appointment to see me. I don't have an appointment to see him. Give him coffee. Tell him I've been delayed. But stop fucking phoning me.'

She pushed her thumb so hard against the keypad she broke a nail. The acrylic split in a white blister and the tip skittered into the shadows of the car park floor. 'Fuck!' she spat angrily.

The couple glanced doubtfully at her and, if she hadn't been so frustrated by Julia's call, Andrea would have found it amusing that they thought they had been given a further instruction. She watched them for a moment longer; envying the way the girl's nipple was being squeezed and tugged; jealous of the pleasure the boyfriend was receiving from his deft, illicit wrist job. Yet, as much as she tried getting back into the spirit of what the couple were doing, her mood had been broken. The scene no longer ignited any fires of passion within her and she knew that she no longer intended to get the pair of them to satisfy the arousal they had awoken inside her.

'Stop that now,' she said flatly. She glared at their wary expressions, silently challenging either of them to say anything out of place. 'Stop that now. It's unseemly. There's a time and a place for everything and a dirty car park is only suitable for rutting vermin and cockroaches.'

Neither of them was able to mask their obvious incredulity but they obeyed. The girl's hand fell away from her boyfriend's length. His hands slid swiftly away from her buttocks and breasts.

'Get dressed. Get off to your respective desks and don't let me catch you doing this ever again.' She shook her head, despising the fact that her mood of passion was now being replaced by a darkening cloud of crimson rage. She could see the couple were stunned by her sudden change of instructions and listened half-heartedly as they mumbled confused apologies and returned their clothes to some semblance of normality.

Sniffing indignantly, Andrea began storming away, heading toward the lift. She paused and turned. Snapping her fingers for their attention she remembered how she had concluded such encounters previously. 'One other thing,' she called. 'I want you both to remember, I've just done the pair of you a massive favour by not contacting your line managers regarding your inappropriate behaviour. You both owe me big time and I don't expect you to forget that. I won't be calling in the debt today. I won't be calling in the debt tomorrow. But, when I do call it in, I expect you both to repay me.'

They exchanged worried glances, neither hiding their lack of comprehension.

'How do you expect us to repay you?' the girl asked meekly.

'Two words,' Andrea replied. 'With interest.' She laughed without humour and added, 'I don't know how you'll repay me. But, one day, you will.' Not bothering to enlighten the pair further, not sure she could answer any other questions they might have even if they had thought to ask, she headed toward the lift door and stabbed the button for the fourteenth floor. She hit the key so hard she broke the acrylic from her index finger. As the sliver of red popped up and then dropped to the floor, she realised her sour mood had grown worse.

Andrea fielded a further couple of calls from Julia (*'Two words, Julia: more coffee. If he's that desperate to see me, he'll wait'*) before settling herself behind her desk. More important than her appointments – more important than the strategy planners' meeting or the report on the latest marketing offensive – was the need to deal with her broken fingernails. She called her usual salon, demanded they send a manicurist to her office and, because the salon was in Andrea's debt, no complaint was made about the urgent demand. Andrea wasn't best pleased at having to wait for two hours for the junior nail technician to arrive, but she made a concentrated effort to quell her annoyance.

Being blonde, blandly attractive, and having just started her first week at the salon, it was difficult to recall the manicurist's name. Andrea thought, if she hadn't worn a badge with the name 'Stacey' on her left breast, it would have been impossible to remember what to call her.

Without hurrying, Stacey stripped the scarlet polish from Andrea's hands, removed the acrylic from the two broken tips, then reapplied new index finger- and thumbnails. Andrea's regular manicurist could usually manage to sculpture all ten nails in less than thirty minutes. Stacey took the best part of an hour and a half to manage the two, simple repairs.

But Andrea was content to relax while her hands were pampered. Memories of the young couple in the car park continued to stir sultry warmth between her legs and the temptation to deal with that dull craving gnawed incessantly. She had already entered their names in her PDA, and flagged their personnel files so she would be notified about developments in their careers within the company, but the desire to exploit one of them for immediate satisfaction was almost irresistible. However, knowing the benefits would be greater if she decided to capitalise on the pair for profit rather than pleasure, she resisted the impulse. She contented herself with imagining how rewarding it would be just to call one of them up to her office and have them cater to her burgeoning needs. The daydream was enough to draw a rare smile across her lips and make her forget the slow passage of time as Stacey worked laboriously at painting a final coat of crimson polish on her nails.

It was only when Stacey mumbled a truculent goodbye that Andrea pulled herself from her reverie. She was surprised it was almost lunchtime and wondered how the morning could have escaped her in a haze of lurid fantasies. 'Wait a moment,' she snapped. 'I need your help for one more thing.'

Stacey stopped with her hand on the door. She didn't look particularly anxious to help but Andrea put her reluctance down to the slothful ways of the younger generation. Holding her fingers in the air, showing off the polished tips that still glistened wetly, Andrea said, 'I have to use the room next door.'

Puzzled and uncomprehending, Stacey said nothing.

'I have to use the room next door,' Andrea repeated, 'and I don't want to spoil the nearly adequate job you've just done on my nails.' She climbed from her chair and walked to the office's en suite bathroom. 'Come on, girl. Follow me and do as I tell you.'

Rounding her shoulders, Stacey followed.

Standing with her back to the toilet bowl, continuing to splay her fingers, Andrea waited expectantly.

Stacey stared at her. 'How do you want me to help?'

'I need to pee,' Andrea explained bluntly. 'And, if I start to move my panties down while my fingernails are still wet, I'm going to spoil the polish.'

Stacey took a backward step toward the door. 'They'll be dry in two minutes. Five at the most. Surely you can wait that long?'

Andrea nodded. 'Yes. I could wait that long. But I won't have to because you're going to do what I tell you. You're going to help me.'

Even though the blonde was shaking her head, she made no further move toward the door. Andrea could see the cowed glint burning dully in Stacey's eyes and knew, without needing to make any threats or hints at repercussions, the manicurist would do as she was told. There was something in Stacey's sullen acceptance of the situation that said she was used to being on the receiving end of instructions. Andrea could even see that the girl secretly craved the domination of others. Throwing her shoulders back arrogantly, unconsciously making her posture more imposing, Andrea said, 'Lift my skirt and pull my panties down. Don't make me tell you twice, girl.'

There was an undeniable pleasure in issuing the command but Andrea didn't smile. She contained the urge when Stacey dropped to her knees and allowed no amusement to touch her lips as her skirt was pushed up to her waist. Cool fingers stroked against the bare flesh of Andrea's hips as Stacey slipped her thumbs inside the cotton and began to draw the panties down. The blonde had to position herself close, almost pressing the swell of her breasts against Andrea's knees, and the tension that grew between their bodies made the air heavy and difficult to breathe.

Andrea's thighs were caressed by Stacey's hands as the underwear was pulled away from her cleft and down to her ankles. For the first time since she entered the office that morning, Andrea found her thoughts were focused on something other than the couple she had encountered in the car park. She stared down at the top of Stacey's head, savouring the sight of a woman kneeling beneath her. Her upper thighs were touched by the whisper of the manicurist's nervous breath.

'Was there anything else?' Stacey asked, glancing meekly up.

Andrea settled herself on the toilet seat and held Stacey with her gaze. They were almost on eye level, Andrea's position slightly superior, and the thickening tension between them augmented every sound. When Andrea told Stacey to wait where she was, the whispered command echoed from the tiled walls. When she began to release her golden stream into the toilet bowl, the flow sounded like a torrent.

They held each other in silent rapture, neither speaking until the flow had tapered to a trickle, then dissipated to a triptych of droplets. Andrea could see her own gaze reflected in Stacey's large brown eyes and believed her smile was sparkling with scarlet bursts of mounting excitement. She couldn't decide whether that sight was real or imagined but it never failed to thrill her when she saw her fury burning like acid through someone else's hope.

'Do you want me to pull your pants back up?' Stacey asked.

Andrea grinned and removed two squares of paper from the toilet roll. 'You can pull my panties back up in a moment,' she allowed. 'But I'll need patting dry first.'

Obediently, Stacey took the offered paper. Whatever hesitation or reservations she did have were brief and transitory. As soon as Andrea parted her thighs, and raised herself slightly from the seat, she did as she was told.

Trembling with excitement, Andrea revelled in the thrill of the submissive gently towelling her pussy lips. The sensitive labia bristled to the caress of another woman and, even though she was only being touched by dry paper, Andrea could feel herself warming excitedly.

Stacey dropped the paper into the bowl and removed her hand.

'Dry me properly,' Andrea insisted. She tugged two more squares of paper from the roll and handed them to the blonde.

With only the slightest display of reluctance, Stacey accepted the offered sheets. She glanced nervously into Andrea's imposing frown, then pushed her hand where it was needed and gently patted along the squirming length of pussy lips.

Teeth gritted, carefully tensing her fingers but trying hard not to spoil the polish, Andrea relished the intimate towelling. She drew a deep, satisfying breath and savoured every dry caress against her sex. They both knew the exchange had gone from being an act of cleansing, and had moved on to something far more personal, and she wondered how many other instructions Stacey would obediently follow.

The shrill ring of her mobile cut through her thoughts.

Stacey snatched her hand away as though they had both been caught.

Andrea glared at the phone in her breast pocket, her fury deepening when she saw Julia's name on the caller display. Her acquisition of her father's company had been a comparatively recent move and she had yet to employ a secretary who was competent enough to deal with the workload and thick-skinned enough to cope with her temper. She held her hands away from her and silently gestured for Stacey to finish her chore and pull the panties back up.

With obvious relief, Stacey obeyed. She was running from the en suite and out of the office before Andrea had a chance to press one knuckle against the phone.

'Wait!' Andrea called.

Stacey hesitated in the doorway.

'Leave your name and number on the pad on my desk,' Andrea instructed. With a knowing smile, she added, 'I think I might use you again.'

The fearful expression on Stacey's face was enough to make Andrea smile as she finally accepted the call on her mobile. 'Yes, Julia,' she said wearily. 'And what is it now?'

'The same as it's been all morning.' Julia sounded frustrated. 'The guy from Sinners is –'

'Two words,' Andrea snapped bitterly. 'My office.'

'You want me to send him up?'

'No. I want you to come up here. Give him another coffee, tell him you've got to be somewhere else, then come up here. I'll see you in two minutes.' She severed the connection before Julia could ask any further questions.

'That guy from Sinners is blazing,' Julia confided. 'He's as mad as a wasp.'

'He's probably been drinking too much coffee.' Andrea grinned. She waved the matter to one side and said, 'I'll get round to seeing him shortly. Before I deal with him, I want something from you, Julia.'

Julia paled but held herself with dignity as she stood facing Andrea. 'What do you want from me?'

'Repayment,' Andrea said sombrely. 'Repayment with interest.'

Julia remained rigid.

Andrea knew the woman would have made a good poker player – possibly a successful one – if they hadn't been dealing with cards that Andrea had already marked. She thought there was a completeness to the way events were working out. On the same day she had earned debts of gratitude from the couple in the car park, she was going to allow Julia the chance to repay a due she had incurred earlier. It was almost like catching a glimpse of some great Zen balance that controlled her life. Guessing Julia wasn't going to break the silence, Andrea spoke first. 'What can you tell me about the Pride of the Company?'

Julia sniffed. 'That's an urban myth. A convenient conspiracy theory. The Pride of the Company are just a rumour to make the company's executives think there's someone above them.'

Andrea pursed her lips. 'They meet a couple of times each month at Sinners. They're exclusively male, with one rather gullible exception, and they still believe, even since I took over my father's position here as managing director, that they are in control of the company. Now, answer my question with a little more candour, Julia. What can you tell me about the Pride of the Company?'

'It sounds like you have all the answers you need.' Julia turned her back and started toward the door. 'I'll go and tell your appointment that you're free to see him now.'

Andrea climbed from her chair and took the three brisk steps needed to position herself between Julia and the door. 'How's your backside?' she asked. Boldly she placed a hand on Julia's rear and squeezed the plump flesh of one buttock.

Julia flinched as though she had been reminded of a discomfort. It was only a subtle tightening of her eyes, a grimace that was gone before it could be properly seen, but it was enough to tell Andrea that her assessment of the situation was correct. Staring into Julia's large brown eyes, concentrating on the warmth beneath her fingers, Andrea believed she could almost read the woman's mind. There was a blazing heat emanating from Julia's rear and, because Andrea knew the Pride of the Company had met the previous evening, she thought it was easy to guess why Julia appeared so sensitive. If she had closed her eyes she knew she would have been able to picture the bruised and reddened cheeks. Keeping her hold firm, but careful not to apply too much pressure, she asked, 'Did it help when I loaned you that balm? Did it help when I wiped away your tears? Or would you say it was a greater help that I've kept your secret to myself?'

Julia glared at her. 'Are you blackmailing me?'

Andrea laughed and squeezed the buttock. She could have buried her nails into the skin but it was enough to simply clutch the mound of flesh. Julia shut her eyes and grimaced unhappily. 'I'm not blackmailing you,' Andrea said honestly. 'I'm just asking you to repay an old debt. You have no qualms about doing that, do you?'

Unhappily, Julia pulled herself from Andrea's grip.

It was annoying to lose the febrile, feminine warmth she had been holding, but Andrea kept her temper, knowing she was about to win a bigger victory. She returned to the seat behind her desk and waited patiently for Julia to gently sit herself down.

'What do you want to know?' Julia asked.

'I want their names. All of them.'

'Why?'

It was frustrating to have the questions barked at her but Andrea kept a rein on her mounting anger. She would rather have dominated Julia as she had Stacey but the proud woman on the other side of the desk was too wilful to submit so easily. Contenting herself with the knowledge that she was the one in control, and that Julia would eventually bend to do her bidding, she sighed heavily before answering. 'It says managing director on my door,' Andrea started, 'and that means I should be the one running this company. I should have been running this company since the day I forced my father to retire and hand me the reins of his empire. But, as long as the Pride of the Company is in existence, there's always a danger that I'm not the one in control. I want membership names for the Pride of the Company so I can methodically disband the group.'

Julia glared at her. 'What if I say no?'

Andrea smiled and shook her head. 'Did I tell you that Ted's moved in with me?'

Julia glowered. 'I was never that bothered about Ted York. You did me a favour by taking him off my hands. The new man in my life is far more capable than Ted ever was.'

Andrea made no attempt to hide her scepticism. 'Does the new man in your life have a name?'

Julia shook her head. 'You wouldn't know him. He's called Robert and he owns a string of auction houses.'

'He sounds thoroughly charming,' Andrea said flatly. 'And I only mentioned Ted to illustrate a point. Since I started here I've taken your man, I've taken the coveted position you fancied occupying and I've taken away every opportunity you've ever had to improve your position here, or in any other company. I've done all that, even though I have no grudge against you. Do you really want to see what happens if you piss me off and refuse to give me those names?'

Julia held her gaze but only long enough for Andrea to watch the last flicker of defiance die. Lowering her head, nodding sullenly, she said, 'I'll have the list of names sent to you before the end of the day.'

Andrea shook her head. 'Send it directly to Personnel. I'll forewarn them that you're faxing through a list of candidates for my new streamlining drive. If you manage it before three they should have their dismissal notices in the morning post.'

'What about me?' Julia asked. 'I'm a member of the Pride of the Company. Does that mean you'll be firing me as well?'

Andrea threw back her head and laughed. Tears of genuine mirth spilled down her cheeks as the sound of her merriment rang from the walls. When she eventually regained her composure she wiped her eyes dry and smiled. 'You think too highly of yourself, Julia,' Andrea explained. 'You're not really a member of the Pride of the Company. Ted's told me what your role in that group is and they all know you're just the club's whipping girl.'

The comment must have struck a chord because she was delighted to see miserable tears start to fill Julia's eyes.

'Don't feel too badly about that,' Andrea assured her. She reached across the desk and placed a comforting hand on Julia's shoulder. 'If you feel the need to be someone's whipping girl once I've dissolved the Pride of the Company, I can always find the time to punish you for your shortcomings.'

Indignantly, Julia pulled herself from Andrea's reach. 'What do I do about the guy from Sinners?'

Andrea shrugged, deciding not to force the issue. Everything she wanted would come to her in time – including Julia's eventual submission. 'I can't see him now. If he's still here when I get back from my lunch, I might see him then.'

'But what am I supposed to do with him?' Julia complained.

Andrea grinned. 'Two words,' she said abruptly. 'More coffee.'

She was amazed to see the couple again, and even more surprised that they were still locked in a passionate embrace. She supposed they must have taken something to heart from the things she had said because, rather than ensconcing themselves in the gloom of a dingy car park, they were now embraced in the doorway of Holy Cross Church.

Andrea sat in a window seat of the bistro opposite. She liked being close to the church because she knew her appearance always unsettled the parish priest. When her father had run the company he had magnanimously invested Holy Cross with a regular, charitable donation. Still carrying a grudge from long, long ago, Andrea had made it one of her first duties to visit the priest and tell him that the company would no longer be giving him a single penny. Now, whenever he saw her, he fixed her with a glare of venom that she wouldn't have believed could be in a priest's repertoire. Reaping the benefits of her malicious drives, she thought it rewarding that she had managed to provoke such passion from the dusty old cleric.

But, watching the couple grind dryly together, enjoying the sight of them as they kissed and embraced, she wouldn't allow herself any of the usual cruel indulgence that came from thinking about the revenge she had exacted against the priest. There was something intrinsically exciting about the way the pair held one another and hungered for each other and her need to experience that intense passion became an overwhelming desire.

Her lunch appointment had been nothing more than a date with her best friend, but Wendy had disappeared to use the lavatory and, from previous experience, Andrea knew her friend was likely to be some time. Scratching her mobile number on a napkin, she hurried out of the bistro and crossed the road toward the church.

As before, they remained oblivious to her approach, even when her heels were sparking loudly against the graves that lined the path. The pair didn't even look up when she was standing right next to them and resting one hand against the church door. 'You two can't seem to get enough of each other, can you?' she marvelled.

They broke apart as though touched by an electric shock. Both were blushing and trying to correct their clothes.

'Have you been following us?' the boy asked indignantly.

She sneered at him. 'Don't flatter yourself.' Glancing at the girl, noticing two buttons of her blouse were unfastened and the shape of one plump orb was visible in the shaded sanctuary beneath, the heat between Andrea's legs began to grow more profound. 'I haven't been following you,' she said honestly. 'But I've been thinking about the pair of you all morning.'

They exchanged unsettled glances as she stepped between them.

'Perhaps that gives you the wrong impression,' she whispered. 'It would be more correct to say, I've been thinking of what I could do with you.'

The boy opened his mouth and she placed a finger against his lips. 'Two words,' she said firmly. 'Shut up. Let's not trample over established ground. You both know you're in my debt, and you know you're going to do exactly as I tell you. Neither of you have any qualms about that, do you?' As she asked the question she reached out to touch them both. With one hand she cupped the girl's breast. With the other she reached down for the swelling of the boy's erection. She could feel their urgent pulses beating through her fingertips and was caught up in the waves of pleasure that came from their expressions of loathing and the continuation of their arousal.

The breast in her hand heaved with the girl's inhalation. The nipple stood hard and its stiffness didn't abate when Andrea kneaded the plump orb of flesh. The erection in her other hand was solid and its pulse quickened as she tightened her hold. Layers of clothing and fabric stopped her fingers from properly enjoying the couple but she knew nothing could detract from the feeling of absolute power and control.

'What do you want?' the boy asked.

She stared at him, wishing she could remember his name, then decided it was unimportant. His girlfriend posed the same dilemma but Andrea's arousal had taken her beyond such trivialities. If she was that desperate to find out what they were called she knew she could consult her PDA.

'I want the pair of you,' she decided. Her fingers squeezed around him, relishing the perfect shape of his hardness and the way his shaft thickened at her touch. She smiled for the girl, tightening the hold on her breast and teasing the shape of the fattening bud. 'I want both of you and, this afternoon –'

She didn't get to complete the sentence. The church door began to creak open and it was all she could think to do to push the couple behind it and hide from whoever was coming out of the church. The door didn't open all the way and she quelled the urge to sigh with relief, hoping her presence at Holy Cross would remain undetected. Voices on the other side of the door snatched her concentration away from the unexpected pleasure of being pressed against the young couple and she listened intently, needing to hear what was being said.

A woman's voice spoke first, hushed with conspiratorial concern. 'What's wrong, father?'

'Sister Pandora!' Andrea recognised the grating tone of the elderly priest. 'You startled me,' he continued. Laughing at himself he said, 'I thought we were about to have a visit from that hellion woman. My eyes must have been playing tricks.'

'Hellion woman? Who's that?'

'Perhaps I'm being too harsh. I suppose there's good and bad in everyone, but it's difficult to see what good the likes of her could ever achieve.' He sounded bitter and angry and Andrea grinned to herself when she heard his normally pious voice tainted with both of those emotions.

'Who is she?' Sister Pandora asked. 'And what's she done to upset you so strongly?'

'She's responsible for the parish's current lack of funds,' the priest said sadly. 'She's the woman who's directly responsible for my having to send you back to the convent where you came from.'

Andrea grinned. She could see the couple were both repulsed by her smile of approval but their chagrin didn't affect her enjoyment. Perversely it added something to her satisfaction to know that they were genuinely disgusted by her cruelty. She also thought it would make them both more pliant.

Through the thick bulk of the church's door, Sister

Pandora sounded concerned. 'I can't go back to the convent,' she exclaimed. 'The Abbess . . .'

'The Abbess has forgiven whatever upset caused your expulsion,' the priest assured her. 'She and I have exchanged several letters on the topic. Rest assured, Sister Pandora, you'll be welcomed back to your convent. My only regret is that you're going to have to go back there soon.'

'And you, father?'

'I managed here before you arrived, and I'll manage quite well once you've gone, although I'd appreciate a letter every now and again.'

Andrea spat an angry curse under her breath. The priest's equanimity was galling and she would have been happier to hear him sobbing bitter tears of exasperation. Knowing there was little else she could do, and sure she would be reaping the pleasures of breaking someone else before the day was over, she pulled the boy into her embrace and kissed him.

His face was flushed with surprise and Andrea switched her gaze between his shock and his girl-friend's helpless indignity. She kept her lips pressed against him, using her tongue to taste and explore his mouth, until the church door was drawn closed. As soon as she heard the heavy latch falling from within, she released the boy and embraced the girl.

This time she met with less resistance. The girl didn't just allow Andrea to test her with a penetrating kiss, she responded with eagerness and curiosity. Andrea traced the swell of the pert, young bosom, pressed herself against the lithe, feminine frame, and enjoyed the attention of another woman who was just as eager to experience whatever pleasures Andrea deemed fit. When they finally parted, they were both grinning and their cheeks were flushed. Andrea knew her own blush was caused by excitement and greedy need; she expected the girl's high colour was also down to an acute case of embarrassment.

'What is it that you want from us?' the boy insisted. His girl reached out to hold his hand and he grudgingly allowed her fingers to intertwine with his own. Glaring angrily at Andrea he asked again, 'What is it that you want?'

She winked. 'One of you two will come to my office this afternoon,' she decided. 'I won't badger you with threats about dismissal or the loss of prospects. I'll just remind you that one of you will visit my office, or both of you will suffer.'

'Which one of us?' the girl asked.

Andrea wondered if she could hear a note of arousal tainting the question. She shook the thought from her mind, sure the speculation was immaterial. 'You can decide between yourselves which one of you visits me. Whoever it is, you'll spend the entire afternoon in my office and, while I imagine it will be demanding, you won't be doing anything that can be classified as work.'

Her mobile phone rang and she saw Wendy's name on the caller display screen. Sighing softly, deciding the fun was over, for the moment, Andrea waved a finger between the pair of them and said, 'One of you needs to be in my office by two thirty at the latest. I'll see you then.' Not allowing them the chance to reply, she skipped happily out of the church yard and returned to her meal with Wendy.

'We had an appointment.'

Andrea turned at the sound of the bellowing voice, not overly startled to see the man from Sinners. The car park was deserted, no lovers clinching in the dingy corners, and she was momentarily unsettled to think he might intend to harm her. His face was flushed with rage and she supposed, given the way she had avoided him throughout the day, it was easy to understand his annoyance. Still, Andrea held herself with dignity, shoulders squared and jaw set with characteristic determination. She met the challenge of his gaze with placid equanimity.

'We had an appointment at nine o'clock this morning,' he roared, storming toward her.

'We did,' Andrea agreed. 'But I've had more important things to deal with today. Perhaps you'd like to contact my office and reschedule?'

He shook his head as he pushed his face in front of hers. 'Rescheduling isn't good enough for me. I need an answer today.'

Andrea laughed lightly. 'I'm in no position to make decisions now. I don't have the –'

'I have creditors. I have a business to run.' He raked his fingers through his hair, transforming his appearance from cultured ire to dishevelled wrath. His voice lowered from the raging bellow he had been using and somehow the whispered hiss of each sibilant seemed that much more menacing. 'I've asked your company to extend me an advance on a loan. I've explained that the money would be vital lifeblood to the continuation of my business. I employ staff –'

'You only employ one person,' Andrea broke in curtly. 'You only employ that fat woman in your kiosk.'

'She's all I need,' he replied defensively. 'She acts as my secretary and girl Friday.'

'Tell her to come to my office,' Andrea said stiffly. 'I've been looking for a secretary and she might fit the bill.'

His jaw tightened and his frown grew deeper. 'Fine, rob me of my staff, and keep me waiting all day for an appointment that was meant to happen this morning.' With mounting vehemence he said, 'But my creditors are growing impatient and I need an answer today. I need an answer *now*.'

Andrea fixed him with a withering stare. She reached into her purse and retrieved a cigarette. Taking the time to light it and draw two breaths from the filtered tip before replying, she asked, 'Who the hell are you?'

'You know who I am.'

She shook her head. 'I've got staff here who tell me you're a kiosk attendant. I've got senior executives who refer to you as the guy from Sinners. But I don't know your name, and I don't believe it's on any of the contracts that cover the business arrangement you had with my father.'

He fixed her with a threatening frown. 'You know who I am,' he repeated. 'Stop trying to toy with me and give me an answer.'

She curled her upper lip into a sneer. '*Trying* to toy with you?' she gasped incredulously. 'I'm a mistress in the art of toying with people. Trust me on this. When I toy with someone, I don't just *try*. I damned well succeed.'

'Stop trying to –'

'Get down on your knees,' Andrea barked suddenly. The shrillness of her voice echoed from the car park's crisp acoustics. She could see a barrier of reluctance in his expression and she was determined to smash it away before he hid behind this mindset. Pointing at the oil-stained floor she said, 'You wanted my time today. You wanted my answer about extending your loan. I'll give you your answer as soon as you've grovelled at my feet and apologised for waylaying me like this.'

'I . . .'

The hesitancy in his voice was enough to make her realise she had won. 'Down on your knees,' she insisted. 'Or I'm leaving here now.'

Gingerly he lowered himself to his knees.

Andrea had to bite the insides of her cheeks to stop herself from grinning triumphantly. She sneered down at him, making no attempt to disguise her contempt. 'Now, kiss my feet,' she demanded.

'You don't –'

'KISS MY FEET!' she screamed. The shrill repetition of her voice reverberated from the concrete walls, coming back to her again and again. Before the last echo had died its natural death, the man at her feet was lowering his mouth to her scarlet sandals.

Andrea released a sigh of contentment. She alternated feet, allowing him to kiss one shoe, then the other. The buzz that came with control never failed to charge her with excitement and she watched the bobbing head beneath her while a growing wetness spread between her legs. Containing her tremors, knowing she would have to exercise tact while dominating this man, she waited until he stared up at her before she spoke.

'Now kiss my shins,' she instructed.

He pushed his mouth to just below one knee and landed a gentle kiss against the flesh.

She had enjoyed a lazy afternoon, indulging herself in the pleasure of the spikey-haired youth. Andrea had expected he would be the one to meet her appointment, having seen how uncomfortable he was with the way his girlfriend responded to being kissed by another woman. And, in spite of his reservations and clearly going against the grain of his true desires, he had made for an adequate lover.

But he hadn't managed to satisfy every urge that beat beneath Andrea's breast and she could see there was now an opportunity to exorcise the last greedy desire for satisfaction that still itched between her legs.

'Both shins,' she insisted. Hitching her skirt fractionally higher, she said, 'And then you may kiss my thighs.'

He graced her with a venomous glare but she had received more stinging looks and this one did nothing to upset her. Contrarily it warmed her to think he was being controlled by her will because she didn't doubt he would have been just as domineering if their roles had been reversed. Relishing the sensation of his lips brushing her inner thighs, she suspected he had probably been guilty of wielding control over more than one unsuspecting woman and she supposed there might even be some justice in making the man bend to do her bidding.

'Now kiss higher,' she said again, pulling her skirt all the way up.

The bright red crotch of her crimson panties was revealed to him and she hurriedly pulled the fabric to one side. Her pussy still felt tender from the hours of pleasurable penetration she had extracted from the spikey-haired boy, but she knew her clitoris could cope with at least one more thrill before the day ended. Splaying the lips of her labia, bucking her hips forward so his mouth could meet the engorged bead of flesh, she sighed happily as his tongue connected with the centre of her need.

He was gifted, she had to grant him that, and his mouth eagerly devoured her sodden hole. His hands clutched her buttocks, pulling her closer and lifting her slightly so he was more able to use his tongue. Ripples of pleasure trembled through her, quickly mounting in size and scale until they were gargantuan waves. She placed her hands against his head, holding him tight where he was needed as she wallowed in the bliss that came from having her sex so expertly kissed. He chased the shape of her labia with his tongue before plundering her sopping pussy. His nose was buried in the thatch of her pubic mound and she marvelled that anyone could be so good at the simple art of cunnilingus. Briefly considering the idea of complimenting him, then deciding he probably already knew he was good, she cursed him to work harder. The words came out in a roar of bitter fury and she felt sure she was on the verge of another wonderful release.

The thought was astute and, as soon as she had spat the instruction, he took her to the brink of a climax that she knew would be devastating. His tongue lapped hungrily at her sex, invoking a wetness that knew no bounds. And, each time she thought she had passed the plateau of orgasm, she felt his mouth returning to her hole and taking her to new, undiscovered worlds of joy. The pleasure was so sudden and immense that, as she revelled in the final, climactic thrill, she briefly lost consciousness.

She came back to her senses to find herself on her haunches in a gloomy corner of the company car park. The perfumed scents of pleasure, passion and excitement were quickly replaced by the darker odours of filth and stale petrol fumes. Andrea briefly wondered how she had been so easily able to surrender herself in such a dismal environment but it was only a passing thought and of no real interest. 'That was good,' she breathed honestly. 'That was so good I almost forgot where we were.'

'We were discussing my loan,' he whispered. 'You were going to tell me if you'll give me an extension.'

She glanced at him, the memory flooding back. 'That's right,' she agreed. And I can give you my answer in two words.'

He looked up, his hope disappearing when he saw the cruel glint in her eyes.

'Two words,' she said again. 'Extension denied.' Leaving him grovelling on the floor, Andrea returned to her car and drove back home.

She had Ted take her again as soon as she returned. There was no appetite for an evening meal; no hunger for anything other than a need to satisfy the demanding itch that now seared in her loins. All she wanted was to feel his heat inside her and all she needed was the satisfying release that came from his passionate embrace and the powerful pulse of their shared climax. Exhausted, her bare body still tingling with the memory of her most recent climax, she reached out and stroked fingernails against one of his gouged shoulder blades. 'Two words,' she said quietly.

He glanced quizzically up from his semi-slumber.

'Two words: thank you.'

'Thank you?' He couldn't keep the wonder from his voice. 'What are you thanking me for?'

'What you just did,' she explained. Light had faded from the room and it was easier to talk in the twilight shadows without him seeing her expression. 'I'm thanking you for what you did just now, what you did this morning, and what you'll do tomorrow morning. I need that. And I'm saying thank you.'

'You don't need to thank me.'

'I do.' She laughed bitterly. 'I really do. If you didn't give me that release on a morning, Christ knows what sort of a bitch I would be throughout the day.'

NEXUS NEW BOOKS

To be published in August

FIT TO BE TIED
Penny Birch

When submissive minx Penny Birch finds herself chastised by the matronly Marjorie Burgess at a dinner party for university colleagues, the situation is so outrageously old-fashioned that Penny assumes the older woman is playing an erotic game with her. Penny is doubly humiliated when she is caught gratifying herself over the experience, only to find that Marjorie was entirely serious. Kinky councellor Gabrielle Salinger comes up with a face – and job – saving solution, but can Penny resist being drawn into Gabrielle's circle of perverted associates?

£6.99   ISBN 0 352 33825 3

THE OBEDIENT ALICE
Adriana Arden

Restless eighteen-year-old Alice Brown discovers to her amazement that the world of Wonderland (renamed Underland, and definitely no place for children) has begun to take young women – or 'girlings' – from our dimension as its sex slaves. In a quest to liberate them, she encounters the perverse wiles of the White Rabbit, Hatter and Hare, and a less than regal Duchess and Queen of Hearts. And it's not only the Cheshire Cat's smile, Alice finds, that lingers once the rest has vanished . . .

A highly original and downright filthy fantasy tale.

£6.99   ISBN 0 352 33826 1

THE DISCIPLINE OF NURSE RIDING
Yolanda Celbridge

When Sloaney Prudence Riding has a sudden fall from grace as her trust fund runs out, she decides to get a job – and what could be more worthy than becoming a nurse? The training at Cloughton Wyke Hydro is rather more severe than she is prepared for, however, involving as it does strict discipline, tight rubber uniforms and an education in the application of bizarre and erotic treatments. Nurse Riding's further instruction in the sophisticated use of medical restraints is interrupted by a hunch that her long-lost twin sister is nearby. Can Prudence ever hope to find her? A Nexus Classic.

£6.99   ISBN 0 352 33827 X

To be published in September

NATURAL DESIRE, STRANGE DESIGN
Aishling Morgan

Natural Desire follows the efforts of the pagan Nich Mordaunt and the unprincipled lothario Anderson Croom to locate the legacy of notorious cultist Julian Blackman. Each has his own agenda, and their search takes them through a series of ritualistic and outright perverse erotic encounters towards the climax. Mothers, their daughters, and sadistic mind games feature in this novel of erotic ritual.

£6.99   ISBN 0 352 33844 X

PUNISHING IMOGEN
Yvonne Marshall

Charlotte and Imogen, the young debutantes who featured in *Teasing Charlotte*, were childhood friends whose fascination with the mysterious society beauty known as Kayla led them into a bizarre vortex of submission and domination. Now Charlotte herself is 'Kayla' – never a real name at all but the moniker for a *very* particular, very kinky high-class courtesan. Imogen, however, thinks there's room for a rival, and Charlotte must take stern measures against her old friend if her dominance is to be assured.

£6.99   ISBN 0 352 33845 8

SUSIE IN SERVITUDE
Arabella Knight

Under the stern tutelage of Madame Seraphim Savage, Susie is in training to be a *corsetière*. A keen student of fashion, Susie soon discovers that at the Rookery – Madame's private establishment – discipline, correction and other special services are always in vogue. Madame's clients, it seems, appreciate the bite of the cane as much as they do the cut of their clothes. That's just as well, as Madame's cardinal rule – that the customer always comes first – is strictly enforced.

£6.99   ISBN 0 352 33846 6

If you would like more information about Nexus titles, please visit our website at www.nexus-books.co.uk, or send a stamped addressed envelope to:
  Nexus, Thames Wharf Studios,
  Rainville Road, London W6 9HA

Nexus

NEXUS BACKLIST

This information is correct at time of printing. For up-to-date information, please visit our website at www.nexus-books.co.uk

All books are priced at £5.99 unless another price is given.

Nexus books with a contemporary setting

ACCIDENTS WILL HAPPEN	Lucy Golden ISBN 0 352 33596 3	☐
ANGEL	Lindsay Gordon ISBN 0 352 33590 4	☐
BARE BEHIND £6.99	Penny Birch ISBN 0 352 33721 4	☐
BEAST	Wendy Swanscombe ISBN 0 352 33649 8	☐
THE BLACK FLAME	Lisette Ashton ISBN 0 352 33668 4	☐
BROUGHT TO HEEL	Arabella Knight ISBN 0 352 33508 4	☐
CAGED!	Yolanda Celbridge ISBN 0 352 33650 1	☐
CANDY IN CAPTIVITY	Arabella Knight ISBN 0 352 33495 9	☐
CAPTIVES OF THE PRIVATE HOUSE	Esme Ombreux ISBN 0 352 33619 6	☐
CHERI CHASTISED £6.99	Yolanda Celbridge ISBN 0 352 33707 9	☐
DANCE OF SUBMISSION	Lisette Ashton ISBN 0 352 33450 9	☐
DIRTY LAUNDRY £6.99	Penny Birch ISBN 0 352 33680 3	☐
DISCIPLINED SKIN	Wendy Swanscombe ISBN 0 352 33541 6	☐

DISPLAYS OF EXPERIENCE	Lucy Golden ISBN 0 352 33505 X	☐
DISPLAYS OF PENITENTS £6.99	Lucy Golden ISBN 0 352 33646 3	☐
DRAWN TO DISCIPLINE	Tara Black ISBN 0 352 33626 9	☐
EDEN UNVEILED	Maria del Rey ISBN 0 352 32542 4	☐
AN EDUCATION IN THE PRIVATE HOUSE	Esme Ombreux ISBN 0 352 33525 4	☐
EMMA'S SECRET DOMINATION	Hilary James ISBN 0 352 33226 3	☐
GISELLE	Jean Aveline ISBN 0 352 33440 1	☐
GROOMING LUCY	Yvonne Marshall ISBN 0 352 33529 7	☐
HEART OF DESIRE	Maria del Rey ISBN 0 352 32900 9	☐
HIS MISTRESS'S VOICE	G. C. Scott ISBN 0 352 33425 8	☐
IN FOR A PENNY	Penny Birch ISBN 0 352 33449 5	☐
INTIMATE INSTRUCTION	Arabella Knight ISBN 0 352 33618 8	☐
THE LAST STRAW	Christina Shelly ISBN 0 352 33643 9	☐
NURSES ENSLAVED	Yolanda Celbridge ISBN 0 352 33601 3	☐
THE ORDER	Nadine Somers ISBN 0 352 33460 6	☐
THE PALACE OF EROS £4.99	Delver Maddingley ISBN 0 352 32921 1	☐
PALE PLEASURES £6.99	Wendy Swanscombe ISBN 0 352 33702 8	☐
PEACHES AND CREAM £6.99	Aishling Morgan ISBN 0 352 33672 2	☐

PEEPING AT PAMELA	Yolanda Celbridge ISBN 0 352 33538 6	☐
PENNY PIECES	Penny Birch ISBN 0 352 33631 5	☐
PET TRAINING IN THE PRIVATE HOUSE	Esme Ombreux ISBN 0 352 33655 2	☐
REGIME £6.99	Penny Birch ISBN 0 352 33666 8	☐
RITUAL STRIPES £6.99	Tara Black ISBN 0 352 33701 X	☐
SEE-THROUGH	Lindsay Gordon ISBN 0 352 33656 0	☐
SILKEN SLAVERY	Christina Shelly ISBN 0 352 33708 7	☐
SKIN SLAVE	Yolanda Celbridge ISBN 0 352 33507 6	☐
SLAVE ACTS £6.99	Jennifer Jane Pope ISBN 0 352 33665 X	☐
THE SLAVE AUCTION	Lisette Ashton ISBN 0 352 33481 9	☐
SLAVE GENESIS	Jennifer Jane Pope ISBN 0 352 33503 3	☐
SLAVE REVELATIONS	Jennifer Jane Pope ISBN 0 352 33627 7	☐
SLAVE SENTENCE	Lisette Ashton ISBN 0 352 33494 0	☐
SOLDIER GIRLS	Yolanda Celbridge ISBN 0 352 33586 6	☐
THE SUBMISSION GALLERY	Lindsay Gordon ISBN 0 352 33370 7	☐
SURRENDER	Laura Bowen ISBN 0 352 33524 6	☐
THE TAMING OF TRUDI £6.99	Yolanda Celbridge ISBN 0 352 33673 0	☐
TEASING CHARLOTTE £6.99	Yvonne Marshall ISBN 0 352 33681 1	☐
TEMPER TANTRUMS	Penny Birch ISBN 0 352 33647 1	☐

THE TORTURE CHAMBER	Lisette Ashton ISBN 0 352 33530 0	☐
UNIFORM DOLL £6.99	Penny Birch ISBN 0 352 33698 6	☐
WHIP HAND £6.99	G. C. Scott ISBN 0 352 33694 3	☐
THE YOUNG WIFE	Stephanie Calvin ISBN 0 352 33502 5	☐

Nexus books with Ancient and Fantasy settings

CAPTIVE	Aishling Morgan ISBN 0 352 33585 8	☐
DEEP BLUE	Aishling Morgan ISBN 0 352 33600 5	☐
DUNGEONS OF LIDIR	Aran Ashe ISBN 0 352 33506 8	☐
INNOCENT £6.99	Aishling Morgan ISBN 0 352 33699 4	☐
MAIDEN	Aishling Morgan ISBN 0 352 33466 5	☐
NYMPHS OF DIONYSUS £4.99	Susan Tinoff ISBN 0 352 33150 X	☐
PLEASURE TOY	Aishling Morgan ISBN 0 352 33634 X	☐
SLAVE MINES OF TORMUNIL £6.99	Aran Ashe ISBN 0 352 33695 1	☐
THE SLAVE OF LIDIR	Aran Ashe ISBN 0 352 33504 1	☐
TIGER, TIGER	Aishling Morgan ISBN 0 352 33455 X	☐

Period

CONFESSION OF AN ENGLISH SLAVE	Yolanda Celbridge ISBN 0 352 33433 9	☐
THE MASTER OF CASTLELEIGH	Jacqueline Bellevois ISBN 0 352 32644 7	☐
PURITY	Aishling Morgan ISBN 0 352 33510 6	☐
VELVET SKIN	Aishling Morgan ISBN 0 352 33660 9	☐

Samplers and collections

NEW EROTICA 5	Various ISBN 0 352 33540 8	☐
EROTICON 1	Various ISBN 0 352 33593 9	☐
EROTICON 2	Various ISBN 0 352 33594 7	☐
EROTICON 3	Various ISBN 0 352 33597 1	☐
EROTICON 4	Various ISBN 0 352 33602 1	☐
THE NEXUS LETTERS	Various ISBN 0 352 33621 8	☐
SATURNALIA £7.99	ed. Paul Scott ISBN 0 352 33717 6	☐
MY SECRET GARDEN SHED £7.99	ed. Paul Scott ISBN 0 352 33725 7	☐

Nexus Classics

A new imprint dedicated to putting the finest works of erotic fiction back in print.

AMANDA IN THE PRIVATE HOUSE £6.99	Esme Ombreux ISBN 0 352 33705 2	☐
BAD PENNY	Penny Birch ISBN 0 352 33661 7	☐
BRAT £6.99	Penny Birch ISBN 0 352 33674 9	☐
DARK DELIGHTS £6.99	Maria del Rey ISBN 0 352 33667 6	☐
DARK DESIRES	Maria del Rey ISBN 0 352 33648 X	☐
DISPLAYS OF INNOCENTS £6.99	Lucy Golden ISBN 0 352 33679 X	☐
DISCIPLINE OF THE PRIVATE HOUSE £6.99	Esme Ombreux ISBN 0 352 33459 2	☐
EDEN UNVEILED	Maria del Rey ISBN 0 352 33542 4	☐

HIS MISTRESS'S VOICE	G. C. Scott	☐
	ISBN 0 352 33425 8	
THE INDIGNITIES OF ISABELLE	Penny Birch writing	☐
£6.99	as Cruella	
	ISBN 0 352 33696 X	
LETTERS TO CHLOE	Stefan Gerrard	☐
	ISBN 0 352 33632 3	
MEMOIRS OF A CORNISH GOVERNESS	Yolanda Celbridge	☐
	ISBN 0 352 33722 2	
£6.99		
ONE WEEK IN THE PRIVATE HOUSE	Esme Ombreux	☐
	ISBN 0 352 33706 0	
£6.99		
PARADISE BAY	Maria del Rey	☐
	ISBN 0 352 33645 5	
PENNY IN HARNESS	Penny Birch	☐
	ISBN 0 352 33651 X	
THE PLEASURE PRINCIPLE	Maria del Rey	☐
	ISBN 0 352 33482 7	
PLEASURE ISLAND	Aran Ashe	☐
	ISBN 0 352 33628 5	
SISTERS OF SEVERCY	Jean Aveline	☐
	ISBN 0 352 33620 X	
A TASTE OF AMBER	Penny Birch	☐
	ISBN 0 352 33654 4	

- - - - - - ✂ -

Please send me the books I have ticked above.

Name   ....

Address   ....

              ....

              ....

              .... Post code....................

Send to: Cash Sales, Nexus Books, Thames Wharf Studios, Rainville Road, London W6 9HA

US customers: for prices and details of how to order books for delivery by mail, call 1-800-343-4499.

Please enclose a cheque or postal order, made payable to **Nexus Books Ltd**, to the value of the books you have ordered plus postage and packing costs as follows:

UK and BFPO – £1.00 for the first book, 50p for each subsequent book.

Overseas (including Republic of Ireland) – £2.00 for the first book, £1.00 for each subsequent book.

If you would prefer to pay by VISA, ACCESS/MASTERCARD, AMEX, DINERS CLUB or SWITCH, please write your card number and expiry date here:

....

Please allow up to 28 days for delivery.

Signature ....

Our privacy policy

We will not disclose information you supply us to any other parties. We will not disclose any information which identifies you personally to any person without your express consent.

From time to time we may send out information about Nexus books and special offers. Please tick here if you do *not* wish to receive Nexus information.   ☐

- - - - - - ✂ -